SLIPPE

Rachael H Dixon

To

Eleanor

Thank you for the
Reading :)

Rachael
x

www.slipperysouls.co.uk

Published by FeedARead.com Publishing – Arts Council funded

Cover art by Rachael H Dixon.

A CIP catalogue record for this title is available from the British Library.

For Derek; my soulmate

Acknowledgements

Firstly, I'd like to thank my mam and dad for fuelling my desire to write by buying me a Petite typewriter one Christmas in the mid-80s, and for letting me read James Herbert novels at such a tender age – it's where it all stemmed from.

I'd also like to thank my brother Eddie for the creative time we spent drawing and writing together, whilst lying on the living room floor, as kids – it helped to warm my imagination.

A big thanks also to my family members and friends who offered words of encouragement throughout this project. There's too many to list individually, but you know who you all are!

The book would never have been complete without a good edit, for which I'd like to thank my sister-in-law Hannah Thompson, who has been an absolute star – (thanks for watching out for those pesky gaping whales and those horrible homophones!) And I'd like to thank my auntie, Elizabeth Bage, for being the first person to read Slippery Souls.

Finally, but most importantly of all, I'd like to say a massive thank you to my husband Derek who made this project possible. He's been a constant source of inspiration, encouragement and support throughout – believing in me, when sometimes I didn't even believe in myself.

shouted, "I'm off now. Dunno what time I'll be back. Probably going for a drink with the lads straight after work."

The door slammed shut behind him, as abrupt as his announcement had been. There was no goodbye kiss, no goodbye hug. Not even a goodbye. Libby tried to recall the exact moment when things had changed between them. They were worlds apart these days.

"Don't bother coming back," Libby snarled, hurling the milk bottle at the bin, imagining it was Alex's face.

His late nights were becoming more and more frequent. These, combined with his earlier-than-usual mornings where he spent ages coiffing and waxing his hair into place, ironing his shirts to within an inch of their lives, and not to mention the eye-watering trail of aftershave he left behind, had Libby wondering of late whether her boyfriend was some kind of philandering scumbag. She recognised all the tell-tale signs which would suggest he was having an affair, but she also recognised it could be wishful thinking on her behalf. Presently she'd like nothing more than for him to pack his bags and piss off with the eighteen year old secretary from work. The girl who smoked like a chimney, wore her skirts too short and answered to the name Trixie. Libby suspected she was probably the kind of girl who wouldn't mind Alex's farting and snot-flicking ways.

Stomping back upstairs to get ready, Libby knew that being optimistic about the possibility that Alex might be messing around behind her back was not the normal rationale of somebody in love. If anything, it was the point of no return. The beginning of the end for their three year relationship, and she didn't even flinch as she imagined the final nail being driven into the proverbial coffin that it had crawled into. If she listened closely enough, she reckoned she'd be able to hear the funeral procession marching closer. And what's more, she was willing to roll up her sleeves and help dig the hole, if need be – all six feet of it.

The glowing flame that had ignited their passion in the first spells of romance had long since extinguished. There'd been nothing dramatic or spectacular about it either. It had fizzled out like a tea light underneath a soggy flannel.

In truth the major crux of the problem, for Libby, was boredom. She was fed up. Bored rigid. And although he irritated the life out of her, she wasn't even blaming Alex for the ensuing tedium – she just felt restless. It seemed like young love had run its course, and now they were just treading water because neither one of them dared to make the break, for whatever foolish reason. Both were taking the easy option and hanging out in the comfort zone. It was becoming too much to bear now though, she wanted excitement, and she craved adventure – neither of which was being provided by their life together. Laughing out loud she realised the irony as she placed her neatly folded pyjamas underneath her pillow.

"Yep, I'm *so* rock 'n' roll."

Lifting the pair of jeans she'd worn the day before from the laundry basket, she held them in the air and gave them a shake as though all of the creases would fall away like crumbs.

"See? If I wasn't, I wouldn't be doing this," she said to herself. "In fact, what the hell, let's live dangerously." After shimmying into the jeans, she plucked yesterday's plain black t-shirt out of the basket too. It was skin-tight, so when she pulled it on the creases instantly smoothed out.

Now fully dressed, she needed to make a phone call. Moving to the pair of large, plastic red lips sitting on top of her bedside cabinet, Libby picked up the top half and jabbed at the keypad. Twiddling her tongue bar and clacking it between her teeth (a habit of hers that Alex found annoying, which, in turn, made her do it all the more), she listened to the dialling tone and waited for an answer.

"Good morning, Dial-A-Drive."

"Hi Dad, it's just me. Do I have any jobs on this morning before my ten o'clock pick-up?"

"No pet, we've got the school run just about covered. You're fine till ten."

Libby's father, Dennis, owned his own taxi firm Dial-A-Drive – fondly named specifically for its acronym DAD. Chauffeuring Libby and her younger sister Izzy round as teenagers had been the inspiration behind the small but successful venture.

Libby had a casual arrangement with Dial-A-Drive, covering busy hours as and when required for a bit of extra cash, though it wasn't her chosen career path. She'd been laid off from her long-term job at the local salon, only weeks ago, after it had gone bust - something to do with Sharnie the manager preferring designer shoes and handbags over paying the rent. Libby had mainly worked as a hairstylist, but sometimes lent a hand out back doing tattoo art and body piercing. God, she'd loved that job. Where else could you go for a haircut and come back out with a tattoo and a pierced navel as well? It was the kind of salon Libby aspired to run one day, but for now ad-hoc taxi driving would have to do.

"Aw thanks Dad, you're a star."

Pulling on a pair of black pumps, Libby bounded back downstairs, then taking a dog leash from the coat peg in the hallway, she yelled, "Rufus!"

She immediately heard claws *clink-clinking* on the wooden floor, then with tail wagging and mouth open in anticipation, a black wiry terrier-cross scuttled into the hallway.

"It's time to relieve your bladder and address the milk shortage, mister."

Libby had adopted Rufus from a rescue shelter two years ago. She had no idea how old he was, but his tufty grey eyebrows and unruly grey goatee beard, which gave his face comedy value, made her think he must be at least middle-aged. At that moment he looked up at her with the excitable look only dogs can do when they're promised *walkies*.

"What would I do without you?" she chuckled, patting the top of his head. "You love me, don't you? And you wouldn't dream of using all the milk in the house so that nobody else could have breakfast, would you?"

Bending down she clipped the leash onto his collar, creating a renewed wave of excitement from him. His feet scrabbled on the floor's smooth surface as he tried to move closer to the front door. Like a cartoon dog trying to chase a cartoon cat, his legs were going fifty to the dozen, but he hardly moved anywhere.

"You do some pretty obnoxious farts, mind you," Libby pointed out, allowing herself to be yanked over to the door. "But hey, at least you don't laugh about it."

Rufus whined impatiently, his feet having found purchase on the doormat. He sat down and crossed his legs.

"Alright, alright, keep your hair on. You must be busting. Come on then, let's go."

Outside the sky was unspoilt blue and the sun was picking out startling reds and oranges and yellows from the autumnal trees that lined the street. Nature's own fashion show. It was a beautiful start to what should have been a beautiful day – how could she have known Death was doing his rounds and was almost at her door?

"No dawdling mind, straight there and back. Are you listening?" warned Libby.

Rufus didn't take a blind bit of notice. He stopped and sniffed every lamp post they passed. This was his religious routine of lamp post pit stops. *Lamp post piss stops more like*, she thought, checking her watch. Eventually they reached the shop, and having collected a bottle of milk they began retracing their steps. The sun, although still low in the sky, glared in shop windows and bounced off passing car rooftops. Libby squinted her eyes and made a mental note to dig out her sunglasses and sun-lotion when she got back home. The day was going to be a scorcher for sure, and being fair-skinned she knew from experience not to take chances. Resembling a crabstick wasn't exactly a desirable look.

The High Street was already bustling. Truck-drivers unloaded heavy pallets from their vehicles in no particular hurry, relishing the warmth in short-sleeved shirts. People ambled about their business – buying the morning paper;

strolling to work; taking dogs for walks. And joggers paired up, chatting. Along with vests and flip-flops the sun had brought cheerful optimism, springs in steps and whistles on lips. Libby sincerely hoped this was the beginning of the fabled Indian summer. If it weren't for the pesky breeze, which animated her hair, it would be a damn near perfect day.

And she knew what would make it even *more* perfect – by getting rid of Alex. He was the fly in her ointment, and they needed to stop plodding along, pretending things were okay. It was a day for change. Either the sun's positivity had spurred her into action or the empty milk bottle on the kitchen table had been the straw responsible for snapping the camel's back in half. Whichever way, she'd made up her mind. He was too straight-laced, and she had a wild side somewhere underneath that was bursting to be free – she was sure of it, and she just needed to discover how to set it free. She'd spent her whole life feeling restless and it was now pretty obvious Alex wasn't helping her feel any better. She didn't know *what* it was she sought, or what the yearning and longing in her heart was for, but at least one decision was made – she'd wait up for Alex coming home and tell him it was over. She imagined he wouldn't be too surprised, or even upset. In fact, she visualised them both sighing with relief. Of course, they'd then have the awkward discussion about who stayed in the house and who left, but that was no big deal. Her parents would welcome her back with open arms if need be. They'd probably drive her nuts and it would feel like a step backwards, but she was only twenty-two, there was still plenty of time to start over again – or so she'd thought.

Stepping from the pavement to cross the road, she tried to remember where the large black suitcase was. Whether it was stored away in the loft, or whether they'd lent it to somebody. Goodness knows *they* hadn't used it in ages. Either way, one of them would need it very shortly, and if it was Alex she wouldn't even mind helping him pack. Happy thoughts of ramming the suitcase full of his clothes and

15

belongings were cut short when she saw something large and silver speeding straight towards her.

A car that could not, or would not, stop.

Libby didn't have time to move, and when her legs connected with the bumper, she was bowled up into the air like a splintered skittle, and Rufus disappeared somewhere underneath the vehicle. The bottle of milk left Libby's hand and arced through the air, bursting open on the road and creating a Friesian cow pattern on the black tarmac surface.

The whole tragic episode didn't hurt as much as Libby would have expected. Indeed, by the time she had catapulted away from the road, thus crashing back down to her gravelly demise on the pavement, she hadn't felt much at all. And as she'd windmilled through the air, she hadn't even seen who was responsible for ending her life either. Afterwards she'd say she didn't care. What had happened had happened, and that was all there was to it. Her new philosophy was *what's the point in crying over spilt milk?*

"Hmmm. Somebody with an entry code, perhaps? Or somebody who has ways and means of gaining access through the tiniest of spaces?"

"Or someone Seth on reception was familiar with," Flatbrook added, shrugging his shoulders.

Krain felt a headache coming on. He was beginning to feel agitated, and he could do without this new fiasco right now. Closing his eyes and pinching the bridge of his nose he asked, "And what about the prisoners?"

"Prisoners up on the ground floor were undisturbed, sir. In fact most of them are still sleeping now."

"Lucky them," Krain said, rolling his eyes derisively. "I expected as much since all the drama seems to have taken place down here."

Bristling and motioning with a nod of his head towards the large iron door, leading to the underground detention cells, he asked, "What about *them*?"

Flatbrook shifted uncomfortably on his feet, blood squelching beneath his shoes.

"Er...they're all gone, sir."

"*What*?" Krain raised an eyebrow, his annoyance suddenly evident, betrayed by flared nostrils. He'd had an inkling that might be the case.

Flatbrook shrank away.

"The cells have been busted open. They're all empty, sir."

Krain's jawbone clenched, his temples throbbing. He trod carefully towards the iron door, wary of slipping on the wet tiles in his black grip-less brogues. Anger *and* worry dominated him, and he wasn't sure which would take precedence. When he entered the narrow passageway beyond, he could see that what Flatbrook had said was true. Krain instantly cursed the fact he didn't have something to hand which he could throw, so instead, he threw back his head and made a long-drawn-out noise like a wounded animal. His calm was well and truly in tatters now.

Flatbrook, who was standing in the doorway behind Krain, winced. Witnessing Krain throw a hissy fit was never ideal.

"Where've they gone?" Krain barked, his jaw still vice-like and his eyes bulging. Flatbrook wasn't sure if it was a rhetorical question or whether he actually expected an answer, so he answered anyway.

"We're not sure, sir, but we're trying to find out."

Now pacing back and forth like a dog in a kennel, Krain rubbed his facial hair as though it suddenly irritated him. The immaculately groomed short beard and moustache combo, which was setsquare sharp, was solid black – contradicting the thick mop of hair on his head that was threaded with silver. Krain looked every part the charismatic older gentleman, and going on looks alone it was easy to see why members of the general public had readily embraced him as mayor. With a mincing gait and a penchant for dinner gloves, his outwardly impeccable manners and etiquette made him a very likeable character; if a tad barmy. On the other hand, there were those, including Flatbrook, who knew better – that Krain harboured an inherent darker side. To his nearest and dearest, he was comparable to a ballet-dancing weasel perhaps. Dangerous and hypnotic, with a definite touch of peculiarity. He mesmerised the people of Sunray Bay as though they were a colony of bunny rabbits (and pity the idiots who mistook his love of lace doilies and Earl Grey tea as signs of weakness). Flatbrook knew he must tread carefully.

"We're not sure of motive at this stage, sir," Flatbrook added. "Do you have any suggestions in that respect? I mean, I'm not sure this can be linked with the incident at the archives yesterday. The council officers there were bled dry – but the wardens in here – well, as you can see..."

Krain's black eyes burned like coals and Flatbrook knew he'd just stoked the flames.

"Do *not* take anything for granted, Flatbrook!" Krain hissed in disbelief.

unweathered we'll be okay." She held aloft a blue biro and a tube of strawberry lip balm. "Oh and I have some cash in my purse too. I might get that cup of tea after all."

"Good stuff," Rufus said, failing to hide his look of disappointment at the lack of foodstuff in the bag. "Shall we pop our heads outside then, see if we can find out where we are?" he added, hopeful that there might be other food opportunities nearby.

"Come on then," Libby said, looping his dog leash around her wrist. "We can't sit around here all day, I suppose."

When she opened the door, revealing a new world beyond, they were hit by an unexpected wall of immense heat. Instantly loving the belting hot sunrays that engulfed them, she smiled. It was shorts and bikini weather, her favourite kind – though, her smile was soon replaced by a frown when she looked down at the jeans and black t-shirt she wore. *How completely inappropriate, and bloody typical,* she thought.

"Flipping heck, it's hot out here," Rufus gasped, echoing her thoughts.

She tried imagining herself in a white cotton sundress instead, thinking that if it was a dream she *should* be able to make anything happen. Nothing happened. Though, it was hardly surprising in all honesty, her subconscious was not usually the cooperative type. If she really did have the power to control her dreams, she doubted she'd dream about anything other than going on dates with Johnny Depp – possibly two-timing him with Orlando Bloom every now and then. And she certainly couldn't see either of them anywhere, so she resigned herself to the fact that jeans and black t-shirt it would have to be.

Shielding her face from the sun, she squinted and saw that they were standing on the porch of a banana-yellow beach hut. The hut was one in a neat row of possibly hundreds of others, all brightly coloured. Steps led down from the hut to a paved promenade, which was currently swarming with people.

The walkway itself traced the line of a large horseshoe bay, which was lined on both sides with identical beach huts. The huts stopped in the middle where the promenade wall ended and opened up onto the beach, and a path led in the opposite direction towards whatever lay beyond. The hut from which Libby and Rufus had emerged was set on the left-hand side of the semi-circular esplanade, and Libby noted that they were only a short walk away from the beach access point. If they walked in the opposite direction, away from the beach access point, she saw that they'd reach a long pier. Straining her eyes, she could make out a big wheel spinning at the very end, and carried on the air she could hear the faint ringing of amusement arcades and the whirring of other fairground rides, interspersed with distant squeals of glee.

At the farthest point on the right-hand side of the esplanade, Libby could just about make out another pier. This one was much shorter, and dancing in a wide band of pixelated heat, she could see that it was home to a solitary red and white stripy lighthouse.

Indigo sea edged the horizon, gently rolling forth and spraying the shore with white sprinkles, to the apparent delight of paddlers. Libby could smell its salty freshness, and was almost compelled to rush down and splash about in the frothy cool water to invigorate her rapidly swelling feet.

"Ha! Who'd have thought death would be a beach holiday?" she marvelled, a delirious grin pasted to her face once again. "People would pay good money for this."

"Are you thinking business opportunities already?" Rufus asked.

Libby laughed.

"I'm not getting *that* carried away. Besides it might not be as good as it looks, and we have no idea what the accommodation options are yet. I would like to presume the dead aren't left to roam the streets and be homeless bums, but hey, who knows. Just don't be too surprised if they cram us into hostels and workhouses, or something as equally crap. My dad always taught me to expect the worst in any given situation, and that way I would never be too disappointed with the overall outcome."

"Your dad really knew how to put a positive spin on things, didn't he?" Rufus said.

"Hey, it's very realistic advice. And, anyway, even if it does turn out to be like a giant holiday resort here, I've seen plenty of those holiday uncovered documentaries to give you sleepless nights for months. In fact, in Spain I once got stuck in a Norman Bates style self-catering apartment."

"Were you assaulted in the shower?"

"No, smart arse. But it had ominously stained bed sheets, a dysfunctional kettle and a poolside cabaret singer who thought he was Elvis. It was the kind of place where you had to sleep with your clothes on and shower in your shoes in case you ended up going home with more than you bargained for – and I'm not talking about cheap souvenirs either. I'm talking about stuff you need anti-fungal cream and a good dose of penicillin to get rid of."

"Lovely," Rufus grimaced. "Shall we just ask if we can go home in that case? And anyway, *what's wrong with Elvis?*"

Libby shook her head and rolled her eyes but before she could respond a middle-aged man in a white vest and black knee-length shorts, sporting the biggest dreadlocks Libby had ever seen, stopped at the bottom of the beach hut steps and called up to her, "Alright missus? Wanna buy a hat?"

In his left hand he balanced a tall pile of baseball caps of varying colours, all stacked one on top of the other. The one at the very top had the slogan *Reality Bites*, and the cap he twirled on his right index finger had the slogan *Kiss Me Quick.*

"Er, no thanks, I don't have any money." Libby replied, patting her pockets for effect.

"Liar, liar, your bum's on fire," Rufus chanted quietly, with a glint of mischief in his eyes.

"Shut it, you." Libby cast him an evil glare.

"*Excuse me?*" the cap man asked, his smile turning into a scowl.

31

"Oh I wasn't telling you to shut up. I was talking to my dog."

The cap man eyed Rufus warily. "What're you up there with a dog for anyway?"

At that moment, people passing by on the walkway looked up at them, and Libby suddenly felt as though she had an audience. She blushed and hoped he wasn't going to cause a scene.

"Just hanging about," she replied, with as much nonchalance as she could muster.

"Well, you should already know you aren't meant to have dogs on the promenade."

Libby sighed. He was getting on her nerves. She wished he would just sod off.

"Why not?"

"What do you mean, *why not*? It's a dog-free zone, are you an idiot or something?" He pointed to a sign further up the promenade which displayed a matchstick dog inside a red circle with a strike through it.

"Oh, I didn't realise."

"You'll be shot with shit if POM catches you down here with it, an' all."

"What's POM?" Libby's brow furrowed in puzzlement, and she could see that he was now growing impatient by the way he tapped his foot loudly on the bottom step.

"Peace & Order Maintenance, for God's sake. Look, do you want a cap or not?"

"No! I already said."

"Suit yourself, I hope you don't *burn*." And with a glowering expression off he stalked, the enormous explosion of mousy-brown knots that sprouted from his head bouncing as he went.

"Are you *sure* you don't want a cap?" Rufus asked with a wry smirk. "After all, your hair's sticking up like a telephone wire."

Still smarting from having been insulted by a random stranger, she said huffily, "I wouldn't be seen dead in one."

32

"Oh you sad, lovable fool. Was that your attempt at being funny?" Rufus groaned, shaking his head in despair. "That was especially bad, even for you."

Libby smiled weakly. "Ha ha, very funny. Now come on, let's hit the beach."

Rufus didn't move.

"What do you mean my sweet deluded one? Didn't you listen to what he just said? Which part of 'dog-free zone' didn't you understand?"

"He said you aren't allowed on the *promenade*, he didn't say anything about not being allowed on the beach."

"So what are you going to do, toss me over the promenade wall onto the beach?"

"Very tempting." Libby bent down and scooped Rufus into her arms. "But no. I'm going to carry you."

"Aw that's not fair, I wanted to walk along the beach wall," Rufus said as he was hoisted up into the air.

"If you walk along the wall we might be shot with shit, as *Mr Kiss-Me-Quick* so nicely put it."

"Hmmm yeah, I don't much fancy that. I wonder what Peace & Order Maintenance is. I mean, I suppose it sounds fairly obvious what they must *do*, but I wonder who they are," he said. "Although, when all's said and done, I arrived on the sodding promenade, so what the hell do they expect me to do? Magic myself over onto the beach? Whoever POM are, they can kiss my hairy arse."

"I can assure you it won't come to that," Libby shook her head and kept a firm hold on Rufus. "Anyway, what do you reckon to all these beach huts?"

"I'm loving the colours and layout. They're rather quaint, aren't they," Rufus replied.

"No, you pudding head, I meant do you reckon they're like portals between life and death or something?"

"Oh right," Rufus pondered. "Well I suppose it's a good possibility."

"It's all quite exciting, isn't it?" Libby beamed, content to carry on dreaming. "I love a good adventure."

"Erm, can I just remind you that we're *dead*. I'd hardly call that an adventure, you fuzzy-headed wombat. And anyway, shouldn't we perhaps ask somebody where we can find some nice food and a five star hotel for the night? We could maybe worry about hostels and workhouses tomorrow?"

"But where's the fun in that, Rufus?" she harrumphed.

Libby had longed for adventure for a good while now, and she loved problem solving (unless it was related to relationships, of course, where she tended to bury her head in the sand for a year or two). She was damned if she was going to ask for help now. Not this soon anyway. And besides, if it *was* just a dream she would go with the flow and see where it took her.

"Hey, what's up with him?" Rufus suddenly asked.

Libby followed his gaze directly across the walkway. A gaunt-looking man stood on the beach, propping himself up against the promenade wall, and he was looking straight at them. His stare was so intense it was, quite frankly, unsettling. His dirty-blonde hair clung to his sweaty face and neck, and his bony shoulders poked out from under the grey sleeveless top he wore. Libby thought he looked like a burnt-out rock star, a vagrant or a druggie – or perhaps all three combined. Just behind him stood a small pace of donkeys, looking hot and bothered in brightly coloured sequin-edged saddles and harnesses, and the man himself wore a leather money pouch around his waist. Libby presumed the donkeys must be his.

"God only knows, maybe he wants to sell us a donkey ride," she replied. "We should probably go, before he tries."

She bounded down the steps without further ado, Rufus weighing heavy in her arms, and all the while the man didn't take his twitchy eyes off them for a second.

"Maybe he's looking at us funny because I'm talking to you," Libby said, without moving her lips much. "For all we know, it might not be commonplace for dead dogs to talk. Perhaps we should keep it low key, just in case."

"Are you kidding?" Rufus snorted. "I hate to point out the obvious, Libby dearest, but here at Costa del Heaven there are beach huts instead of clouds and donkeys instead of harp-playing angels – so enlighten me, *what's so odd about a talking dog?*"

"Well, he's still bloody well watching," Libby hissed, merging herself into the steady throng of people on the walkway, hoping to mingle in and lose his unwanted attention. Nobody else round about seemed to notice that Libby and Rufus were having a conversation – or if they did, they didn't seem to care.

Quickly swallowed up by the crowd, Libby was soon satisfied that they were safely out of reach of Donkey-man's watchful gaze, and it was only then she noticed there were quite a few people on the promenade wearing pyjamas. She thought that, unless it was a charity event, they all must have died in their night attire, which in turn made her think longingly about her own pyjamas. Loose, baggy and light. How she wished she was wearing them. Why oh why hadn't she been the type to make trips to the corner shop in her pyjamas, she wondered. Plenty of other people did. She'd been too worried about appearing slobby and uncool, that's why – yet, evidently, it would have paid off in the long run. Nevertheless, there she was. Uncomfortable and sweating in her jeans, with little she could do about it.

She'd always loved everything seaside-related and wondered, again, whether this was some kind of subconscious mind play. Maybe she was in a coma and her brain was delivering the most vivid dream of her life as she lay in a hospital bed. This was all well and good, she thought, so long as she didn't wake up before Johnny Depp had at least made a cameo appearance in a pair of Speedos.

They passed by a small stall packed to the rafters with seaside paraphernalia. Multi-coloured plastic windmills that blew in the wind, buckets that looked like flamboyant jelly moulds with matching spades, and portable beach mats, the type that leave criss-cross marks on bare skin. All of it feel-good tat which filled Libby with nostalgic memories of

35

childhood family holidays to the seaside; an amalgamation of snippets from a life that seemed so distant now. In her mind's eye she could see herself and Izzy giggling as they buried their dad up to his neck in sand on Blackpool beach. And she had a distinct memory of plodging along Scarborough's shoreline, where she'd accidentally stepped on a starfish with her bare foot. She'd cried about it for at least an hour afterwards until her dad had bought an ice-cream to placate her. It had had hundreds and thousands sprinkled on top, finished off with a big squirt of monkey's blood. The first lick had banished the yucky feeling of the starfish between her toes in an instant. And her dad had beamed at her, amused at how easily pleased she'd been.

It was only now that Libby began to realise the enormity of being dead, if that were in fact the case. She wouldn't see her friends and family again, well at least not for a long while yet, and the idea was suddenly terrifying. Although she could take some small comfort in the fact that, if this all was *really* real, she now knew for definite that death wasn't final and there was more to it than just earthworms and ashes.

Her thoughts were dashed when the owner of the stall, who'd been lurking behind a giant inflatable crocodile, thrust a red beach ball into her face.

"Wanna buy a ball, love?" His big moon face was almost as large as the ball he presented.

"No thanks," she replied. It somehow didn't seem appropriate to sit and build sandcastles at that moment in time. Though she thought if she was still there after a couple of days she might be back with a beach towel slung over her shoulder and a sugar dummy strapped round her neck.

Rufus wriggled excitedly in her arms. The promenade wall had now given way, opening up to the wide stretch of beach beyond.

"Can we go and dig in the sand? Can we, can we?" he asked, his tongue lolling from the side of his mouth.

Funny, Libby thought, *how you can have a dog with an apt understanding of the human language yet deep down he's still just a dog.* She smiled, delighting in the fact that his tail was wagging furiously. Pleased to lighten the load from her arms, she set him down onto the sand. Then standing up straight and stretching her back, she looked up and saw a massive sign above them. She wasn't sure how she'd missed it before. Nevertheless, in big cheery yellow letters the sign read, *Welcome to Sunray Bay.*

And underneath, scrawled in red spray paint, were the words, *Don't be afraid...be VERY afraid!*

Chapter 4

His breathing was slow and steady, despite the carnage. Outside the night was warm and humid, as it always was, but inside the prison chilly air stroked his exposed skin with unwelcome icy fingers. His muscular arms were bare and tense, but smooth and without goose-bumps – he didn't respond to the encompassing coldness one bit. Spatters of blood flecked his forearms and face, and had he not been wearing a black shirt and black trousers then sprays of red would have been visible on his chest and legs too.

Only now, when everything was still, did he survey the damage. Blood saturated the floor and speckled the walls and ceiling making the room look like an abstract painting; slumped bodies spoilt the contemporary effect and denied it from being an agreeable work of art. The stench of death gripped the back of his nasal passage like a rusty, pungent perfume. A smell that was all too familiar; a smell that could be his signature fragrance.

His right fingers throbbed from firing the gun in quick succession, and his fist pounded from punching teeth out. By rights, he should have been tanked-up on adrenaline, but his heart kept a slow and steady *duh-dum, duh-dum, duh-dum* rhythm. He hadn't known adrenaline for a long while now.

There were three dead in total and one just as good as. He watched the remaining prison warden cowering on the floor and knew things would go either one of two ways. If the prison warden was happy to indulge information, he'd secure himself a relatively pain free death – but if he resisted, he'd get a mouth full of bloody gums, time to reflect, and then a snapped neck.

It was a necessary evil.

He, more than most, knew all about difficult choices. How it was sometimes pure shitty luck that the choices

38

presented weren't always good ones to choose from – yet, one way or another, a decision had to be made. He'd made his own choices that night, from which he knew there'd be repercussions. Weren't there always? It was the story of his life.

Now here he was giving the prison warden two unspoken choices – it was the least, or most, he could do. And the minute the prison warden looked him in the eye and cried, "Fuck you, you freak," he'd made the choice without even realising it...

9:52am: The beach, Sunray Bay

Opening his eyes he saw that it was daylight, and he wondered how long he'd lain there. Before he had time to gather his thoughts into some form of coherence, the silhouette of a boy fell across his upper body, shadowing his whole face from the sun.

Laughing, the boy kicked sand at him.

As it rained down over his face, he snarled and swiped his arm out to grab the boy's leg.

The boy jumped backwards in shock and yelled, "Mam look, there's a man over here and he's trying to beat me!"

The boy's mother didn't come to look. Instead she shouted back, "Well if he doesn't, I will! Now hurry up, else I'll be late for work."

Kicking more sand up, in cheeky defiance, the boy stuck his tongue out and scarpered off.

Looking up at the sky he lay completely still and, without dusting himself down, he thought, *Shit, I'm still here.*

Chapter 5

Krain emerged from the underground detention area wearing a look of thunder; narrowed eyes smouldered beneath low black eyebrows, and thin lips were drawn tighter. Taking the stairs two at a time his long legs ensured a swift, effortless motion. He reached the top in four seconds flat. Flatbrook followed not far behind, his short legs doing overtime trying to keep up. Gasping and wheezing for breath he was surely on the verge of a heart attack.

"I want all of those prisoners accounted for, Flatbrook," Krain bellowed. It was an order, not a request.

"Yes, sir. Most of dayshift are already on to it."

"Well I think they need to get *on to it* a bit better, don't you?"

Krain stopped dead in his tracks, having stridden only six paces from the top of the staircase. A sudden and unexpected look of hopefulness had spread across his face. Flatbrook almost crashed into the back of him, but managed to side step at the last moment. Seeing what Krain saw, Flatbrook's expression also changed – to one of profound relief, mingled with a hint of horniness. Walking towards them, across the ground floor foyer, were three figures. Two of them were Krain's personal assistants, Red and Kitty.

Red, of average height, build and looks, had closely cropped mousy hair and a blast of ginger-brown beard. His black, thick-rimmed rectangular glasses, his only fashion assertion of which Krain approved, offered him a bookish quality. In total contrast, the striped brown suit he wore made Krain cringe. Underneath the vile suit jacket, Red wore a plain white shirt teamed with a large knotted tie of garish nature; burgundy with a light green paisley pattern, to be more precise. It was totally obscene, and lucky for him that Krain didn't employ on the basis of fashion sense.

Regardless of the fact Red looked like a harmless colour-blind librarian, he had a mouth like a sewage plant and a tongue as sharp as broken glass. Indeed, the local library might benefit from having a set of brass balls like his working in the department. Instead of dissuading late returns by issuing pitiful fines, Red would be more likely to dole out alternative punishments of a violent nature. Of course, the removal of fingers with a set of rusty secateurs would be deemed less than civilised, but a very effective method all the same. One finger would equate to one day of lateness, and he'd probably move onto toes for really late returns. It was because of this irascible nature that Red had been Krain's personal assistant for around five years now, he fit the required protocol to a tee.

Kitty, on the other hand, was a woman of few words. Seething in nature, but quietly so. She seldom spoke, and when she did it was as though she was pissed off with the entire world. Her real name was Sakura Namakura, but for reasons unbeknown to Krain, she preferred the pseudonym, Kitty. She'd been Krain's personal assistant for just under two years, and even though Krain had had no need for another personal assistant (Red more than sufficed), his wife Morgan had talked him into taking her on.

Morgan was agoraphobic and never left home. Kitty was a good friend of hers, and was always making social visits to the lighthouse. Krain had no idea how the friendship had come about in the first place. He'd wondered if they'd clicked because they were both from ethnic minorities. Kitty, with her geisha-white skin, from the Far East, and Morgan, the exotic toffee-skinned woman, from origins unknown. That was as far as his ponderings on the subject went though; in truth he didn't really care about such trivialities. If Morgan wanted to have coffee mornings with hamster-eating, fire-breathing dwarves he'd let her get on with it.

That wasn't to say he was comfortable with the current set-up. Sometimes, he caught Kitty looking at him in a smug, knowing kind of way. A look that wasn't comfortable for a boss to receive from any employee. This made him wonder

41

whether Morgan dished the dirt on their personal life. In fact, who was he kidding, Kitty probably knew about all of their domestic disagreements – maybe even their latest one. She probably even knew he preferred tanga briefs over boxer shorts and that he had a birthmark the shape of Australia on his left buttock.

Despite his unease with the situation, he grinned and bore it. He seldom said no to Morgan, and besides, Kitty was a damn sight more pleasing to the eye than Red was. Even anti-social Red hadn't complained when he'd acquired Kitty as a partner. Though Krain supposed if Red so much as looked at her the wrong way she'd eat his balls for breakfast.

Hailing from Harajuku, in Tokyo, Kitty was on the opposite end of the spectrum to Red in the fashion stakes; though neither of them portrayed a professional appearance per se. Red looked like a stand-up comedian and Kitty like a superhero's nemesis – usually wearing outfits of the tight-fitting catsuit variety. Krain reasoned this might be the clue to her feline nickname.

Today her shocking white hair was back-combed into an obscenely large do and it paled into her flawless skin, falling down onto the shoulders of her white PVC catsuit. The outfit stuck to her well-proportioned body like it had been sprayed on. Flatbrook was practically swimming in his own drool – his eyes alternating between the impressive swell of her cleavage to the perfect curve of her hips. He paid little attention to the third person walking towards them.

The third figure was a slight man who walked with his shoulders hunched and his hands cuffed behind his back. He was wearing a red Sunray Bay prison overall, which undoubtedly made him one of the escapee prisoners.

Krain clapped his hands together, "Ah, I wondered where you two would be." He moved forward to greet Red and Kitty.

"Found this one sleeping under the viaduct, sir. Member of the public reported him," Red said. "Some bloke going to work thought he'd stumbled across a dead body, but it turns out this stupid bastard was just taking a nap."

The prisoner didn't raise his eyes from the ground, his composure crestfallen.

"Horrible little shite hasn't said a word since we picked him up," Red added.

Krain looked at an angry purple swelling on Red's cheekbone. Noticing, Red shrugged his shoulders and said, "Aye, put up a fair fight though."

Krain looked at the prisoner and said, "I hope you're in more of a talkative mood now, I want to know what happened here last night."

The prisoner raised his head, for the first time since his arrival, and looked Krain in the eye. His gaze was a look of loathing.

"Go fuck yourself," he hissed, saliva flying from the sides of his mouth like a rabid dog.

Krain looked disgusted and unimpressed.

"Now really, that's no way to speak in front of a lady."

On cue, Kitty cuffed her hand hard against the back of the man's head, echoing her thoughts of disapproval. As a rule Krain didn't care for bad language much, he was old school like that. He tolerated it from Red, but that was only because half the time he couldn't understand what the Glaswegian was talking about anyway, and when he did understand him, the cussing seemed like second nature.

The prisoner grunted in frustration and jerked his head away from Kitty.

"Bring him to the Affliction Suite," Krain said, motioning with his hand for them all to follow. "We'll get some answers out of him there."

The prisoner's body tensed and he dug his heels into the floor. His bare feet squeaked as he was dragged forward, and he groaned in protest. All the while a smile played about Kitty's black glossy lips.

The Affliction Suite, as Krain called it, was in the lower depths of the prison, at the opposite end of the building to the underground detention cells. Rarely used, these days, it was merely a safeguarding implement for times like this. Krain wasn't keen on the brashness of the term torture chamber, and he'd named it otherwise so it had a more professional ring to it.

Inside, the Affliction Suite was relatively small with just enough room to fit all five of them in comfortably. In the centre of the room stood a chair that wouldn't have looked out of place in a dental surgery, and positioned near the back wall was a heavy metal iron-man (a device similar to an iron-maiden, but without the spikes inside). The fluorescent strip-lighting was harsh, and as Red closed the iron door behind him, shutting them all inside, the prisoner suddenly looked like a rabbit caught in the headlights.

"Get him in the chair," Krain ordered.

The prisoner resisted, but Red and Kitty heaved him over to the chair and shoved him down hard. They then set to work strapping down his wrists and ankles. Kitty leaned over and undid the buttons on his prison jumpsuit, wearing a look of sheer disgust on her face as though she were cleaning dog muck off the bottom of her six inch stilettos. In turn, the prisoner snarled, his anger evident and his pride wounded. Once the buttons were undone to waist level, Kitty ripped open the red fabric to expose his naked spindly torso.

On the few occasions when the Affliction Suite had been put into use in recent times, it was Kitty who had enjoyed administering the devices. She'd taken up role as chief torturer without even having been asked. This was fine by Krain though. It was good to see an employee so assertive, proactive and passionate about their job.

Clutching the two clamps which dangled from the back of the chair, Kitty brought them round to the front. With obvious delight, she then clamped them firmly onto the prisoner's nipples. Sweat had formed a light sheen on his forehead and was glistening wet along his hairline. Kitty relished every moment, and when she took hold of the device's handset from under the chair arm, she waved it in front of his nose, goading and teasing. Her cocoa bean eyes conveyed pure indulgence and something of wickedness.

Satisfied that everything was set to go, Krain crouched down so that he was at eye level with the prisoner and asked,

"So, are you going to tell me what happened last night? Of course, you'll have already figured out that it will be in your best interests to do so. I'll give you one chance before Kitty switches this thing on."

Pointing casually to the prisoner's chest he leaned in and added, "By the way, do you have *any* idea how sensitive a person's nipples really are?"

The prisoner simply shook his head in defiance and hissed, "Pretty pointless all the same. A bit like you really."

Flatbrook took the opportunity to glance in Kitty's direction and murmured to himself, "That depends on who they belong to."

Luckily for him Kitty was too preoccupied to care.

Krain sighed, a long-suffering sigh. He'd expect no less from Flatbrook. With a simple nod of his head, he signalled for Kitty to commence with electric shock treatment, thinking they should have rigged an extra clamp to a certain part of Flatbrook's anatomy. The vulgar little man would get his comeuppance one of these days, it was only a matter of time before Kitty snapped and kicked his arse all the way to kingdom come – and Krain wouldn't stand in her way, it was the better alternative to ploughing through a pile of Sexual Harassment in the Workplace forms.

Turning a small dial on the handset, Kitty proceeded to press the red power button. The prisoner immediately cried out in pain, sending strings of spittle flying from between his clenched teeth.

"Are you ready to talk *yet*?" Krain asked. "You know, the voltage goes quite high on this thing and Kitty isn't squeamish. In fact, she quite likes the smell of cooking flesh."

The prisoner tried to look stern, but his eyes expressed an element of pleading which ruined the effect. He simply shook his head.

"Have it your way." Krain nodded to Kitty once again.

The prisoner writhed in agony as Kitty went through the motions of increasing the voltage three more times – and each time he still refused to speak. Eventually Krain looked more bored than frustrated.

"Loyal to your rescuer, hmmm? I can't help but wonder though," Krain said, with a malicious smile, "whether you'll still be so loyal when I put you in the iron-man."

The prisoner's eyes grew wide and he shook his head wildly. "I don't know anything."

"Well, we'll see. Red, Kitty, prepare the iron-man and untie him from the chair."

With the threat seemingly too much to bear the prisoner suddenly yelled, "Okay, okay, I'll tell you what I *do* know."

"Finally, we're getting somewhere." Krain hunkered down again "So tell me, who *was* your saviour?"

"I don't know," replied the prisoner warily.

Krain looked dubious, "Don't play games. How many of them were there? And what did they look like?"

"There was just one of them," the prisoner answered, then glaring up at Flatbrook, he added, "He's one of your lot."

Flatbrook gasped, "Peace & Order Maintenance?"

"Yeah."

The prisoner was grinning now, pleased to see the look of horror on Flatbrook's face. He'd well and truly set the cat among the pigeons.

"So, how else did he look exactly? Remembering, of course, that if you're lying to me about any of this I *will* kill you. And if I have to take matters into my own hands," Krain said looking down at his white-gloved hands, "I will kill you for that also."

"I dunno. He was sort of tall, maybe."

"Well that really whittles it down, doesn't it?" Krain sighed, "Don't try my patience, you imbecilic scoundrel, that could be just about anyone in the department." Looking round at Flatbrook, all five feet of him, he quickly added, "Well *almost* anyone."

With his patience pushed to the limit, Krain puffed out his cheeks and said, "You're toying with me, aren't you?"

Gripping the nipple clamps between his fingers, he squeezed down hard until tears appeared in the prisoner's eyes.

"Alright, alright. He was *really* tall," cried the prisoner, "With a shaved head."

"Now, that wasn't so hard was it?"

Krain stood up straight and, in thoughtful gesticulation, stroked his beard. A twinkle of recognition sparked in his eyes.

"Sir, that's hardly helpful," Flatbrook snorted. "Half the team would still fit that description."

"No Flatbrook, it was most helpful. In fact, I believe I know who the perpetrator was." Nodding his head, Krain was cocksure of his presumption. He balled his right fist and pounded it into his left palm. "It's confirmed *one* of my notions."

Leaning down, he set his face within inches of the prisoner and asked, "Did he wear sunglasses, this man? And did he have a large tattoo on the side of his head?"

Poker faced, the prisoner answered, "I can't remember."

In a swift, but violent movement, Krain pinched the clamps again, twisting them round until blood seeped down the man's belly and pooled into his navel. Flatbrook turned away not wanting to see if the man's nipples had come away with the clamps, he hadn't had time for breakfast as yet and his stomach was decidedly queasy.

In an eye-opening scream of agony, every single muscle in the prisoner's body tensed and he squealed, "*Yes! Yes!*"

Releasing his grip on the clamps, Krain was dismayed to see the fabric of his gloves now blotched burgundy.

"You've been most helpful," he said, smelling his fingers before wiping them on the prisoner's overall legs. "Thank you."

Standing up, he turned to Red and Kitty and said, "Put him in the iron-man."

The prisoner's head snapped up, his face a mixture of disbelief and horror.

"No, you can't! I told you what you wanted to know, didn't I?"

"You did indeed tell me everything I needed to know, but it was rather like getting blood from a stone," Krain replied. "And as much as I admire your sense of loyalty, I can't imagine for one minute why on earth you would feel a duty to protect the person in question. But that is by-the-by. The main reason I'm killing you is because I don't like liars."

The prisoner looked outraged.

"This wasn't about loyalty. It was about me not wanting to cooperate, nothing more and nothing less than that. I owe *him* nothing, and I owe *you* nothing," he spat, his face hardening. "But when all's said and done I told you the *truth*, didn't I?"

As Red and Kitty prepared the iron-man, Krain answered, "On the contrary, you knew very well the name of the person you sought to shield from me, but you insisted on beating around the bush. His name is Grim, and you damn well knew that already – since he was the one who put you *here* in the first place!"

Turning and walking from the room Krain then added, "And let's face it, I was always going to kill you anyway, you ridiculous fool."

Chapter 6

Brushing the sand from his clothes, Grim finally stood up. He'd been looking at the boards of the pier above him since the little boy had left, making patterns and faces in the wood grain. The sun had heated the front of his black uniform so it was burning hot. His back, on the other hand, was damp from lying in the tide-sodden sand, and his shirt clung to his skin. He had far greater concerns though; concerns that didn't afford him the luxury of worrying about whether he was comfortable or not. The prison saga, a failed suicide attempt and his new escape plan all occupied the front of his mind, his soggy clothing taking a definite backseat.

To make matters worse, he was standing like a scolded puppy with his tail between his legs underneath the pier of all places – this certainly didn't help matters. He cursed himself for having not fled Sunray Bay while he'd had a good head start, but the overwhelming feeling of despair he'd felt when he'd left the prison earlier was still raw and chewing on his nerve endings. And he knew the attempted suicide had been worth a shot.

Grim had had a constant anguish in his heart and gut ever since he arrived in Sunray Bay. It was an internal pain that gnawed at his insides like a malignant tumour, every so often escalating to an excruciating level. Usually when the emotional pain peaked he'd hide himself away for a day or two until it settled back down to a nauseating tooth-achey kind of throb, but today it was worse than ever, to the extent where he'd tried to relieve his emotional burdens completely. He couldn't stand it anymore. Life was a living hell.

Christ, I can't even get that right, he thought, looking out to sea. He'd often wondered what lay beyond the crisp horizon of Sunray Bay, though he surmised it was something

49

he would never know. Even the sea didn't want him, it had spat him right back out onto the beach.

He could feel the pull of the walkie talkie hanging from the belt loop of his Peace & Order Maintenance uniform. It felt heavy and damp, and he suspected it probably wasn't working. Not that he needed to use it. That would be ridiculous. It wasn't as though he was going to radio Krain and ask him how his day was going. On second thoughts, he'd actually love to do that. Hearing Krain's distraught voice would be like music to his ears. Maybe he *would* call Krain later, when he'd got himself far out of town. Although there was a distinct possibility that Krain might not be alive by then, of course, but that would be sweet all the same.

Retribution, that's what it was all about.

Thanks to Krain, Grim's life was mapped out before him again with not even so much as a glimmer of light at the end of the tunnel. He felt isolated and alone. Nobody else could possibly know what it felt like. He was a complete outsider, and as such he was going to get the hell out of Sunray Bay. There was nothing there for him, there never had been. The most Sunray Bay had ever offered him was trouble. And, of course, forever-ness.

Before he scarpered, he needed to see Gloria one last time. Lovely, sweet Gloria. She'd been the only person in Sunray Bay to whom he'd felt an inkling of friendship, or whatever it was their encounters would be deemed. He would tell her everything, it was only right, and if she decided to snub him then he wouldn't blame her. If she could possibly find it in her heart to understand his predicament, and provided that she didn't rip his throat out, he hoped she might even let him stay at her place until dusk. He'd have more chance of making it to the borders of Sunray Bay without being caught once it was dark.

He planned to venture to The Grey Dustbowl; a large desert made up of a grey gritty substance. It reminded Grim of the contents of an ashtray. He knew the air would aggravate his respiratory system, irritate his eyes and skin, and make him sneeze – but he certainly wasn't going there for comfort. Besides, he'd suffered worse.

Stretching on for miles and miles, nobody knew exactly how far The Grey Dustbowl went, since nobody had ever endured it. Or at least, no survivors had ever come back to tell the tale. Heat exposure, thirst, loneliness, and who knows what else – it was a recipe for insanity. Grim was willing to brave it. If anybody could reach the other side it would be him. And if it drove him crazy in the process, well that might be no bad thing.

Looking up the crowded beach toward the promenade, he realised he was going to be exposed and in full view. There was a huge possibility that he'd be swarmed by armed Peace & Order Maintenance Officers as soon as he stepped from under the pier. But it was an unavoidable risk, and he needed to get moving.

Wiping the lenses of his sunglasses on the front of his shirt, he put them back on and moved off up the beach toward the promenade wearing a new bold look of determination on his face.

Chapter 7

Sunray Bay, huh? Libby thought, *So much for the pearly white gates. And where's St. Peter with his accompaniment of angels?*

In fairness, given the absurdity of that day, she wouldn't be too surprised to learn St. Peter manned the ferris wheel at the end of the pier, a bored look on his face disguised by a long billowing beard. Or perhaps he was heartthrob Pete, who brandished tattoos on his forearms and spun waltzer carts filled with screaming teenage girls. With a cigarette dangling precariously from the corner of his mouth Libby imagined he'd glide effortlessly around the uneven flooring and, whichever cart he stopped to spin, the admiring girls inside would shout *faster, faster*. Libby smiled at the idea. So far she liked what she saw in Sunray Bay, and it seemed that Rufus did too. He was already digging a hole in the sand nearby – much to the annoyance of a woman who was lying sunbathing on a beach mat a couple of feet away from him. Sand flicked up in all directions, showering down much too close to her oiled skin for comfort, and so Libby urged him further down the beach before he got them both into trouble.

They weaved around deckchairs and windbreakers, drawn to the sea with its playful waves that licked the beach like countless preening salty tongues.

"So, what did you make of that message?" Rufus suddenly asked.

"What message?" Libby replied, carefully stepping around someone's picnic basket.

"The one on the welcome sign."

"Oh the *'don't be afraid, be very afraid'* one? I didn't reckon much to it at all to be honest. You get graffiti everywhere you go these days, and I've seen a damn sight worse than that written on bus stops and in toilet cubicles, I can tell you."

Rufus nodded his head, he supposed she was right.

"So what's the plan? Do we have one?" he asked, his tail subconsciously wagging as he watched two gulls dip and soar overhead.

"I dunno, let's just have a walk about eh? Maybe get an ice-cream?"

Rufus licked his lips. "Oh Miss Hood, I thought you'd never ask."

On the promenade they'd noticed numerous stalls selling all the old favourite seaside snacks and confectionaries. The sugary aroma of fresh doughnuts and candy floss mixed with the mouth-watering smell of fish and chips. It wafted down the beach and played about Libby's nostrils. Her stomach groaned with the promise, and Rufus's saliva glands were going into overdrive. As much as Libby was loving the idea of greasy fish-shop chips with a splash of vinegar, since she hadn't eaten all morning, an ice-cream seemed far more appealing in the implacable heat. In fact, a cold dollop or two presented in a waffle cone with a flake of chocolate sticking out the top would be even better than a cup of tea. She only hoped raspberry ripple would be up there on the menu; her favourite in life and in death. As though reading her mind, Rufus smacked his lips with his long parched tongue and said, "Mmm, triple chocolate for me."

Libby had never allowed Rufus chocolate before, apart from the time he'd gobbled a whole box of chocolate Brazils from under the Christmas tree. She'd blamed Alex all day for snaffling them, until she'd taken Rufus out for walkies later that evening – then it was fairly evident who'd *really* eaten them. She'd heard chocolate was harmful to dogs, toxic or something like that, but she couldn't see any harm now that he was dead. In fact, he could knock himself out and have two if he wanted.

"Let's go and have a quick plodge in the sea, then we'll head back up to the promenade for ice-creams," she suggested.

She removed her pumps and sighed with relief. The sand squelched between her toes and felt wonderful. It was surprisingly cool and soothing on her clammy feet.

Nobody round about made a fuss over Rufus, so Libby presumed either dogs were allowed on the beach or else nobody cared enough to mention that they weren't. When they arrived at a clear section of the shore, Rufus chased the waves and Libby stood letting them lap gently over her feet. She purred quietly in pure bliss, and was again taken back to memories of family holidays as a child; building sandcastles with Izzy; investigating rock pools and flying kites with her dad; and her mother hiding beneath parasols, guarding their picnic and her pale skin from the sun. Libby was like a carbon copy of her mother, tall, slim and redheaded, whereas Izzy was like their dad – short and thickset with dark curly hair. She realised that she was going to miss her family an awful lot. On the flipside she didn't dare think about what they must be feeling right now, if this was all *really* real – and if it was, she wondered if there was any way of letting them know that she was okay.

Rufus came splashing back to where she stood and shook his wet body next to her. Water sprayed up her legs.

"Hey what's up, Dolly Daydream?" he asked, noticing the fretful look on her face.

"Oh nothing," she replied, shaking her head dismissively, not wanting to get too depressed and wrapped up in morbid thoughts. "Come on, let's go and get those ice-creams." She beckoned for Rufus to follow her. "We'll find a nice shaded spot to eat them."

"Good, it's about time," Rufus panted. "Have you ever heard of canine combustion?"

Libby rolled her eyes and was just about to laugh at him when her heart stood still. Up ahead plodded a slow trail of donkeys, and she was certain she recognised a white and grey one with *Polly* embroidered on its pink harness. It looked like one of the donkeys owned by the strange donkey-man they'd seen earlier. Surveying the area Libby couldn't see him anywhere though, thankfully. She sighed with relief. Not that there were laws against hanging around looking creepy, of course (Christ, half the population would be committing an offence if that were the case), but there was just something indescribably weird about him. Shrugging, she scolded herself for being such a paranoid big girl's blouse. So what if he was around? She'd send him packing if he approached.

Arriving at the promenade once again, Libby brushed down the soles of her feet and pushed them back into her pumps. She and Rufus then moved toward the nearest ice-cream stall and looked longingly at the blue menu with its list of refreshing temptations, each and every one of them tantalising their dry mouths.

"Oh they don't have raspberry ripple," Libby sighed with slight disappointment.

"But they *do* have Mr Whippy," Rufus replied. "Get one of those and ask for monkey's blood on top. It's a bloody good compromise."

"Yeah I suppose so." She nodded. "How about you? You still going with chocolate?"

Before Rufus answered, four people (three men and one woman) stopped right behind them and began a slanging match.

"I can't believe you went and got us all killed," the tallest of them yelled at another member of the group who was wearing an orange shirt. "I'm gonna rip your bloody head off."

The man in the orange shirt bristled and shouted back, "Yeah well, you weren't complaining when I offered you both a lift."

"Well we didn't realise you'd had more booze than the rest of us put together, you bleeding idiot," the tall man cried, as he swung out with his fist.

Quickly moving forward to prevent the tall man from punching the man in orange, presumably her partner, the woman in the group inadvertently ended up taking the full force of the blow to her own face. She immediately crumpled and fell to the floor. Blood poured freely from her nose and it gushed from a nick in her top lip. She lay stunned on the floor for a while, and Libby was surprised there weren't any cartoon stars dancing around her head.

A group of people who'd been watching nearby barged their way over, shoving and shouting. Libby couldn't decide whether they were genuinely horrified at the prospect of a woman having had her lip and nose bust by a man, or whether they just fancied a piece of the action. She knew for some people it's any old excuse for a brawl – and it looked like this was shaping up to be a battle royale. Even the owner of the ice-cream stall swung his shutters closed. Rufus backed up when someone almost stepped on his paws, and Libby tried to shuffle backwards as the rowdy group encircled her as though she was invisible.

Great, I'm going to end up with a bloody nose at this rate, she thought. No sooner had the thought crossed her mind than someone shoved into her fiercely and grabbed her bag. Clutching at the strap tightly she held it to her body and spun round just in time to see a man running away from her, barging his way back into the steadily growing crowd that had congregated around the fight. His limp dirty-blonde hair splayed down onto the back of his grey sleeveless top, and Libby recognised him immediately as Donkey-man. Her heart thumped faster with adrenalin, and she opened up her bag to peer inside.

"Hey, you arsehole! Get back here," she screamed, shaking her fist after him. "You've stolen my purse!"

Furious, she barged her way out from amongst the jumble of arms, legs, fists and blood, and stood on her tiptoes to see if she could see where he'd run off to. It was no use, she couldn't see him anywhere. In fact she couldn't see much past the solid wall of on-lookers. For all she knew, he could be long gone or he could be standing right under her nose. It was hopeless.

"Well that's just effing great," Libby said to Rufus throwing her arms up in the air. "No ice-cream for us now."

Rufus dipped his head and folded his ears back in disappointment. Libby pursed her lips in frustration.

"The way he was eyeing us up earlier, I bloody well knew there was something up with him."

"Well I hate to keep harping on like this, but what now?" Rufus asked.

Libby pulled her hair up with one of her hands and fanned it up and down in an attempt to cool her neck.

"Let's move away from these morons for starters," she said, looking daggers at the group of people who'd started the whole kerfuffle to begin with. If it wasn't for them she'd probably still have her purse. If the man in the orange shirt was still unscathed, she had a good mind to go and rip his bloody head off herself. She elbowed her way over to the promenade wall and sat down on its hot surface with a harrumph. They were in dire need of a plan now they had no money, food or drink.

Rufus jumped up onto the wall and nuzzled underneath her arm. She played with the fur on his neck for a short while, then sat up straight suddenly and said, "Hey, look over there. That man coming up the beach, do you reckon he's one of those Peace & Order Maintenance people?"

Rufus bobbed his head about, failing to see who Libby was actually referring to amongst the crowds of other people around. She pointed to a man walking towards them who was wearing a black uniform with the letters POM unmistakably emblazoned above the chest pocket of his shirt. Libby wasn't sure how Rufus could have missed him, he was certainly tall enough. He wore a pair of wrap-around shades, his head was completely shaven and he had a day's worth of designer stubble on his square jaw. He wasn't Johnny Depp and he wasn't wearing Speedos, but Libby thought he was definitely a fine alternative. She'd already jumped back onto her feet.

"*What are you doing, you maniac?*" Rufus asked. "He doesn't look like he's going to shoot us with shit right now, but if you go wandering over there you might provoke him to."

"Calm down and stop getting your knickers in a twist," Libby said, already starting to move off. "If he's Peace &

Order Maintenance, then I'm reporting my stolen purse. He's probably coming to sort this fight out anyway, so I want to nab him first before he gets too busy."

Rufus shook his head in astonishment as he watched her walk away, smoothing down her hair and brushing dog hairs off her t-shirt as she went.

"Report your stolen purse my arse," he grumbled.

Libby walked right up to the uniformed man and stopped in front of him. She fluttered her eyelashes and smiled, expecting him to stop. But he didn't. He stepped right past her and carried on walking. Clicking her tongue, Libby turned and went after him.

"Excuse me," she said loudly, in case he didn't hear her. It was bad enough that he hadn't seen her, but to be snubbed twice would just be downright embarrassing.

He turned his head, but still carried on walking.

"What do you want?"

Libby rushed on and caught up with him, hand signalling for Rufus to join them.

"I've just been mugged," she said, somewhat out of breath. "Some man ran off with my purse."

"Well that's just shit luck, isn't it?" he replied, his voice uncaring, and rather like sandpaper against pebble-dash.

Libby's mouth dropped open in disbelief.

"Is that all you have to say on the matter? Aren't you meant to do something about it?"

"Look, I'm not on duty, I can't help you."

Libby looked him up and down as she trotted to keep up with his fast pace, Rufus padded along behind with his tongue dangling to the side. She noticed that the man's black uniform had the number twenty-three embroidered on the shoulder panel and that he had a walkie talkie hanging from his belt loop.

"Well it looks like you're on duty to me," she replied, indignantly.

He stopped momentarily and turned his head, giving Libby an unyielding look.

"Leave me alone," he growled.

"Come on, I'm having a bit of a rough day here," Libby pleaded, turning on her smile again. It had never failed her in the past. "Help me out, please."

"*You're* having a rough day?" he snapped. "You have *no* idea."

"So you won't help me?" Libby's smile was now a scowl. She was vexed by his big-headed rudeness.

"No." He turned and started walking again. Then as an afterthought, and without even turning to look at her, which pissed her off even more, he added, "Get used to it. Shit happens a lot round here."

Libby stood still with her hands on her hips and her nostrils flared, and she watched as his tall frame disappeared into the crowd.

"What an arrogant arsehole," she said.

Chapter 8

Grim had half expected the pretty redhead to follow him; she'd seemed like the persistent type. Thank God she hadn't though. The last thing he needed right now was someone hanging around, slowing him down. He supposed that was the thing about being in Peace & Order Maintenance, some people had the false preconception that you actually gave a shit. He had a good mind to burn the damn uniform when he got to Gloria's – providing, of course, she supplied him with spare clothes.

He now knew he'd been unwise in accepting the job with Peace & Order Maintenance in the first place; hindsight the useless perception that now taunted his credibility. He'd never fitted in, like a zebra with spots instead of stripes, because he just wasn't the same as his colleagues. The only unity they shared was that they hated him as much as he hated them. Of course, if it hadn't been for Krain's deal he never would have joined the team. In retrospect, Grim could see he'd been on a fool's errand anyway. He was loath to admit that he'd been naive in his desperation. And naivety wasn't something that could be afforded in Sunray Bay. It would get you into trouble. When Krain hadn't held true to his part of the deal, Grim had confronted that trouble square on. It was a dangerous game he was playing, but he'd been too angry to feel scared and too frustrated to be cautious, and so he'd released all of the prisoners back into the streets – the very prisoners he himself had captured. His actions would probably signify the end of Sunray Bay as he knew it, and it was almost tempting to stay behind and watch the trouble unfold, but what would be the point? He'd certainly earned himself no favours, and was quite possibly one of the most hated men in Sunray Bay. Even Gloria might despise him once he told her about everything that had been going on behind the scenes. But she deserved to know the truth. She was a good woman.

He remembered the first time they'd met. He'd been in a bad way and she'd literally come along and scraped him up off the floor. She'd been persistent, just like the redhead. Muscling her way into his life, making it her business to make sure he was taking care of himself and urging him to open up and tell her things. There were still many things that she *didn't* know, he'd never open up to anyone that completely, but she knew more about him than anybody else in Sunray Bay. That is, she knew more than just the rumours – the rumours which he'd never admitted to being true, though neither had he dismissed them as being bullshit. Gloria had always tried to make him feel better; she said that everyone deserved a second chance. It never made him feel better, but he appreciated the sentiment. Today he'd put her notion to the test – would *she* give him a second chance?

A slight vibration at his hip stirred his thoughts, and he heard a faint crackling. Unclipping the walkie talkie from his belt he raised it to his ear and stood still. Static white noise fuzzed and as he twiddled with the volume button, he strained to hear anything coherent above the chattering din of the beach-goers all around him.

Krsh krsh krsh blockade krsh krsh border krsh krsh krsh immediately krsh that's krsh krsh officer twenty-three...

And that was all Grim needed to hear.

"Shit," he muttered, fixing the walkie talkie back onto his belt loop and looking around, preparing himself for a confrontation with one of his fellow employees at any moment. *So*, he thought, *Krain's worked it out*. He was hardly surprised – but then, he'd dared to hope for longer.

He considered stripping off his shirt to be less obvious in case he was spotted by one of his preying colleagues, but realised he'd probably draw a lot more attention that way. A strapping six foot five, Grim was not easy to miss and would stand out like a fox in a chicken coop. He *had* to make it to Gloria's, she was his only chance. Not only that, but she was

Sunray Bay's hope of a revolution once he told her Krain's secrets.

Heading away from the promenade, Grim kept his head low and walked towards the row of restaurants and guesthouses that graced the very front of the seaside town. All of them looked the same, but with differing names and colours, all offering the same things and all of them competing with each other. Signs outside offered the lowest unbeatable prices, even though they'd already been trumped a few doors along. Luckily for the vendors, the beach was always teeming with people so competition was never too fierce – there was always enough business to go around.

Grim set his sights on an alleyway leading down the side of Ye Olde Seafarer Guesthouse and decided he'd get away from the hubbub of the seafront that way, working his way to Gloria's place through the backstreets. He knew all of them well enough; he'd lived on them plenty in the past. And he'd know where to hide if need be.

He estimated there would probably be around twenty Peace & Order Maintenance Officers on duty that morning – not including Krain's two personal assistants, Red and Kitty. Currently they'd all be ransacking Sunray Bay looking for him, and Grim didn't doubt that Krain would probably pull in extra hands if the search wasn't fruitful in the first hour or so. Time was ticking like a faulty bomb, and he knew things could blow up in his face at any minute.

It wasn't that Grim was scared of confrontation (any man capable of doing what he'd done in the past didn't have much time for fear), and given half the chance, he'd take on the entire Peace & Order Maintenance team all at once and gladly fight to the death. Alas, it wasn't that simple. If Krain managed to get an advantage, Grim wasn't sure what horrors would pan out for him. And it wasn't strictly Krain that Grim was wary of either (although he was bad enough), his wife Morgan was even worse. It made him uneasy to think of what she would do to him if he wound up in her clutches. Shuddering, he had a pretty good idea...

Morgan had a reputation for being a man-eater. There'd been a scandal a couple of years back, when a number of missing members of the community (all men), had been discovered within the realms of the lighthouse. The discovery was made when Krain himself had confronted her on the whereabouts of the electrician who had come to sort out some loose wiring and had never left the premises again. Subsequently, Krain had found a handful of men within the confines of his own home. They were all in varying states of hypnosis and were being used as what could only be described as sex slaves. Krain had tried his best to keep it all under wraps, but news had leaked out somehow, and the whole of Sunray Bay had lapped up the headlines. Apart from a tidal wave that had annihilated the north pier, it had been the biggest news story of that year – which was hardly surprising really, given that it had all been going on right under his nose. What *was* surprising, however, was that Krain had stuck by his wife. They'd attended numerous marriage counselling sessions and eventually the whole incident had been swept into a pile and kicked underneath their thick Persian carpet, so to speak. Grim thought it was only a matter of time before all the dirt started to get trodden back out.

With the thought of Morgan wanting to jump his bones, Grim quickened his pace. He'd rather take his chances with The Grey Dustbowl than allow his body to be used like an activity centre by the mayor's wife whilst his zombified brain did as it was told – even if she *was* sexy as hell.

Chapter 9

"You can put your tongue away now," Rufus said, looking up at Libby.

"What's that supposed to mean?" Libby averted her eyes from the section of crowd that the Peace & Order Maintenance Officer had disappeared into so she could look down at him.

Rufus shook his head distastefully. "You were pretty much slobbering all over him, you weak-willed wretch."

"No I wasn't." Her forehead creased in the middle. "I was just asking for help."

"Yeah whatever, you could have fooled me," Rufus said, rolling his eyes. "So what do we do now?"

Libby glowered at him.

"Look, if you ask me that *one more time,* mister, you'll get a foot up your arse."

Libby was feeling tetchy. She was hungry, thirsty, hot, sticky, and moneyless. And what's more she'd just been rudely shrugged off by a rather dishy, albeit obnoxious, bloke in uniform. *Could things get any worse*? she wondered.

She knew Rufus was right, though. They needed a plan. There was a severe lack of welcoming facilities in Sunray Bay; the dead were just left to wander clueless. An arrival kiosk would have proved handy, even leaflets in the beach huts would have been better than nothing. On first impression everything seemed so badly organised, and Libby was already planning a complaint – whenever she found out *who* she should be complaining to.

Scouring the long line of townhouse-style guesthouses and restaurants up ahead, Libby supposed the best idea would be to head in that general direction, towards town – whatever and wherever that may be. The tall buildings were casting lengthy shadows that beckoned to her. She thought if they headed that way they could at least hide from the sun for a while. Her eyes wandered along the line of garish vinyl overhangs and brightly coloured signs that were plastered all over the eateries and B&Bs. With menus on walls and vacancy signs in windows, the variety of contrasting colours and typefaces made the whole scene look like a mish-mash of newspaper and magazine clippings. Sunray Bay was loud and hectic, both visually and audibly.

Jutting out on the very end of the row, Libby noticed a building that didn't look like it belonged with the others. It was a lot shorter and newer in build and so its bricks weren't yet weathered by the sea air. Its white sign outside displayed a simple italic *I*.

"That's where we're going," she said, marching off and suddenly sounding more assertive. She pointed to the mismatched building. "Surely it has to be an Information Centre."

When they arrived outside the orange brick building, Libby could feel blisters forming where her swollen feet had been squeezing against the rough edges of the heels of her pumps, each step was a pinching agony, and Rufus had slowed to a snail's pace, his paw pads dry and cracked from the heat of the pavement.

"I'm not cut out for this," he complained.

"Oh stop whinging, Rufus."

"I'm getting on, you know. It's alright for you, young whippersnapper."

Libby stood outside the Information Centre's door to let him catch his breath. She leant against the brickwork while she wiggled her feet in the air; first her right one and then her left. It felt good to take the pressure off for a short while. As she balanced on one foot, she turned her attention to a cork notice board on the wall near her hand. One poster in particular caught her interest. Inside a scarlet border was a picture of a juicy-looking burger with text next to it stating, *Black Dog Burger Co. – Baying For Your Blood.*

"Ugh," Libby's nose wrinkled in disgust. "What on earth's one of those? It sounds horrible."

"*Black Dog* Burger?" Rufus whimpered, his eyebrows raised. He liked the sound of it even less than she did.

Seeing small print at the bottom of the poster, Libby read aloud, "Made from only the best ingredients of fine black pudding. Rich in iron and protein, these puppies will be sure to put hairs on your chest. Available in white or wholemeal bap with salad garnish and a choice of relish – please note, cheese can be added at an additional charge."

"Actually," Rufus said, looking thoughtful, "that sounds bloody lovely." Libby disagreed, she couldn't think of anything worse.

Pushing at the double glass doors to the Information Centre, she urged Rufus forward and they both stepped inside. They sighed in harmony as a waft of chilled air breezed down from the vent above their heads, welcoming them in. Enjoying the coldness too much to proceed any further, they stood still for a moment on the doormat and looked about them.

Libby had been correct in her assumptions, it was indeed an Information Centre. It was bright and airy with rows upon rows of leaflets, maps and guides – all of which were marked with white price stickers. Libby even noticed there was a rack of picture postcards too.

"Who the hell do you send those to?" she asked, moving over to pick one up. A donkey wearing a sombrero looked back at her with a speech bubble caption that read, *Wish you were here!*

"Your enemies if that one is anything to go by," Rufus snickered. "It's a rather polite way of saying *I wish you were dead.*"

Libby chuckled along with him. A man in the next aisle, who was wearing a straw trilby, raised his head and looked at her disapprovingly. She shrugged her shoulders at him and put the postcard back on the rack. *Some people have no sense of humour*, she thought.

Rufus tittered loudly again, "Hey, look over here, Libby. You can buy Sunray Bay tea towels and mugs too."

She grinned, but didn't laugh this time – she was conscious of an old couple nearby perusing a shelf of Sunray Bay fridge magnets, and didn't want to attract any more looks of disdain.

To the rear of the shop she saw a woman standing behind a tall counter. The woman wore a navy suit jacket over a plain white blouse, and she looked like she'd rather be anywhere but there. She offered Libby neither a welcome nor a smile; her customer service was obviously as bland as her uniform. In fact, she looked so unapproachable, Libby reckoned if she asked for help she'd probably get a middle-fingered salute in return.

"I wonder if Sunray Bay has *any* nice people in it," Libby muttered to Rufus, as the door opened behind them. The bottom of the door brushed against the wiry doormat, making a long *swooshing* sound, and Libby looked round to see who had entered. Stunned and mortified just about summed up her reaction when she saw that it was Donkey-man. His greasy hair moved like large worms underneath the air conditioning vent, and his curled lip twitched. The dilated pupils of his bulging eyes locked onto her. Only a thin sliver of blue around the edges of his pupils gave evidence that his eyes weren't completely black. He looked as though he was high on something.

"Oh my God," Libby gasped.

Rufus snarled, and the hair on the back of his neck bristled. He wasn't an aggressive dog by nature, but he didn't want to run away now that danger had presented itself either. Appearing to be nervous at the display of Rufus's beared teeth, Donkey-man held both of his hands out infront, in a peaceful gesture. He looked from Libby to Rufus, then from Rufus back to Libby.

"Can I have a word?" he asked, taking a large gulp. The pointy Adam's apple in his throat bobbed in and then back out again. His voice seemed surprisingly deep for someone so thin, Libby thought, and she couldn't understand why he was acting more nervously than she was. She edged further back into the shop, using small shuffling movements, so as not to goad him into any kind of action. The last thing she wanted was a conversation with a drugged up handbag snatcher. She shook her head slowly at him.

"Look, I won't hurt you," he said, stepping from the doormat.

Libby's heart felt as though it had jumped up into her throat. *Fight or flight; which will it be?* she wondered. The way his eyes penetrated hers, she rather liked the idea of flight. Scanning the room for witnesses and escape routes, she noticed that the old couple who'd been looking at fridge magnets were now standing at the counter speaking to the miserable-looking shop assistant. All three of them distracted and unaware of the scene that was unravelling near the doorway. The man with the straw trilby was nowhere to be seen now; he must have slipped out when Libby and Rufus were looking at tea towels.

Libby quickly weighed up her options, and the best idea she could come up with was to ask the shop assistant to raise an alarm and get help – which didn't instil her with any kind of hope, because old misery guts looked like the most unhelpful person in the world. Nevertheless she carried on creeping backwards, keeping an eye on Donkey-man all the time in case he rushed at her.

"Look, I don't have anything else," she said, trying to keep her voice steady. "You already took my purse. That was all I had."

"Sorry about that," he replied, moving forward and closing the gap between them, which prompted more growls from Rufus. Putting his hand deep into the front pocket of his jeans, Libby dreaded to think what he was about to pull out. To her surprise he produced her purse and a spurious smile, as though he'd just performed magic. "Here, you can have it back."

Libby tensed up even more.

"If you don't want that then what the hell *do* you want?" she asked.

"Come with me," his poppy-out eyes were still affixed to hers, and he wagged his fingers trying to coax her to him. "You can have your money back, just come with me."

"No way," Libby said, shaking her head defiantly.

Flipping the purse over in his hand, so only Libby could see what he held underneath it, she yelped in shock. Nuzzled into the leather of the purse and the grip of his fingers was a pen knife.

Spurred into flight, Libby yelled, "Help!"

Finally, the old couple and the shop assistant all directed their attention to the unfolding drama.

"He's got a knife," Libby gushed, as she raced towards the counter. She was followed closely by Rufus, who scarpered with his tail between his legs. His bravery had ended when Libby's own nerve had dropped.

Donkey-man let Libby's purse fall to the floor and he stood with the pen knife held aloft. The shop assistant made a gasping noise as though her head was deflating, but an element of excitement gleamed in her eyes as though she'd been waiting for something interesting to happen all morning. Reaching beneath the counter she pulled out a cordless telephone and began tapping onto the keypad with her manicured fingernails.

"Stop! Don't do that," Donkey-man barked.

The shop assistant halted and eyed him suspiciously.

Thumbing a small badge on the breast of his shirt, Donkey-man's eyes narrowed and he communicated with her silently. The badge was a simple black circle with a white circle inside of that. Libby had no idea what it meant, but the shop assistant evidently knew, because her excited eyes sparked brighter with enlightenment.

"You don't want her sort roaming around here, do you?" Donkey-man asked her.

The shop assistant cast a sideways glance at Libby and shook her head.

"*My sort?*" Libby asked. Her face was a mask of disbelief, she wasn't sure why the shop assistant was looking so accusingly at her when there was a man in the shop who

69

was obviously off his tits on something whilst waving a knife around.

The shop assistant replaced the telephone back under the counter and nodded her head once at Donkey-man, as though she was giving him the go ahead to do whatever he'd intended in the first place. Meanwhile, the old couple were now cowering at the side of the counter obviously not able to decide which was worse – a knife-wielding crackhead or a talking dog and its owner of indiscernible *sort*.

Without wasting any more time, Libby bundled Rufus into her arms and barged straight through a door marked *staff only* at the back of the shop.

"Hey, you're not allowed back there," the shop assistant screamed, scrabbling from behind the counter.

Libby could hear Donkey-man already coming after her. He was yelling, "Hey come back! Come back here."

Her shoes screeched on the lino floor as she ran, and all the while her blisters screamed silently. She quickly surveyed her options, noting that off to the left was an open door revealing a toilet and to the right was a closed door. Ignoring both of these, she saw a fire exit at the end of the corridor which seemed to be the most promising option out of them all. As she hurtled towards it, she lost her footing and stumbled forward. Releasing Rufus from her grasp, they both flew through the air. He landed much further up the corridor, and she landed heavy on her left arm.

Yelping in pain, tears welled up in her eyes. Her arm pulsed and throbbed furiously. She didn't think she'd done any lasting damage because she could still move it, but she reckoned she'd end up with a whacking great bruise all the same. Pushing herself up to look behind, her whole body tensed when she saw Donkey-man launching himself into the air. Right on target to land on top of her, his face was a flurry of panic and he made a long *yeooowwww* noise, as though the sound would propel him faster. Flipping over, so that she lay on her back, Libby swiftly turned into a violent hell-cat. With her arms and legs thrashing, she clobbered him in the face and neck just as he crashed down onto her stomach.

"Stop fighting me," he snarled, bringing the pen knife up and nicking her arm with it. Libby wasn't sure whether it had been intentional or accidental. But either way, she poked him in the eye with her left thumb, and then as he reared up clutching his face, she brought up her foot and kicked him hard in the nether regions. Donkey-man yowled like a cat, and Libby scurried from under him like a crab on all fours until she was clear of him. They both picked themselves off the floor at the same time, Libby clutching her arm and Donkey-man cupping his crotch, and the chase began again. This time she was at an advantage, because the pain she'd caused between his legs had slowed him down considerably.

Rufus was already standing by the fire exit when Libby arrived, and he stood to one side as she shoved hard on the door's push bar with her hip. Heat exploded all around them as they burst out into a back street, and Libby almost knocked a boy off his bike as she bowled straight out into the middle of the road. Luckily there was no other traffic.

Risking a backwards glance, Libby saw Donkey-man emerge into the sunlight after them. He thrust his hands out and pushed the fire exit door in frustration, it cracked against the outside wall and bounced back inwards. His contorted face was an image of rage.

Dashing to the other side of the road, Libby and Rufus ran onwards down a cobbled alleyway that was nestled between a tattoo studio and a guesthouse. Her breathing was coming in short, painful rasps and she grasped at her side, cursing herself for being so unfit – she couldn't believe she had a stitch already. Her feet pummelled the uneven cobbles. Each impact stinging and shooting up her shins, and the slapping noise of her soles echoed around the alley. Her foot twisted awkwardly on the jagged edge of a cobble, and once again she fell to the ground with a clatter. This time her hands took the brunt of it.

She shrieked in pain, and hoped that somebody else was around to help her. She fully expeced Donkey-man's pen

71

knife to be driven into her back at any moment – but it didn't come. Instead she heard a familiar gravelly voice ask, "What the hell are you doing?"

Looking up she saw the face of the Peace & Order Maintenance Officer glaring down at her – and there was no sign of Donkey-man at all.

Libby was stunned into silence at first, but then she spat, "No thanks to you, the bloke who stole my purse came back to finish me off."

The Peace & Order Maintenance Officer shrugged his shoulders and then disappeared back round the corner he'd come from without another word.

How bloody rude, Libby thought, gritting her teeth. She picked herself up off the floor and dusted her grazed hands on her jeans. Looking at Rufus she asked, "Are you ok?"

"Suppose I'll live," he panted.

"Good." Libby nodded. Then swinging her handbag back over her shoulder, she marched round the corner to confront the Peace & Order Maintenance Officer. She was furious at how she was being treated in Sunray Bay, and since he'd been less than helpful she intended on giving him a piece of her mind.

"I'm going to report you..." she began mouthing off, but her words petered out when she saw him standing next to a silver car, looking through the driver side window with a brick in his hand.

"What the hell are *you* doing?" she asked.

"What does it look like?" he replied, coldly.

"It looks like you're about to vandalise someone's car. Or steal it."

"Well, there you go then..."

"Which part of peace and order don't you understand? I know you said you weren't on duty, but that's taking the piss a bit isn't it?"

He laughed, a dry, humourless laugh, and looked at her with contempt.

"Look, I'm not Peace & Order Maintenance okay. Just leave me alone."

"Well why are you wearing that uniform?"

Libby had no idea what a Peace & Order Maintenance uniform even looked like, but arguing with him at least meant that she wasn't being chased by Donkey-man anymore, and although he was a moody arsehole she at least felt safe around him – and, regardless of how irritating he was and how much it dismayed her, she realised again how undeniably sexy he was. She took the opportunity to look him up and down once more.

He lowered the brick to his side, and one of his eyebrows protruded from the top of his sunglasses.

"Look, I *was* Peace & Order Maintenance, but I'm not anymore. Is that alright with you? *Now* will you just go away?"

"Have you been fired or something?" Libby asked, stepping closer to him; close enough to see pumped up veins snaking down his forearms to the backs of his hands. He was acting too erratically for someone who had just knocked off shift. "That would explain your shitty mood."

Irritation marred his face, and he answered, "No. Not even close. Now if you please, I'm in a bit of a fucking hurry here."

Libby's eyes widened as he lifted his arm in the air and brought the brick crashing down to the car. Glass from the window imploded all over the driver's seat, and reaching his hand into the car, he pulled up the button to release the lock and flung the door open. He swiped tiny shards of glass from the seat and sat down in front of the steering wheel.

"What the hell kind of a car is this anyway?" she asked. She'd never seen one like it before. It was all angular and retro looking, with a sleek rectangle affixed to the top.

"A solar powered one," he grunted unenthusiastically.

Libby stepped closer and watched with interest as he set about fiddling with the front panel, to the side of the steering wheel.

"I take it you are trying to steal it then?" she asked.

"Look woman, just go away will you."

Libby was intrigued for reasons she couldn't fathom, and she wasn't about to go away just yet. Like greenfly attracted to yellow, there was something about him that was exciting and fascinating, and not just because he looked hot either, there was something underlying that made her want to know who he was and why he was being so difficult. She wanted to scratch the surface to see what it was. Bending down to peer into the car window she said, "Looks to me like you're having trouble. Do you even know what you're doing?"

"What, and I suppose you do?" he snapped.

She stood up and crossed her arms over her chest.

"Well no – but maybe I could help."

She could see that he was trying to remove tiny pins from the front panel, his large fingers too bulky for the intricate job and his fingernails too short. He huffed and didn't even bother looking up.

"There's an immobiliser switch behind this panel..."

"Well shove over, let me see if I can get at it," she said, signalling for him to move over into the passenger seat.

He looked up at her, bemusement clouding his face.

"You said you were in a hurry didn't you?" she urged. "We'll be waiting around till Christmas at this rate."

"What do you mean *we*?"

"Because when I help you steal the car, I want *you* to help *me*. You know that old saying, you scratch my back and I'll scratch yours? Well that applies here."

Rolling his eyes, he sighed and negotiated his long legs over the gear stick and handbrake, then hoisting himself over into the passenger seat he hit his head on the ceiling. Libby flipped the driver's seat down and Rufus jumped up onto the back seat.

"By heck, it's like a bloody oven in here," Rufus complained.

The Peace & Order Maintenance Officer groaned and looked round at Rufus in disbelief.

"For fuck's sake, this is just great." Running his hands over his head in exasperation, he said, "Get your dog and get out of the car."

Libby was by now already sitting in the car, her fingernails going to work on the pins.

"Oh come on," she said, "That's a bit harsh isn't it? It *is* bloody hot in here. You must have got out of bed on the wrong side this morning."

Sweat trickled down her spine and she felt flushed, yet when she looked at the Peace & Order Maintenance Officer she was surprised to see that his skin was matte, and he seemed to be completely unmoved by the heat.

"I'm not joking, get out," he said again, firmly. He reached over and put his hand on hers to stop her fiddling. At the touch of his skin, her breath caught in her throat and she made a wheezing sound.

"My God, you're *freezing*," she cried.

He jolted away from her, snatching his hand back as though he'd been stung. Libby looked at him with growing concern and laid her hand below his shirt sleeve so that their skin touched once again. His arm was stone cold.

"Don't touch me," he growled, shrugging her hand away.

"Are you ok?" Libby asked. "Do you need to see a doctor?"

Without responding he tried to open the passenger door. It banged against the brickwork of the building it was parked outside and wouldn't open enough for him even to squeeze out.

"I'm fine," he snarled. "Now just get out and leave me alone."

"Look mister," Libby snapped, prodding her nails into the pins again and working them loose. "I don't know what your problem is today, and I certainly don't know what your problem is with *me*, but you're beginning to piss me off."

Giving the panel a final yank, it fell off in her hands, and upon seeing the immobiliser switch she flicked it off. She'd never stolen anything in her entire life, and to start with a car was pretty thrilling. *It won't harm to have some fun for once,* she thought.

"Now stop bloody well arguing and tell me how to start this thing," she said, lifting her eyebrow and flashing him a grin.

He banged his head off the back of the headrest in defeat and puffed out his cheeks.

"You really don't give up do you?"

Leaning forward he pressed a yellow button in front of the handbrake and the car instantly purred to life.

"Not easily," she said. "I know you said you were having a pretty crappy day, but really, so am I. I could do with some help right about now. For starters I'd like to know where the hell I am and what I'm meant to be doing. Oh and it'd be nice to know why my dog can sodding well talk all of a sudden."

At the mention of his name Rufus poked his head between the front seats, but before the Peace & Order Maintenance Officer could respond a loud roar filled the alleyway and a black car, similar looking to a Bentley, pulled up alongside them.

"Ah shit," groaned the Peace & Order Maintenance Officer, slamming his balled hand against the dashboard. Then with a sense of urgency he yelled to Libby, "Go, *go!*"

Libby hesitated too long, and the black tinted window of the other car rolled down. Sitting within arm's reach, in the other car's passenger seat, was a woman with shocking white hair which hung down over her left eye. She was biting her lip in concentration, one side of her black mouth turned up in a haughty smirk, and she was pointing a gun straight at the Peace & Order Maintenance Officer.

In a moment of unthinking madness, Libby flung her handbag at the other woman, making the gun clatter from her hands to the floor, and then slamming her right foot down onto the accelerator pedal, hoping to God the logistics of cars in Sunray Bay was the same as back home, she cranked the handbrake off and sped down the alleyway with a screech; tyres wheel-spinning on the hot road.

"Who the hell were they?" she gasped.

"Never mind, just keep driving."

The Peace & Order Maintenance Officer was now leaning out of the passenger side window, and Libby watched in the rear-view mirror as he shot out the tyres of their would-be pursuers. It all happened so fast, Libby hadn't even noticed him pulling the gun from the holster at his waist.

"Are they after you?" Libby asked.

He settled himself back into his seat and faced forward.

"Why would they be after *you*?"

"How should I know?" she retorted. "I've had a psychotic donkey-keeper following me with a knife since I arrived, so nothing would surprise me."

As they rounded the corner at the end of the alleyway, they headed up a quiet side street, signed Mariner's Way, and Libby pointed out of the side window.

"And speak of the devil, *there he is*!" she cried.

Standing on the corner watching them intently, with his unnerving globular eyes, was Donkey-man.

"No, that's not the devil," the Peace & Order Maintenance Officer corrected. "But he will kill you."

Chapter 10

11:16am: The streets of Sunray Bay

The buildings got grubbier the further inland they headed, and as they zipped through tight back streets she was sure they weren't even meant to be driving a car down most of them. Twice already she'd scraped the wing mirrors against stonework.

"I'm Libby," she said, eventually, chancing a look to her left and hoping to break the silence. "Libby Hood."

"Just keep going and I'll tell you when to turn off," he replied, sullenly. "They've seen us with the car now, so we'll have to be quick."

Libby still didn't have a clue who *they* were exactly, and she didn't bother asking again either, since she had a feeling he still wouldn't tell her.

"So what's your name?" she probed.

He clacked his tongue in a way that seemed usual for him now, in that everything appeared to be bothersome, and he said, "It's no concern of yours."

Libby's nostrils flared.

"Are you having a laugh?" she retorted. "I just stole a car for you *and* I saved your arse. You would've been blown into the middle of next week if I hadn't intervened. So excuse me, *mister high-and-bloody-well-mighty*, I have to disagree with you on that one – I think it's *every* concern of mine who you are."

He puffed out his cheeks and looked at her. The wind was rushing in through the broken window making her red hair thrash about as though it was alive, and her jaw jutted forward in anger.

"Grim," he sighed.

"What's grim?" she asked, narrowing her eyes and wondering if he was being a smart arse.

"I am."

"What, is it your name or are you making a statement?" Libby still wasn't sure. She remained facing front, afraid to take her eyes off the tapering lane they were headed down. Washing hung low between the two buildings sandwiching them, and she cringed as the car clipped the bottom of a white sheet.

"It's my name."

"What, so is it your first or last name?"

"Neither," he said gruffly. "It's just my name."

Pointing up ahead he then added, "Take a right here, and then there's a sharp left. Keep going and I'll tell you when to stop."

"So where are we going, *Grim*?" she asked, pulling the steering wheel right.

"*I'm* going to see an old friend," he answered.

She waited a moment to see if he would say more. He didn't. Checking the rear-view mirror she didn't think they were being followed, and she saw that Rufus had curled up into a ball on the backseat. How he could snooze at a time like this was beyond her.

"Not much of a conversationalist, are you?"

When he didn't acknowledge her question, she looked at him. His profile was angular and his solid frame completely consumed the passenger seat. Because he was sitting so close, she could smell him, (saltiness with a citrusy tang of aftershave perhaps), and she wondered if the stubble on his strong jaw line might be unintentionally sexy. She scolded herself for finding him so annoyingly attractive.

Particularly interesting was the large cursive *D* tattooed in black on the side of his head; a bold statement that she suddenly wanted to know more about. She thought it might be evidence of an expressive side, and she wondered just how much flirting she'd need to do before she broke through his stony facade to reach it. And on that note, she decided she would find out. She'd never chased a man before in her life, it was against her ethics – but she couldn't see a problem with a bit of harmless fun. Besides he was proving to be a real challenge – and a welcome distraction from being dead.

"Nice tattoo," she said, raising her eyebrows and flashing her best smile. "Have you got any others?"

But she may as well have been talking to the steering wheel. Ignoring her question, he said, "Pull over behind that derelict building on the left."

Sulking, but not yet defeated, she did as instructed and mounted the mossy kerb at the side of the building, which looked to have been a pub at some stage. Before the car even came to a standstill, Grim's hand was already twitching on the door handle. He turned to her with a dour look on his face, and, as though it pained him to offer gratitude, he said, "Thanks."

"No problem." Libby smiled thinly.

Rufus stirred in the back of the car as Grim threw open his door. Libby opened her door and popped the seat forward, watching as Grim made off down the street. Stroking Rufus on the head, she said, "Come on, sleepyhead."

He yawned and stretched his back legs, then jumping out into the street he looked around curiously at their new surroundings.

"Ugh, where are we? I think I much preferred the beach."

"I've no idea where we are, but we'd better be quick or else we're going to lose him."

They jogged after Grim who was walking briskly, clinging to shadows as though trying to make himself invisible.

"So who is this friend of yours?" Libby called after him, puffing hard and out of breath already.

He stopped walking and turned to face her. Yet another look of annoyance resided in his thin-lipped grimace. Ducking into the dingy doorway of a rundown shop, he grabbed her by the wrists and pulled her in next to him.

"What are you doing?"

"What do you mean?" Libby asked, confusion marking her eyes "We're coming with you."

She was all too aware of the nostril-stinging smell of ammonia all around them in the urine-stained doorway, but she was distinctly more aware of how close they were standing together. Her hot sticky skin was mere inches away from his frosty body, and the thought made her feel giddy. Invisible bands of cold on her wrists tingled from where he'd touched her, and if it wasn't for the smell of piss she thought she'd like to reach up and kiss him. Daring and spontaneous; to taste his lips and see how cold they'd be. She imagined, at that moment, they'd be more refreshing than raspberry ripple ice-cream. Her senses were amplified, and she could hear his heart beating – or was it her own? And she could see the jagged edge of a thin scar that was barely even there running down his left cheek, protruding from beneath his sunglasses. She wondered how far up it went, but couldn't see beyond the blackness that shielded his eyes.

And then he shattered her thoughts...

"You can't," he shook his head. "You have to go your own way."

In an instant Libby's brown eyes sparkled with anger, he had her head in a spin.

"What about our deal?"

"I didn't make any deal," he said, looking skyward and running his hands over his rough stubble in exasperation. "*You* were the one who was going on about scratching each other's backs. I'm sorry but I really don't have time for this. I appreciate your help, but I have to go now. *On my own.*"

"Well that's gratitude for you," she said, frustration pricking her eyes with tears. "After all I've just done for you, you're just going to leave me stranded, knowing that I have no money and that some maniac with a knife is trying to kill me."

Grim put his hands out to hush her, and he peered from the shop doorway hoping that their argument hadn't attracted attention. In seeing that it hadn't, he turned back to her and said, "Look, the bloke who's been following you is called Jarvis Strickler..."

81

Interrupting him, Libby waved her arms about and said, *"And?* Why are you telling me that? It wouldn't matter if his name was Mickey-bloody-Mouse. I don't want us to be introduced, he's trying to kill me not take me out for a drink."

"Well if you'll just let me finish." The corners of Grim's mouth curved upwards in the hint of a possible smile. "He doesn't target just *anybody*."

"What's that supposed to mean? Who does he target?"

Grim eyed her coldly once again, the smile well and truly lost, and it was hard to tell whether it had even been there in the first place.

"He's part of a group called The Ordinaries. They target people just like you."

"People like me? Could you expand a bit on that please, and stop talking in bloody riddles?" she said, fighting the urge to grab the front of his shirt and rag him in frustration.

He looked down at Rufus, who was sniffing with great interest at a dark ominous looking stain just outside the doorway, but then shook his head.

"For God's sake alright, just come with me. Right here isn't the time or place to be discussing this."

Libby smiled triumphantly and followed his lead believing she'd just made a small breakthrough.

"You can talk to Gloria when we get there," he said over his shoulder.

The smile vanished from Libby's face in an instant. *Who the hell's Gloria?* she thought. But then she remembered Grim had referred to her as an old friend, reasoning that Gloria couldn't be his girlfriend or wife in that case. Astounded, Libby couldn't believe how irrational and ridiculous she was being – she didn't even know anything about him apart from his name, and she suspected it wasn't even a proper one anyway. Her face blushed with embarrassment and for once she was pleased he was facing the other way. She was behaving like a schoolgirl with a crush, and she told herself to get a grip.

For the next few minutes she openly looked through all of the windows they passed by, trying to form an impression of what life was actually like in Sunray Bay – and trying to distract herself from looking at Grim's backside. The further away from the seafront they'd come, the more she noticed everything was dirtier and more unpleasant. Window panes were filthy black, probably inside and out, with blue bottles heaped up on every single sill. Graffiti of a vulgar nature was emblazoned on any and every surface that was available, and the gutters were litter strewn. Libby found herself hoping she didn't end up living at that end of town. She was far from snobby, but still, she had standards – and her gut feeling told her it was not the safest or friendliest of places. Most of the buildings appeared to be dilapidated, and she couldn't tell whether they were being occupied or not.

Finally, after they'd travelled a couple of streets, Grim came to a stop outside a grimy three storey building. Through yellowed windows and grey cafe style net curtains, Libby could just about make out tables and chairs inside. And mounted just below the building's top floor windows, a seedy-looking sign flickered red in the daylight, spelling out the words *Knickerbocker Gloria's*.

Libby's initial thought was that Grim's old friend must own an ice-cream parlour – which was pretty handy. Although, judging the state of place, she wasn't entirely convinced Gloria was too strict on hygiene regulations. Then again, she was so hungry and thirsty, she'd have taken food from a sewer rat at that moment in time.

Following Grim round to the side of the building, into an enclosed alleyway with cracked paving stones and weeds, Libby was careful not to stand in any of the dog shit that was copiously dotted about. They carried on until they reached a rusty wrought iron gate to the rear of the property. Grim led her through a concrete yard to the back door, and without knocking, he opened it and stepped into a large murky kitchen that smelled nothing like an ice-cream parlour should. Deep fat fryer fumes and cigarette smoke enveloped Libby as she stepped inside, making its stamp in her hair and

83

on her clothes; a stink, she imagined, that would only come out after a vigorous wash. Her appetite took a sudden nose-dive, but as she looked around the kitchen she realised the greasy smell was the least of her worries. A tall gorgeous brunette leant against the brown rim of a stainless steel sink, dragging on a cigarette and holding a mug of something steaming. Libby noted that the content of the mug wasn't the only thing that was steaming – the other woman's body was tanned, taut, and wearing very little. A rhinestone encrusted bra top cupped her large rounded breasts and a matching stringy thong sat high on her hips. Libby instantly felt ugly and frumpy in comparison, and began to wonder what the hell kind of ice-cream parlour it must be exactly.

"Hey." The brunette shot Grim an effortless, yet heartbreaking, smile. And Libby told herself to forget about the flirting, because she didn't stand a chance now.

Chapter 11

"Grim, flowerpot! What do I owe the pleasure?"

A woman's gruff voice rolled in from the kitchen's open doorway, like marbles over asphalt. Libby watched as its unlikely owner, a petite woman with a square peroxide blonde bob, followed it through. Her blue doll-eyes, framed with long curled black lashes, looked impossibly large and babyish for her age. Libby estimated she was in her late forties, only because telltale wrinkles ran deep at the sides of her eyes and mouth – apart from these she could have been in her twenties for all Libby knew. She was wearing a candy-pink pinafore that dipped low at the neckline and rode high at the hem, with white canvas shoes. And her fringe was cut so severely it had to be a fashion statement. Between her thin cerise lips, she gripped a cigarette, and when she saw Libby her eyes grew wider than a bush baby's.

"Oh, and who's your girlfriend?"

"Gloria," Grim said sheepishly, "I'd have let you know I was coming, but..."

Gloria took a draw from her cigarette and then waved it at him, "Don't be daft, sweetie. You're welcome here any time. You should know that by now."

She moved over to Grim, a small pink flurry of energy, and gave him a light slap on the bum.

"Go and grab yourself a seat and I'll get you a coffee, and while you're doing that you can introduce me to your girlfriend."

Gloria turned to Libby with renewed interest and winked. Grim leaned against the kitchen counter, making no attempt to sit down.

"She's not my girlfriend," he said impatiently. "Look Gloria, I need to talk..."

85

Gloria looked at Libby with an apologetic look as though she was thinking, *oh well, never mind eh?* But as Grim opened his mouth to continue, Libby butted in, feeling disgruntled about being ignored.

"I'll introduce *myself* then, shall I?" Looking to Gloria, she said, "I'm Libby. Libby Hood. I only arrived here this morning."

"Oh, sorry to hear it. How are you finding things?"

"Well so far I've been mugged and held at knife point, so I'm not having a very good start to the day. Oh, and by the way that's my dog Rufus, I hope you don't mind me fetching him into the kitchen?" She pointed down to where Rufus was licking at grubby food spillages on the floor tiles. Then looking back at Grim, she said to Gloria, "Is he always this endearing?"

Gloria grinned.

"That's Grim. What you see is what you get.

Libby very much doubted that. What she was seeing she certainly wasn't getting – not in the way she wanted anyhow.

"And don't be silly, the dog's fine," Gloria added. She then cast her attention to the dark-haired minx who was still standing by the sink. All the while she'd been watching and listening with a snooty smirk loitering on her lip-liner perfected pout.

"Lula, are you *still* down here? You'd better hurry up or else Stan'll go mad."

Lula rolled her eyes and dropped the stub of her cigarette into the mug she held, then clanking it down in the sink amongst a pile of other dirty crockery, she slinked over to the doorway, her hips swishing evocatively from side to side and her eyes never leaving Grim. Libby felt like she was witnessing some sort of mating ritual; she thought that if Lula had a feathered tail she'd be flicking it in Grim's face. At that moment, Libby hated her with a passion because she saw how Grim watched until she'd disappeared from view. Libby doubted Grim would even spit on her if she was on fire, never mind look at her like that. Her shoulders slumped.

"Who was that?" she asked, trying to sound nonchalant, and feeling about as sexy as her eighty-year-old winceyette-wearing grandmother.

"One of the dancing girls," Gloria replied, clattering dishes and pots about on the draining board whilst trying to locate some clean mugs.

Kitchens and dancing girls? Libby's face displayed the confusion in her mind, and seeing this, Gloria explained further, "I run the cafe downstairs and my husband Stan runs an exotic dance bar upstairs."

She nudged Libby in the arm jokingly with her elbow and laughed. Then looking Libby up and down, she said, "Actually, you're not looking for a job, are you honey?"

Libby laughed out loud.

"*Me?* God no, I'd be lousy."

"Nah, you'd be ok I reckon. Anybody can take orders and wash up."

"Oh..." Libby's face reddened.

"Oh you thought I meant upstairs?" Gloria patted her chest and laughed awkwardly. "Well, I think you'd do good there too, don't get me wrong. I mean, we don't have a redhead in the group so you'd go down a storm, but we don't let just anybody in. I know you're a friend of Grim's, and any friend of Grim's is welcome here too, but upstairs is quite an exclusive little group. Those girls have something extra special, you know what I mean?"

Grim was by now pouring water from the kettle into a mug Gloria had handed him, and he grunted, "She's not my friend."

Libby was beginning to feel the first twinges of defeat, there seemed to be no give with him, and no man was worth pursuing *that* much – not to the extent where she was beginning to feel uncomfortable. She was thankful when Gloria diverted the conversation.

"How's Rufus doing, anyway? He's such a cutie isn't he?" she asked, clapping her hands together and looking down at Rufus who was sitting on the floor with his nose pointed up in the air. He was sniffing at a large griddle of bacon sitting above him on the counter, which was basking in a layer of white congealed fat and tantalising his taste-buds. He stood up at the mention of his name, turned to Gloria and wagged his tail.

"Well hey there, you're quite a cutie yourself. I'm doing alright, but I'd be even better if I could have some of that bacon," he replied, wandering over to inspect Gloria's proffered hand.

Gloria gasped and withdrew her hand, then looking at Grim she said, "Who are these two exactly?"

"I dunno," Grim answered, he was sipping from the mug now and avoiding eye contact with Gloria, as though he was being scolded by his mother. "They followed me."

Gloria stood in front of him, arms folded across her chest and the lines of her face intensified by her seriousness. "Why did you fetch them here?"

"Like I said, they wouldn't leave me alone, I didn't have a choice."

"Well, do you even know *what* they are?" Gloria took a cigarette from the breast pocket of her pinafore, and rolled it around in her fingers as though deciding whether she wanted to smoke it or not.

"I can't believe you," Libby interrupted, her eyes burning into Grim. "We *followed* you? Is that the extent of it as far as you're concerned? Or don't you remember that I saved your life?"

He stood looking at her coolly, his blasé body language infuriating her more and more.

"Will *you* have the decency to tell me what's going on?" She whipped round to face Gloria. "Perhaps explain why everyone starts talking gibberish around me?"

Gloria looked apprehensive, and then said to Grim, "Is she definitely *something*?"

"Yeah, The Ordinaries are chasing her," he replied.

"Oh great, that's just what I need." Gloria flung her arms in the air. "Okay, first thing's first, let's see what we're dealing with here eh? Now what exactly *are* you?"

Before Libby could respond, Grim clanged his mug down hard on the counter and both she and Gloria jumped.

"Who she is, and what she is, is pretty fucking secondary right now," he snarled. "Like I said, I need to speak to you Gloria."

Libby's fists balled up and she planted them firmly on her hips.

"Look here, you rude, egotistical arsehole, I think I deserve some answers. I've just about had it up to here with you," she said putting her hand up to her forehead for effect. "It's all me, me, me with you, isn't it? Now before you go any further, you can bloody well tell me what it is that I'm supposed to be. Oh and by the way, who the *fuck* are The Ordinaries?"

Both Grim and Gloria were taken aback by Libby's outburst. Gloria lit her cigarette finally and said, "The Ordinaries are a group of people who specialise in killing..." she looked thoughtful. "Erm, well, for want of a better word – monsters."

Libby didn't know whether to laugh out loud or to turn around and leave. It seemed that she hadn't met one normal person since she'd arrived in Sunray Bay. Each person was as crazy as the next.

"Is that a joke?" she asked, her face was serious and she certainly wasn't laughing.

"What's funny about it?" Gloria asked with a definite sting in her tone. Hostility had swooped into the kitchen and everybody stood in deathly silence for a moment.

"*Monsters*?" Libby asked, trying to clarify the absurdity of the situation. "Are you saying I'm a monster? And, just to be clear, are we talking metaphorically or literally here? Though, not that it matters, I can assure you I'm not a monster in any way, shape or form."

"Everyone in Sunray Bay is a monster of some kind, darling," Gloria said. "If you hadn't noticed already, it's hardly heaven is it? If you aren't a monster physically, then chances are you're a murderer, a rapist, a thief or some other kind of scumbag. It's all one and the same thing here. I like

89

to think of Sunray Bay as a type of sieve for heaven, and we're all the lumpy, unsavoury bits that don't get through."

"Well that's just ridiculous," Libby snorted. "I'm not any of those things."

Gloria looked apprehensive, and then said to Grim, "Is it possible she doesn't know?"

"I would say that's highly unlikely," he replied. "How could you not know?"

"Look sweetheart, quit with the bullshit and tell us what you are, or else leave," Gloria said, pointing to the back door. "You're obviously not just a normal run of the mill criminal, not with that...with that soul issue going on." She nodded at Rufus.

"*I'm* not normal?" Libby spluttered. "That's rich coming from you lot. And what the hell's that supposed to mean? What's wrong with my soul?"

Gloria turned to Grim, who looked about ready to explode. She shrugged her shoulders and said, "She probably doesn't know the physics of Sunray Bay since she hasn't been here that long." Then to Libby she said, "An abnormal soul goes hand in hand with an abnormal person, such as yourself. And by abnormal, I obviously mean a monster. Now when anybody, normal or abnormal, leaves their earthly existence and arrives here there's a lot of mystical energy at work, and for abnormal people, their physical bodies can't contain the abnormal soul during this process, for whatever reason – I suppose it's rather like shaking a can of fizzy pop just before you open it – it comes bursting right out."

"So are you telling me you don't think I have a soul on the basis that you think I'm abnormal?" Libby asked.

"Not at all," Gloria said. "I'm saying that your dog has your soul, because you're abnormal."

"*Rufus* has my soul? Oh right, now I see. Yeah that makes perfect sense," Libby said sarcastically. "Why didn't I think of that?"

"It does make sense," Gloria snapped. "When you arrived here his body obviously absorbed your soul because your own body couldn't contain it. His was the next best thing."

"Well if that's true, what would have happened if I'd arrived alone?" Libby challenged.

"In that case, you probably wouldn't have had this problem, because chances are your soul would've bounced back into your own body when there was nowhere else for it to go. It's a classic example of being *abnormal*. Believe me, I know, there are plenty of abnormalities in Sunray Bay!"

"This is getting silly now," Libby said, walking to the door. "I think I've heard enough."

"Take your head out of your own arse, for crying out loud! Why else do you think your dog can talk?" Gloria snapped, riled at being dismissed. "You can't tell me he talked beforehand? You're either in denial, or else you're trying to hide something. Whether you like it or not, your soul has slipped out of you and into your dog – and that would only ever happen for one reason."

Libby halted at the back door.

"And what reason is that?" she asked.

"That you're a *monster*, for Pete's sake!" Gloria cried, "Weren't you listening?"

This time Libby did laugh. "Oh my God, what are you two on?"

Gloria and Grim both stared at her, and she suddenly felt as though she were treading on very thin ice.

"Christ, you're absolutely serious aren't you? That's just ridiculous. I'm not a monster at all. In fact, it's the most insane thing I've heard in all my life. There are no such things as monsters."

"Look, I couldn't give a shit whether you're a vampire, a werewolf, a ghoul or a fucking witch," Grim suddenly yelled, standing up straight to assert some dominance. "It's the least of my worries. Now Gloria, I *really* need to talk to you."

Gloria stood still like a mannequin, only now taking in the look of seriousness on his face.

91

"Oh hell's bells, what have you done?"

Grim bent over the kitchen worktop and cradled his head in his hands, showing a more vulnerable side.

"I have to leave town..."

"Why?" Gloria squeaked, her voice not so husky when she was alarmed.

"I'm going to The Grey Dust Bowl as soon as it's dark."

His sunglasses were completely unnecessary in the gloom of the kitchen, but they remained in place, blanking emotion from his face. "I'd really appreciate it if you'd let me stay here till then."

"But that's absurd. Why would you want to go to The Grey Dustbowl? Surely things aren't that bad?"

Libby quietly wandered back into the centre of the kitchen, away from the door. She listened intently as he finally started to open up, and decided she was going nowhere just yet.

"There's nothing here for me, Gloria. Nothing at all."

"What about your job?"

"I'm not with Peace & Order Maintenance anymore."

Gloria grimaced. "Ah, why do I get the feeling that's what this is all about?

Grim looked down at his shirt with his mouth pinched tight and in a swift angry movement, which seemed impossible, he ripped it from his body and threw it away from him in disgust. His chest and abdominal muscles underneath were well defined like a handcrafted sculpture, and as buttons sprang to the ground, Libby's mouth just about hit the floor too.

"I take it I was right then?" Gloria asked.

Grim plunged his hands into his trouser pockets and stood towering above her. He'd rapidly regained his composure of slight brooding, rather than full-on fury; the level of brooding that got Libby in a lustful tizzy.

"Krain's coming after me. It's all gone tits up. He backed out of our deal." Grim ground his teeth together in frustration, and his temples throbbed. "A whole fucking year busting my balls for him and that's what he does."

"I knew it," Gloria slammed her palm down onto the counter. "I told you to be careful, didn't I?"

"Not now Gloria, save all your *I told you so*'s, because I don't want to hear them. What was I supposed to do? You'd have done the same..."

"So why is he after you?" Gloria suddenly looked suspicious, and Grim looked discomfited again.

"Well, you know the work I've been doing for him? I never really knew why I was doing what I was doing because he never told me – and I never asked. To be honest, I didn't really care; I had a one-track mind. I only wanted what had been promised to me. Anyway, when he refused his part of the deal I saw red. I went to the prison last night, and well...I found out what I've been inadvertently helping him do."

Gloria didn't seem too comfortable about where his story was headed.

"So, what *have* you been doing? And moreover, what have you *done*?"

"I'll not lie to you Gloria, and you're not going to like it. For the past year I've been taking werewolves into custody. They've been held at Sunray Bay Prison...and not just the criminally insane ones either."

Gloria gasped. She along with the rest of the Sunray Bay populace had been following the news stories for quite some time about how werewolves were dwindling in their numbers, disappearing into thin air from the very streets they walked. Most people didn't give a stuff because it made the streets that little bit safer every time there was a full moon. But on the flipside, it made some people uneasy as to where they were going exactly. Krain hadn't really commented on the issue much in his media interviews, he put it down to a surge in criminal activity amongst the hairy beasts and the fact that The Ordinaries were on the ball and reacting to this. The Ordinaries were a questionable group of monster assassins, but Krain allowed them to operate on the understanding that they left his own elite vampire group alone – anything else was rich pickings. But it was all rather strange, because the way in which the werewolves were going missing didn't seem like the usual trademark of The Ordinaries – and, besides, The Ordinaries themselves denied any involvement.

"Oh Grim, you haven't! *Why?* And what does Krain want with them?"

"It's all to do with Krain's fast food enterprise, his factory over in the Industrial Estate."

"Black Dog Burger Co?" Gloria was so enthralled she was unaware that an inch of cigarette ash had fallen down the front of her pinafore, into the fold of her cleavage.

"He keeps all the werewolves I've brought to him down in the prison cellar, and once there's a full moon coming round he ships them over to the factory in white vans..."

Gloria's hand reached up to her mouth in horror. "Please don't tell me what I think you're about to..."

"Yeah." Grim nodded solemnly, "They're his source of black pudding."

Gloria grabbed the edge of the kitchen counter and her knees became weak. She wretched and mewled, "Oh my goodness, that's horrific. Are you sure? I've eaten those things!"

Grim nodded his head. "A fine vampire delicacy by all accounts. Though to be fair, Gloria, it's certainly no more brutal than his old methods."

"That's hardly the same. The iron-man was for the criminally insane only," Gloria shook her head, correcting him. "By the sounds of it, this black pudding venture is a free for all!"

"Yeah, it is. Though I'm beginning to doubt that his iron-man strategies in the past were kosher to be honest," Grim sighed.

Gloria shuddered and opened her mind to the possibility of what Grim was saying. Torture by iron-man was surely the most horrific death for any werewolf – a device for locking werewolves into on the eve of a full moon. He'd be kept there in the iron casing until the full moon came around, for when metamorphosis took place. With no room inside to accommodate the transformation, the werewolf would die a slow and horrible death; fatally crushed by his own full-moon bodily functions – truly barbaric. And to think that Krain might have been administering that type of torture on werewolves, some of whom hadn't even committed any offences, was just diabolical.

"Who's Krain?" Libby asked, suddenly wanting to be included in the conversation again.

Both Grim and Gloria looked at her as though they'd completely forgotten who she was and why she was sat in the kitchen with them.

"He's the mayor of Sunray Bay," Gloria answered, too stunned by Grim's revelation to be hostile toward her anymore.

"Who happens to be a vampire," Grim added, his voice tinged with hatred. "And there's not much I hate more."

Libby moved closer to the pair of them.

"So if I've got this right, you've been working for the mayor, who just so happens to be a vampire, and you've been capturing werewolves so that he can make black pudding out of them?"

"Give the girl a gold star, she's finally keeping up," Grim snarled, his curled lip baring straight white teeth.

"Wow, you couldn't make this shit up," Rufus said, joining in.

"Well why is Krain after you now? What did you do when you found out about the whole werewolf black pudding scenario?" Libby asked, still confused as to what the crux of the problem was – apart from the fact that monsters were apparently running wild in Sunray Bay.

Gloria nodded. "Yeah Grim, what happened next?"

Grim turned his back on them and looked out of the window above the sink to the yard beyond.

"I killed the night wardens in the prison, and then I let the werewolves out."

Gloria scrabbled for a nearby tumbler of water and took a mouthful.

"Jesus Christ, Grim, now I can see the enormity of the situation, I'm not surprised you're scarpering. You killed some of Krain's vampires and then you unleashed a pack of rabid mongrels back onto the streets. You really are in big fucking trouble, sweetheart."

"Why? What will happen now?" Libby asked. She felt totally drawn into the whole drama now and was beginning to feel like she was part of a weird soap opera.

"It means that the shit will well and truly hit the fan here in Sunray Bay," Gloria answered. "You couldn't have picked a better time for it either, Grim – it's a full moon tonight."

Grim rolled his eyes heavenward and sighed, "I know. But I guess that's no bad thing for me – it'll be distraction enough for me to make it to the borders without being stopped."

"That's just excellent Grim, you stir up a load of shit and then you bugger off," Gloria said. "And what about the rest of us left behind? You might have caused a war, do you realise that?"

As he began to respond, she cut him off and continued, "Of course, I realise that you can't stay now. Krain and his vampires won't stop till they've caught you, and as for the werewolves, well, they won't take too kindly to the part you've been playing in Krain's little delicatessen scheme – and that's putting it mildly."

"Let's be fair though," Grim said. "I was never on anybody's side to begin with. You've always been great to me Gloria, but you know as well as I do that I just don't belong. I know I've caused a big fucking mess, and I know you won't see eye to eye with me over what I've been doing..."

"Too bloody right I don't," Gloria snapped.

"But please, let me stay here until it's dark, and then I'll be out of your hair once and for all." He reached out and put his hands on her shoulders, making her look even smaller and doll-like. "Please?"

Gloria bit her lip.

"Stan would kill me and, I have to say, I do not condone what you've been doing for Krain one jot. It's callous and murderous, and I thought you'd risen above all of that Grim – but you know, right now, I'm not so sure that's true."

Grim dropped his hands from her shoulders and nodded his head slowly.

"But since I know you *are* a good kid deep down in there somewhere, I'll give you a break. God knows why, I must be soft in the head. You can stay till nightfall, but make yourself scarce. And for goodness sake, keep out of Stan's way."

"Thank you," he said quietly, crossing his arms over his bare chest as though having bared all emotionally, he was now feeling self-conscious about his semi-nakedness.

Gloria seemed to notice this and said, "I'll go and grab one of Stan's shirts for you to put on."

As she breezed past, Libby couldn't help but think she was a spoil sport. Amid all the crazy talk of werewolves and black pudding, vampires and torture devices, Libby had been enjoying the view immensely. She had another good look while she could, and just as she was about to ask more about Krain another ridiculously pretty girl walked in, presumably from the exclusive little group upstairs. Her hair hung in waves down to her waist like golden syrup flowing from a spoon, and her skin was vanilla and flawless. She looked displeased to see Libby and Grim in the kitchen (which suited Libby fine – she could deal with animosity better than the flirting Lula had displayed earlier), and as she poured herself a coffee, she stuck her nose in the air and sniffed loudly. Without turning round she stated to nobody in particular, "I can smell vampire."

Grim grabbed a bottle of whiskey from behind a bread basket and skulked out of the room without a word. Libby watched him go.

"What flew up his nose?" the girl asked.

Libby puffed out her cheeks. She felt like a total spare part, standing in a complete stranger's kitchen and not even knowing whether she was welcome or not.

"I dunno, but I suppose I could say the same to you."

The girl smiled and shrugged.

"That time of the month," she said.

Libby rolled her eyes.

"Hey you," the girl said playfully, seeing Rufus sitting on the floor. Bending over to pet him, she asked in a high-pitched baby voice. "Aren't you a sweet little fella?"

Libby could tell that Rufus was grinning from ear to ear, and she looked in disgust at the little traitor.

"Hey *you*," he replied, his stumpy tail beating the floor.

The girl nodded smugly, and looked up at Libby. "I knew you were a vampire."

Chapter 12

Red and Kitty barged through the corridors of the council offices; anyone who saw them would've thought they'd just had a lovers' tiff. Red slammed into a glass door and let it swing back on Kitty with full force, not caring whether it hit her or not. She stomped behind him, burning holes in the back of his head with her glare.

"Why the fuck didn't you pull the trigger?" Red asked for the umpteenth time.

Kitty raised her middle finger at him and said nothing.

Grim had left them in the alleyway looking like a couple of bumbling stooges from a comedy caper, and Red was placing the blame firmly on Kitty. He had no idea how they'd manage to explain it to Krain, but however they did it they would come across as completely incompetent. Red was livid.

They found Krain pacing backwards and forwards in his office, a mobile phone held to his ear. Without knocking they entered and stood before his large mahogany desk like two naughty schoolchildren summoned by the headmaster, both wearing scowls.

Krain was in the middle of a heated conversation too, and he glowered at Red and Kitty.

"What do you mean you've got none left?" he barked into his phone. "You *deal in silverware*! That's like a newsagent running out of newspapers, for crying out loud."

Whatever the response was on the other end Krain didn't like it, and he threw his mobile down onto the desk.

"They're one step ahead of us already!"

He snatched a piece of paper from his desk and scrunched it up in his fist. Throwing it at the wall he said, "The whole town suddenly has a silver shortage, can you believe it?"

"Silver, sir?" Red raised his eyebrows.

99

"Yes, silver! You know, the stuff you make cutlery, jewellery and *silver bullets* out of." Krain slapped his palm down on his desk, making a loud clapping noise. "I do wonder about you sometimes, Red. Did you think we were going to fix this problem with a few boxes of Bonios?"

Red blushed and Kitty bit her lip to hide her smirk.

"Anyway, what brings you both here?" Krain asked, his eyes narrowing in suspicion.

Red and Kitty looked at each other, and Red nodded his head to show that he would take the lead.

"We found Grim, sir. He was stealing a car round the back of the Blue Wahoo Guesthouse. He has an accomplice, some girl with red hair, probably in her early twenties. We hadn't really expected her to be with him, she caught us unaware," Red stopped for breath and he looked awkward. "And they, erm, managed to get away, sir."

Krain scratched his beard. "You didn't follow them?"

"No sir, we were incapacitated at that point."

Krain sat down hard in his high-backed leather chair and held his face in his hands, beyond words at that moment in time. Red looked again at Kitty, then down at the handbag she held.

"We *did* bring his accomplice's handbag though, sir."

Kitty set the bag down on top of Krain's desk.

"Why thank you, it'll go lovely with my new suede shoes," Krain growled.

"We thought you might like to find out who she is," Red offered.

"If you'd both done your jobs properly, then I wouldn't need to," Krain barked.

Red and Kitty hung their heads, keeping their eyes on the black leather slouch bag which was the only peace offering they had. Krain sighed.

"When today's over I want to book some time in with you two. We need to do a performance review."

Red rolled his eyes, and Kitty's lips were pursed tight, like a naughty girl who did not take well to being told off.

Reaching over to the handbag, Krain dragged it across his desk and laid it down in front of him.

"I take it you've checked inside for ID? Surely you can't be that inept, though I am beginning to wonder."

They both nodded their heads once.

"There were just a few bits and pieces of junk in there, nothing much," Red clarified.

Krain removed his black gloves. He kept a spare pair in the drawer of his desk, and had discarded the soiled white ones as soon as he'd arrived in his office – they were now lying in the wastepaper basket. Gloves were as essential to Krain as air. He needed to wear them pretty much every hour of every day in order to keep some level of sanity. He possessed a vivid psychic awareness that was brought about by the touch of anything on his bare skin. If he so much as brushed an inanimate object that had been handled by somebody else, his head would be filled with thoughts of that person. A lot of the time he viewed his ability as being a nuisance, but it was an empowering ability nonetheless. It kept him ahead of the game – but that's not to say he was keen on using it all that often. He found it a mentally and physically draining experience, one which also made him feel dirty. It was as though a small part of the person he was getting an insight into was somehow entering his own personal space, clogging up his brain cells and cloying his senses with their own filth and grime.

Thankfully he got some release when he was with Morgan. She had the ability to block his third eye, and was the only person he'd met who was able to do this. Ultimately, that was the hold she had over him; the reason why she walked all over him and got away with it. Sex between them was mind-blowing, in a sense that he could touch her, skin on skin, without being overwhelmed by her thoughts and presence. Over the years he'd tried having sex with others, but nothing was more off-putting. Touching any other woman's skin was enough to extinguish the fire in his loins when his head was flooded by her tedious thoughts and experiences. And so he praised the day he ever met Morgan, and sometimes he found it difficult to imagine his life without her.

Looking at the object in front of him now he found it difficult to summon the will to touch it. He'd already moved a bottle of hand sanitizer closer to him, ready to ensure that all traces of the bag and its owner could be removed instantly.

Red and Kitty looked on expectantly, and Krain lightly ran his fingers over the soft leather. He closed his eyes to better see the projections he was receiving in his mind's eye, and it was then that he saw her; a young, pretty redhead. His chest tightened, making him wheeze, and he quickly withdrew his hands from the bag. He saw that her name was Libby, (Elizabeth Jane Hood, to be precise), and that she had a dog called Rufus, yet he was completely stupefied about *what* she was – and for the first time in years he doubted his own psychic ability.

Gasping, he murmured to himself, "It can't be...no, it can't be right, surely?"

With a vacant look in his eyes, he rasped to Red, "Bring her to me, immediately. She takes precedence over Grim. And the dog, you must fetch the dog too."

Red looked surprised, but nodded his head in agreement and grabbed Kitty's arm, pulling her to the door with him. When they'd left the office, Krain clutched the handbag in both hands and fell back into his chair, soaking in the presence of the mysterious redhead.

In his head he could smell patchouli and hear a fluttery laugh that didn't even belong to her long after he'd finished holding it.

Chapter 13

12:24pm: Knickerbocker Gloria's, Sunray Bay

"Are you still here?" Gloria came waltzing back into the kitchen.

"Um, yeah. I wasn't sure where else to go," Libby said, feeling embarrassed and wishing she could slide between the cracks in the floor tiles.

"Oh I wasn't talking to you." Gloria wafted her hand dismissively, and looked at the treacle-haired girl instead. "I was talking to Ragdoll."

Ragdoll looked up from her crouched position on the floor, where she was still petting Rufus, and said, "Yeah, I'm racking up some overtime."

"Watch you don't burn yourself out though, eh?"

She stood up, stuck her chest out and pointed to her large boobs, "These aren't going pay for themselves you know."

Gloria rolled her eyes and grabbed a hot-pink apron that was hanging from a hook behind the door.

"Well if you get tired of all that dancing you could always muck in down here with me. The lunch time rush is about to start and I'm short staffed. Jennings is in court and Gretel hasn't bothered showing up yet."

Ragdoll lifted her coffee mug from the counter and slinked off, waiting until she was out of the door before calling over her shoulder, "Nah thanks, waiting on people doesn't agree with acrylic nails."

Gloria scowled after her.

"I'll lend a hand if you like," Libby said, realising the opportunity.

Gloria smiled.

"You're a good 'un sweetie, *whatever* you are."

"Look, about this monster thing, I'm really not you know..." Libby started.

103

Gloria put her hand up to stop her going any further. "Hey look, it's okay don't worry about it." Then pointing to the coat pegs behind the door, she added, "Grab yourself a pinny. We've got about fifteen minutes till rush hour starts, and honestly, it's like feeding time at the zoo."

As Libby tied a heavily stained striped apron round her waist, Gloria said, "So what are your plans for tonight?"

Libby looked down at Rufus, who was enjoying the cool kitchen tiles on his belly whilst his eyes were still looking up to where the bacon was. Seeing this, Gloria tossed all of it into a plastic dish and put it down in front of him on the floor. He sprang up and started to scoff it down as though he hadn't eaten in a month.

"I'm not sure to be honest, what do people usually do on their first night?" Libby asked.

Gloria shrugged and grabbed a couple of chopping boards from a cupboard above her head. Handing one to Libby, she said, "People tend to do whatever they can to get by really. If you have enough money, you could stay in one of the guesthouses on the seafront. But if you don't have much, there're hostels not far from here. Probably only set you back a couple of quid a night."

"I don't have *any* money," Libby sighed. "That bloke from The Ordinaries stole my purse."

Gloria's mouth twisted in sympathy, as she lifted a lettuce from its cellophane wrapper. "Look I can't give you much, but I'll give you some cash in hand for helping out today. It'll help you get sorted for tonight at least." Wagging her index finger, and speaking in a more hushed tone, she said, "I'll give you a friendly word of warning though. There are shelters for the moneyless, and some people might tell you to use them – but between you and me, I really wouldn't recommend it. You'd be better off taking your chances out on the streets than resort to those places, sweetheart. They're always full of *really* nasty sorts."

"Thanks," Libby said, suddenly feeling more alienated than she had when she'd first arrived. The dim reality of

Sunray Bay was beginning to chip away at the sunny facade she'd first encountered.

"So what is Sunray Bay exactly? I mean, where are we?"

"Who knows," Gloria answered bluntly, slamming a wide kitchen knife through the lettuce. "It's purgatory, that's how I see it anyhow."

"If it's purgatory, does that mean there *is* a heaven, and that we'll go there eventually?"

"Hmmm, nobody knows for sure what comes after Sunray Bay." Gloria shook her head, chopping the lettuce into finer pieces. "Some of us will move on *somewhere* eventually, yes, if we work extra hard at it."

"Work extra hard at what?"

"Earning back those brownie points that we were lacking when we first arrived, of course."

"So, you were saying before that not everyone who dies comes to Sunray Bay?" Libby asked, slicing into a large block of orange cheese. Her stomach gurgled loudly.

"Good grief no," Gloria said, reaching for a punnet of tomatoes. "Only us bad apples come here, honey. And before you ask, I've no idea where all the goody two shoes go. Like I said before, Sunray Bay is some kind of filter — sifts out all the riff raff, criminals and monsters."

Libby stopped cutting and looked to Gloria.

"Well I'm *none* of those things, so how did I end up here?"

"Quit denying it, love, it's getting tiresome. Just because you're a monster doesn't necessarily make you a bad person. On the contrary, I've known some really nice monsters in my time. Of course, it's unfair that they all get tarred with the same brush, but that's just life in general, I think you'll find. Anyway, I've given you a job today haven't I? If I had a problem with you, I'd have kicked you out already. But as it is, I think you're okay. So stop denying it and we'll get on a lot better."

Libby didn't bother denying it any more, she couldn't see the point. If Gloria wanted to believe she was a monster, then so be it, so instead she asked, "So which of them are you?"

"Which what?" Gloria asked, popping a cherry tomato into her mouth.

"Well you said that all people in Sunray Bay are either criminals or monsters. Which are you?"

Gloria looked at her sternly and waved her wet kitchen knife in the air, a string of lettuce falling to the floor.

"It's never polite to ask that question. A person's past is a person's past, okay? A lot of us are trying to make a decent living here – trying the best we can to move on."

"Move on *where* though? Why do you even care so much if you don't even know what comes next?" Libby asked, feeling as though she was going round in circles. "And, no offence, but you keep asking what I am."

"Spend a few days in Sunray Bay and you'll see why most folk would like to get out. I for one will take my chances with whatever comes next – it can't be any worse, surely. And yeah, I asked because I wanted to know what kind of trouble Grim had brought to my back door, that's all. It's screamingly obvious that you're more than a criminal, and you'll get into no end of trouble if you don't sort that soul issue of yours out soon. The weight of a soul is a sought-after commodity here – if you don't retrieve it, someone else will, you mark my words. I just don't want any trouble round here, that's all."

Libby had been wondering for the past half hour whether it was possible that there'd been some kind of celestial glitch. She knew for definite that she was just a bog standard girl, who had no shady past of bank robbery, murder or money-laundering to speak of, and she didn't have fangs or claws either. The most she'd ever done wrong was steal a geography textbook from school – but even that had been an accident. If she could prove there'd been a glitch of epic proportions, she wondered if she could make a complaint somewhere to the powers that be. Surely she'd deserve a queue jumper pass straight into heaven – or vouchers at the very least for a comfy residence in Sunray Bay while she waited for the issue to be rectified. She didn't know whether to laugh or cry at the thought, the chances seemed slim that anybody would even listen to her in the first place.

"So what's Grim's story?" she asked, wanting to take her mind off her own sticky situation for a while, but then realising it sounded as though she was prying into his past, she added, "I mean, who is he?

Gloria gave her a knowing look; a tip of the head with raised eyebrows.

"You'd do well to forget about him, honey."

Libby looked blank and feigned ignorance.

"I can see that look in your eyes," Gloria said. "But you're wasting your time, just so you know. I've known him for nearing two years now, and never in all that time have I known him to be involved with anybody, you know, romantically."

"Oh I didn't mean anything like that." Libby blushed, yet she was strangely thrilled at the revelation that he wasn't attached to anyone. "I'm not interested in him that way. I just wondered who he is, and whether he's always such an arsehole."

Gloria laughed; a shrill phlegmy noise in her throat that made Libby want to cough.

"You've caught him on a bad day, that's all. Mind you, he is hard work at the best of times. He isn't the chirpiest or chattiest of people around. But then he has a lot more problems than the average person, you know?"

"Problems like what?"

"Personal ones," Gloria said, her face serious again and warning Libby not to overstep the mark.

"Something to do with the deal he had with Krain?" Libby asked, daring to overstep it a little.

"That's just the tip of the iceberg," Gloria responded, unperturbed by Libby's question.

"So, what was the deal they had exactly?"

"It's a long complicated story," Gloria answered, wiping her hands on her apron. "And I don't have the time, or the inclination, to tell it."

"Well can't you tell me just a *little* bit?"

"Then I'd have to ask you, why do you care? If you're not bothered about him, why the need to know?"

Libby became flustered again and looked down to the slice of bread she had laid before her as though it would offer an answer.

Gloria chuckled and shook her head lightly.

"You're setting yourself up for a fall. He'll only break your heart. Save yourself the trouble."

"No, it's not like that," Libby said in defiance, crossing her arms awkwardly so the butter knife was sticking up towards the ceiling in her left hand.

"Course it's not," Gloria sighed with irony. "I've seen many a young girl swooning over him, and not one of them has got anywhere with him, not even close. He's just not interested. If anybody did ever manage to get into his heart, then they'd deserve a bloody great medal in my books. I mean, don't get me wrong, he *should* be loved, everyone needs to be loved – but he just won't let anybody in."

Libby studied Gloria and wondered whether she'd been one of the women doing the swooning in the past, and as though reading her mind, Gloria said, "And in case you're wondering, no it isn't down to personal experience. Grim is almost young enough to be my son."

Libby smiled back sheepishly, but was pleased to hear it.

"So what about his deal then?"

Gloria sighed, and checked her watch.

"Okay, I'll tell you as much as I can before the lunch mob arrive."

Spurred on by the promise, Libby quickly spread margarine on slices of bread, stacking them up high, and she listened with interest.

"It all boils down to the fact that Grim doesn't have a soul," Gloria began. "I won't go into the ins and outs, or the whys and what fors, because that's nobody else's business – but having no soul means that he can't pass on from Sunray Bay."

"Oh, you didn't actually tell me that bit. How do you pass on from Sunray Bay? Do we all just live another life here and then *die again*?"

"No, not exactly. There's a soul weighing system, a special set of scales that are kept at Sunray Bay's courthouse. Each person's soul is weighed at varying intervals to see whether they are ready to pass on to... well, wherever it is that redeemed people go to. Incidentally, that's where Jennings my chef is today – at court having his soul weighed. If he's been a good boy, he'll be able to pass over. Though I kind of hope he's been a bad boy, otherwise I'll need to recruit a new chef. Hey, are you sure you don't want to work here? There may be a permanent job open if you're interested?"

Libby was far too distracted to talk job applications just yet.

"But how do you redeem yourself in the first place?"

Gloria tapped the side of her nose and said, "Keep *that* clean and your soul should gradually get heavier over time. You can't feel it physically of course. It's something only the scales can pick up on. Basically, you've just got to prove you can be a good girl."

"But what if you die whilst you're still in Sunray Bay? Say if a car knocks you over and you never got round to redeeming yourself."

Gloria made a line across her throat with her thumb and said, "They say it's game over, I'm afraid. Gone forever."

"So does that mean because Grim has no soul and because he can't redeem himself, he's destined to just cease to exist one day?"

"Yeah, pretty tragic, huh?"

"It's awful," Libby said nodding her head, not able to imagine what that must be like for him. "But didn't you say Rufus has my soul? Doesn't that mean I'm in the same boat as Grim?"

"Oh no," Gloria said, "Just because it's not inside your body, doesn't mean you don't have one. All you have to do is figure a way of getting it back from Rufus. Grim just doesn't have one at all."

"So the deal Grim had with Krain, was it to do with his soul? Is Krain able to give him one?"

Gloria stuffed lettuce and tomato into a large plastic dish and mixed it all together with a pair of salad tongs. "Not Krain *exactly*, but yes that's the gist of it. Krain's wife Morgan would have been able to give him a soul."

"Krain's wife? Would she be able to help me get my soul back from Rufus?" Libby asked.

"It's not really the avenue you need to be taking," Gloria said, sprinkling raw onion into the salad bowl. "There's a small department at the council who specialise in slippery souls – you know, abnormal souls. I tend to call them slippery souls sometimes, makes them sound less ominous. They usually extract the soul from the foreign body, in your case Rufus, and then they keep it in quarantine for anywhere up to a year. It's a lengthy process, but at least nobody else can steal it while it's in their possession. Book an appointment first thing, and get it sorted. You should make it one of your top priorities, up there with finding a job."

"So how do they *extract* the soul exactly?" Libby asked.

Gloria squirmed and kept her head down.

"I'm not sure you'd like the answer if I told you. But I don't believe there's another way."

Libby gasped, and Rufus's eyes widened.

"So what about Morgan? If she could help Grim, maybe she could help me and Rufus too."

"Well it's like I said, I wouldn't approach her personally, but hey, go ahead if that's what you want to do."

With slight apprehension, Libby asked, "Is she a vampire?"

"No, she's a witch."

Oh great, Libby thought, *why didn't I think of that?*

"She's one of the oldest residents in Sunray Bay too," Gloria added.

"How old?" Libby asked, her curiosity piqued.

"Anywhere up to three-thousand-years-old I'd say."

110

"And she's still here after all that time? I guess there's no rehabilitating some," Libby said, "She must look pretty dreadful too! How old is Krain?"

Gloria snickered and then coughed into her hand.

"I've no idea how old Krain is, but don't worry, Morgan doesn't look as old as she is – she looks like she's only into her third decade not her third millenia. And aside from the fact she's a witch, and could probably make herself young and beautiful with a few swigs of frogs' legs and bats' eyes elixir, or whatever, when you come to Sunray Bay you cease to age physically." Pointing the salad tongs at Libby, she said, "So, if you end up being here another fifty years, you'll always look just as you do now. I mean, it's a crying shame I didn't die about twenty years earlier than I actually did." Then winking at Libby, she added, "Then I may have had a pop at Grim myself."

Libby forced a smile.

"How old is Grim?"

"I'd say a good ten years on you at least."

"Well, I'm mature for my age," Libby retorted.

"Defensive aren't we? I thought you said you weren't interested?" Gloria laughed, untying her apron at the waist. "Anyway, there's the shop door bell. Can I leave you here to carry on buttering that bread while I pop out front?"

Libby nodded; her face serious with thoughts and questions.

"But why didn't Krain and Morgan give Grim a soul in the end?"

"I dunno, honey. You heard just as much as I did from Grim himself just now," said Gloria, walking from the kitchen.

"Oh Gretel, it's you. *Where've you been?* You should have called to say you were going be late! Now hurry up and get through into the kitchen, will you?" Gloria's voice shrieked just outside the door.

Libby watched the doorway until a short, older woman with stiff hair, reminiscent of a wire pan scrubber, entered the room. Her flip-flops rhythmically thwacked on the hard floor, and as with most other people Libby had met in Knickerbocker Gloria's, Gretel had a cigarette dangling from the corner of her mouth. Smoking seemed like a compulsory thing to do and Libby wondered if she'd be smoking by the end of the day.

"Hello," she offered, "I'm Libby."

The other woman just grunted, and Libby expected that that was the extent of the conversation. Not that it bothered her; she'd quite happily keep to herself. She watched Gretel's large masculine arms reach out for a chequered apron from behind the door, and couldn't help but wonder which category the older woman fit into – criminal or monster. A thick band of hair framed her top lip, and a collection of DIY tattoos climbed up her forearms. Libby decided she could easily be either one – or both.

Gloria popped her head round the kitchen doorframe and said to Libby, "Oh, honey, I forgot to mention, help yourself to a sandwich and take a break when you've finished sorting that bread. You must be starving."

Starving was an understatement, so Libby finished buttering the mountain of bread as quickly as she could, and then after a cheese salad sandwich washed down with a glass of tap water, she told Gretel she was popping out into the yard. Although it was still fiercely hot outside, she needed some non-greasy smelling air to fill her lungs with, and Rufus needed the loo. Leaning her elbows on the low brick wall out in the yard, she absent-mindedly looked down the back street. Her head was spinning and she felt nauseous, she couldn't tell whether she wanted to be sick or not. She guessed the shock of it all was finally sinking in. Fanning her face with her hands, she gave herself a few moments to pull together.

"So, Gloria says that I should make an appointment with the council to get my soul back from you," she said to Rufus, who was cocking his leg against the wall.

"And is that what you want to do?" he asked, fearful of what her answer would be.

"No, of course not," she clucked her tongue. "Gloria seemed to imply that they'd kill you or something. And even if they didn't, they'd still keep my soul for anywhere up to a year! I can't let that happen either, we need to find a way to resolve this whole massive cock-up as quickly as possible. I prefer the idea of approaching Krain or his wife – we might be able to get out of Sunray Bay quicker."

"Well I'm pleased to hear you're concerned for my wellbeing, but are you for real? Krain and his wife don't sound like nice people, Libby. Why would you want to do that?"

Libby frowned.

"Because there's been a mistake, and it's our only option. We shouldn't be here, and if she's a witch then maybe she could even get us home somehow – or at least make it possible to contact my parents."

"And why would she do that? Out of the goodness of her heart?" Rufus chided. "Bloody hell Libby, this needs some serious thought, she's not the sodding Wizard of Oz you know."

"I know, I know, calm down. I was thinking, maybe if I speak a little bit more to Grim..."

Rufus shook his head and harrumphed.

"I can't believe you, that's what this is all about isn't it? You hapless hussy. You'll try anything won't you? When are you going to stop chasing after him?"

Libby looked genuinely hurt.

"I just want to talk to him," she snapped. "He had a deal with Krain and his wife, so he must know how to contact them. And, who knows, he might even know if it's possible for me to contact home. I'm being serious, Rufus, this is really messed up, and I'd like to at least speak to my parents."

Her eyes filled with hot tears, and she felt close to breaking down. At that moment she was twenty-two going on six years old. She was loath to admit it, but she needed her dad to tell her everything was going to be alright.

113

"Okay, okay," Rufus said, brushing his head against her leg in the style of an affectionate cat. "So are you going to go and speak to him now?"

"Yeah, I think so," Libby said, standing up straight and blinking the tears from her eyes. "What about you, are you staying down here?"

"Well I'm certainly not playing gooseberry, if that's what you mean. And don't you worry about me, I'll find something to do," he replied. Then with a wink, he added, "Good luck, tiger."

They both wandered back into the kitchen, where Gretel was plating up sandwiches. As Libby shut the door behind her she was so distracted by her thoughts she failed to notice that a figure had crept up and was leaning against the yard wall outside, watching her. The fabric of his grey sleeveless top ruffled in the breeze, and his brooding expression was framed by dirty-blonde hair.

Chapter 14

1:07pm: Knickerbocker Gloria's, Sunray Bay

Libby ventured into the dimly lit hall. It reminded her of an animal's burrow; brown threadbare carpet like well-trodden soil, and various doors, which led to other concealed rooms and cupboards, could have easily been gateways to a network of tunnels. Fusty dampness invaded her nostrils, and she held the back of her hand to her nose trying to block out the smell because it made her feel queasy. It reminded her of wet dog, only tenfold. Deep nicotine-cream wallpaper with dark stripes running vertically covered each high-ceilinged wall. Libby doubted the place had been decorated in years. A swing door leading into the cafe from the kitchen hung ajar, and she could see Gloria zipping about between customers.

Making doubly certain that Gloria's attention was turned away, she darted to the staircase, praying she wouldn't be spotted. Creeping upwards, she cringed every time the stair boards creaked beneath her weight, and she hoped with every ounce of good fortune she had that Grim was upstairs. She'd heard him going up when he'd stormed out of the kitchen earlier, and she hadn't seen or heard him come back down again.

She wasn't sure what she'd do if she bumped into one of the dancing girls, or even Gloria's husband. They probably wouldn't be too pleased about her snooping about, so she scurried up the stairs as fast as she dared hoping to avoid any such confrontations. When she reached the top she stood in a narrow dreary landing. The same brown carpet stretched forth, and the same shabby wallpaper hung to either side of her. Two closed doors were on her right, and there was an identical one to her left. Dull, bassy music thudded down a narrower staircase which lay at the other end of the landing. Libby expected that was where the dancing girls were,

115

further up in the dismal realms of the building. Crossing her fingers behind her back, she hoped Grim wasn't *that* far up.

Feeling jittery about being caught, she tapped lightly on the first door to her right and listened for a response. None came, and she bit her lip, indecisiveness taking hold.

"Grim, are you in there?" she whispered.

There was no answer.

Turning the handle slowly she pushed open the door, and before it was even fully open the smell of air-freshener enveloped her; a sweet sickly smell that was obviously intended to mask an even more unpleasant odour. In the corner of the room stood an off-white bath with a thick rim of grey sludge about a third of the way up. A toilet was right next to that, its broken seat skewed and hanging on by one rusted screw. And beneath the room's miniscule frosted window was a wash basin which had heaped remains of soap tablets melded onto it. When Libby saw that Grim definitely wasn't there, she shut the door again, not wanting to linger like the offensive smell. Moving over to the door on her left, she repeated the whole process.

Disheartened by the lack of response, she opened the door and squinted into the darkness. Rows of free-standing clothes rails lined either side of the narrow room, each crammed with sparkling costumes, feather boas and hats of a garish nature; obviously a changing room for the girls upstairs. A window was visible, on the opposite wall, behind curtains that were drawn tightly to block out the sunlight. And beneath it was a single bed.

Libby's heart juddered.

On top of the bed with his body propped against the metal headboard and one hand resting on a bottle of whiskey was Grim. His chest was bare and, despite the complete lack of light in the room, he still wore his sunglasses. He didn't move, and Libby couldn't decide whether he was sleeping or not.

"Grim?" she whispered, her mouth becoming dry with trepidation.

Unmoving, he growled, "What do you want?"

"I just want to talk," she answered.

Stepping fully into the room she closed the door behind her, instantly noting how hot and stuffy the room was, and because of the intensity of heat in the confined space, she was once again conscious of Grim's enthralling scent. Her heart skittered erratically, and blood throbbed behind her eyes; she felt as though she'd entered a wolf's den. He was sitting there like a brooding alpha male, motionless and waiting to pounce.

"It's hot in here," she said, not quite sure what else to say in the awkwardness of the moment.

"Is it?" he replied, raising the bottle of whiskey to his mouth and taking a long swig.

"I could do with a good stiff drink myself," she laughed light-heartedly, feigning interest in the railed clothes, and fingering them, as she walked towards him.

When she reached the foot of the bed, he asked, "What do you want, Libby?"

Her voice caught up in her throat. It was the first time he'd addressed her by name, and there were a couple of things which sprang to mind that she could suggest, if only she could find her voice, but instead she just looked at him. Allowing her eyes to wander freely, she followed the neat trail of hair travelling upwards from his trouser waistband to his navel, then further up to the thickening expanse across his large toned chest. Finally, her gaze rested on his expressionless face, masked behind sunglasses. She couldn't determine where he was looking, and she felt her face burning red. Moving to the side of the bed, she sat down by his legs and looked at her hands, not daring to meet his blank, black gaze again just yet.

"I wanted to talk to you about Krain."

He turned his head towards her and said, "What about him?"

"I'd like to know who he is, well, that is, I'd like to know who his wife is exactly, and where I can find them. You see, this is all wrong..."

She lifted her hands in the air to show her despair.

117

"I shouldn't be here. Gloria thinks I'm a monster and Ragdoll thinks I'm a *vampire*, for God's sake. It's just ridiculous. If Krain's wife really does work magic, I'd like to know if she can help me out. I can't stay here. I just don't fit in."

Grim raised an eyebrow.

"Sorry, no offence," she said, bowing her head. "But I don't belong here in Sunray Bay."

Grim issued a humourless laugh.

"That makes two of us."

"*You* believe I'm not a monster, or a vampire, don't you?" she asked. "I mean, I think I would have known about it, if it were the case. I'm a vegetarian for crying out loud, which is about the least monster-ish thing in the whole world. And I don't shrivel up and die in sunlight. Well okay, I burn a little, but that's because I'm ginger!"

Grim remained still and Libby couldn't tell what he was thinking, his body language gave nothing away, and just as she was about to go on further he straightened out his arm and offered the bottle of whiskey to her.

She accepted it and smiled.

"I've never drunk blood in my entire life," she explained. "But a good single malt? Now you're talking. This is my kind of poison."

She brought the bottle to her mouth and, without wiping the top, took a drink from it. Relishing the burning sensation that swept down her throat, she ran her tongue over her lips.

"Look," she said. "Gloria told me..."

"Told you what?"

"That you have no soul, and that's why you had a deal with Krain."

"Oh did she?" Grim said, disgruntled.

Libby brought her feet up onto the bed in front of her, and cradled her knees.

"Can I just ask something out of curiosity? If Morgan is the one who would have given you a soul, then why did you make the deal with Krain?"

Grim's mouth tightened.

"It's complicated."

"But is it true though, that you offered a year's worth of service to Peace & Order Maintenance in return for a soul?"

Grim didn't reply, and Libby took his silence as confirmation.

"Anyway, I'll get to the point," she said. "I'm interested in meeting Morgan, perhaps, to see if she can help me. How did you come to make your deal? And where would I find her and Krain?"

"Like I said, it's not that simple. And besides, I didn't go looking for either of them – it was Krain who approached me. He wanted to get his new venture off the ground, and knew I'd be the best person to help out."

Libby's eyes widened, and she whistled.

"Wow, you must be good," she said, not sure herself whether she was being sarcastic or serious. Looking at his firm biceps, she wondered just how many werewolves he *had* wrestled, and whether the scar on his cheek was an injury obtained from such a scuffle.

"Yeah, I am," he said, without any hint of arrogance.

"What went so wrong then? Why did Krain back out?"

"Because Morgan wanted something from the deal too."

"Oh so it was a three-way thing?" Libby sat up straighter. "What did she want?"

"You've never met Morgan."

"No I haven't, what's that supposed to mean?"

"She has a reputation."

"A reputation for what?" Libby asked.

Grim sighed with irritation and took another gulp from the bottle of whiskey.

"She's a bit of a – slut..."

Libby laughed out loud.

"So in a nutshell, you provided Black Dog Burger Co. with resources for a year, which made Krain happy, and as repayment you were meant to acquire a soul from his wife Morgan, who, in turn, wanted a little bit of *you* to make her happy?"

Grim shuffled uncomfortably and snarled, "Yes."

"Now that's what I call full circle," she chuckled.

"I didn't know anything about *that* part until yesterday," Grim said defensively, his mouth a thin straight line. "And neither did Krain, presumably. She's the reason it all went wrong."

"I think I'm beginning to understand now. Basically, Krain wasn't too happy about the indecent proposal his wife made, so he terminated the deal?"

"Of course he wasn't bloody happy."

"Sounds to me like you should have drawn up a contract, that way everyone would have known where they stood from the beginning. Never mind, you'll know for next time though, eh?"

She smiled at him, but he just scowled back, realising in hindsight how foolish he'd been.

"So would you have?"

"Would I have what?"

"Let her have her wicked way with you?"

"What do *you* think?" he barked. There was nothing playful about his tone.

"I don't know. That's why I asked."

"*No!*" he snapped. "I wouldn't sell my body for the price of a soul."

Libby rocked backwards, clutching her legs close to her.

"Does that mean she probably wouldn't willingly help me out then, since I'm not a bloke and have nothing to offer her?" she asked, looking thoughtful but teasing all the same.

"Probably not," Grim replied, matter-of-factly.

Libby's shoulders drooped, she hadn't expected that answer.

"Well is there *anybody* else in Sunray Bay who can help with soul defects? I mean, you have one and I have one, surely there has to be someone else who can help us?"

"No," he snapped. "And my problem is *not* the same as yours."

"They're both problems, all the same, and you shouldn't just run away. You can't give up like that."

120

"And what the hell do you know? You haven't got a clue. You don't know anything about me, apart from what Gloria told you."

"So tell me," Libby said, fighting an urge to lay her hand on his arm. "I'm a good listener."

His mouth twisted in frustration, but before he answered they heard a loud thud from somewhere else in the building, which resonated through the walls and door, followed by Gloria's gruff voice yelling, "*He's not here, I haven't seen him in weeks!*"

Her statement was met by muffled voices, which Libby and Grim couldn't decipher. "You can't go up there! We're entertaining clients!" came Gloria's panicked response.

A man's voice, which was much clearer and distinct now as it grew closer, replied, "It's Peace & Order Maintenance procedure, Gloria, we're searching the entire town and your place is no exception."

And then a deeper voice belonging to somebody else said, "We're going up whether you like it or not, but you can rest assured that we'll try to cause as little disturbance to your clientele as possible." Whoever it was laughed; a deep guttural laugh.

Libby's eyes locked onto Grim's sunglasses, trying to glimpse his eyes beneath. Her heart started rapping against her breastbone once again, and Grim sat forward.

"Fuck, they've found me already," he rasped.

121

Chapter 15

Bob Swinburn led the way up the staircase, his partner Jack
Fryatt followed close behind. They were both Peace & Order
Maintenance Officers and neither one was a stranger to the
second floor of Knickerbocker Gloria's. When Krain had
issued instructions for the whole town to be stripped down
and searched, Swinburn and Fryatt had made their way to the
areas surrounding Knickerbocker Gloria's, first and
foremost, intending to take his order quite literally. They'd
covered most of the side streets first before heading to the
exotic dance bar – hoping that their ruse wouldn't be
detected. They figured that a quick dance or two from the
Knickerbocker girls, whilst everybody else in Peace & Order
Maintenance was so preoccupied, was certain to go
unnoticed. They knew most of the girls anyway and always
tipped well, so there were no worries of them giving the
game away either.

They knew the layout of the building as well as they
knew their own homes, and when they reached the first floor
landing, Bob said, "Suppose we better check out these
rooms, for formality's sake."

Jack smiled; his gleaming teeth more prominent than
Bob's. Bob had a mouth full of crooked yellow teeth, none
of them looking particularly sharp or fang-like – his biggest
misfortune. He was living proof that not all vampires were
lucky enough to brandish trademark pointy teeth, and he'd
thought on numerous occasions that he might like to get
them fixed one day, replace his own sorry looking set with
white porcelain veneers. The financial aspect was always
enough to put him off though, and although he hadn't been
blessed in the looks department, he supposed he was lucky
that he didn't have an allergy to garlic like Jack did. Life

without pasta and flatbread pizza just wouldn't be worth living.

Looking at his partner, he was also pleased that he didn't have an aversion to sunlight either. Jack's skin was pallid and greasy underneath a thick layer of factor fifty sunscreen, whereas his own skin was the colour of a soaked teabag. Bob was proud of his own strong bloodline because, apart from aesthetically displeasing teeth, he had quite a reputable heritage. Coming from good sturdy stock, he could smell like a shark, see like a hawk, hear like a dog, and he could climb surfaces like Spiderman. The only thing apart from teeth that the Swinburn lineage hadn't mastered yet was immortality, but that wasn't bad going because no vampire bloodline had mastered it, as far as he was aware anyway.

As he stood on the landing he tried hard to focus on the official task at hand, ignoring the pulsing feeling behind his eyes; a feeling that usually accompanied the prerequisite for blood. He could smell the girls already. He'd been such a good boy for such a long time and sometimes wondered how on earth he controlled himself. Though, on special occasions like birthdays and anniversaries he would treat himself on the sly. He would pay the Knickerbocker girls a little extra for a quick bite. If Krain ever found out, Bob knew he'd instantly be dismissed from Peace & Order Maintenance, but the rush he got from doing it always seemed worth the risk. Besides, the girls were forbidden from offering that kind of service – so it was always a discrete exchange that worked well for both parties involved.

The simple truth was that Bob still enjoyed the old, illicit ways. He thought there was nothing better than tasting fresh blood straight from its living source, and that it was a sad state of affairs that Krain had completely changed the natural ways of the vampire social order. As well as believing that sucking on a person's neck was as common as muck, Krain also no longer deemed drinking blood straight from a person a necessary act, declaring that the amount of STDs and viruses crippling today's society made him feel physically sick. Bob thought the mayor was absolutely bonkers – an uppity, middleclass ponce who was forgetting the very foundations of his own birthright – but who was he to argue? Bob wasn't married to the most powerful woman in Sunray Bay. He didn't have any of that weird psychic stuff going on either, so he kept his mouth shut and behaved like a good boy – for the most part – ignoring his natural urges as best as he could to stay in a decent job.

He'd been in the Peace & Order Maintenance team for well over a year now, and he'd taken new recruit Jack Fryatt under his wing only three months ago. The Peace & Order Maintenance Department was primarily made up of vampires – a minor detail that hadn't been disclosed to the general public due to legal issues relating to equal opportunities and human rights – which under Krain's corrupt, one-sided government, were both pretty much non-existent. Krain's saving grace was that it was hard for Joe Public to differentiate a vampire from a non-vampire, so nobody knew – in fact, even vampires struggled to tell the difference sometimes.

Bob knew if he fell off the wagon and gave in to his primal instincts openly and freely he'd be classed as a feral. Ferals were vampires who refused to be dictated to under Krain's new legislations, and Bob harboured a slight envy towards these free-spirited ones. But on the flipside, the threat of The Ordinaries was something that he could live without...

Krain allowed The Ordinaries to operate behind the scenes in Sunray Bay, under the agreement that they kill ferals only, leaving his own elite team of sophisticates alone. It was a win-win situation: Krain could sit back and watch with ease as the streets were rid of dangerous monsters and ghouls, making it appear that he was providing a good service to the public, and The Ordinaries got to do what they enjoyed doing most – killing monsters, violently and mercilessly. So far Krain's master plan had been running smoothly, that is until Grim had gone berserk in the small hours of that very morning. Bob wondered what exactly it would mean for Krain and Peace & Order Maintenance in both the short term and the long term – he wondered just how much Grim had discovered about Krain's refined black pudding enterprise and what he meant to do next. Though he also had a feeling that Grim would be the least of their worries come nightfall and with that in mind, he was more than tempted to splurge his cash and indulge in some pure gluttony while he was at Knickerbocker Gloria's – and while he had the chance to do so. At least when all hell broke loose later, he'd be able to die happy.

He rubbed his hands together in anticipation as Jack opened the door to the first floor bathroom, wanting to proceed to the second floor without further ado.

"Yeah let's get the drudgery out of the way with then we can go upstairs to the real treasure," Jack agreed.

Bob winked at him, and was relieved to see that they hadn't uncovered Grim in the bathroom. He'd never worked the same shift as Grim, but he was wary enough to know that he was more than a handful, even for two men, and right now Bob had better things on his mind.

"So, are you sure we'll be able to squeeze in some *quality time*?" Jack asked. His jittery eyes sparkled, making him look like a schoolboy about to play truant.

"Yeah, who's gonna know?" Bob replied.

Jack grinned wide, his fangs resting in deep grooves on his bottom lip."Which one will you go for?" he asked as they moved to the next door.

"Whichever one's available, I'm really not fussy," Bob chuckled, thinking he might actually be greedy and reckless and ask for them all. He pushed open the door on the left, and they both stopped snickering and stood frozen as they looked into the darkened room before them. A man was lying on the covers of a single bed, his wrists were handcuffed to its headboard and there was a black silk bag over his head. But more noticeable was the woman who was straddling his naked torso. Her long blonde hair fell down to her waist and, from where they stood it looked as though she was wearing nothing but a pair of big white knickers with the words *ho, ho, ho* emblazoned in red across the back.

As the door clanked open, the woman turned her head. Her angry profile was silhouetted against the dimness, and she snapped, "You'll have to wait your turn!"

Bob and Jack looked at each other, dumbfounded, and they both shrugged their shoulders. Apologising, they bowed back out of the room and closed the door behind them.

"Since when did they offer *that* kind of service in here?" Jack asked. His eyes shone even brighter and his fangs had grown slightly longer.

"I have no idea," Bob replied, "But it's about bloody time."

The throbbing behind his eyes had intensified, and if he'd had a decent set of vampire fangs his would have grown even longer than Jack's.

"Mind you, what was with her pants? Did you see them? They weren't very sexy...I mean, is it Christmas or something?"

Jack laughed out loud.

"No, but I bet it is for that bloke she's riding."

They both cackled and Bob slapped him on the back, ushering him towards the second flight of stairs.

Chapter 16

They remained still, breaths held, until the voices of the Peace & Order Maintenance Officers had drifted upstairs, absorbed by the distant beat of music. Then, when she thought it was safe to do so, Libby reached down and pulled the satin bag from Grim's head.

"That's three times I've saved your arse now," she whispered.

"*Three?*"

"The car, the gun and now this," she beamed. "You owe me big style."

Grim's brow creased above his sunglasses, but as he took in the sight of Libby sitting on his stomach wearing nothing but an enormous blonde wig, a black t-shirt bra and terribly uncoordinated big white pants, it smoothed out and he almost broke a smile – *almost*.

Wriggling his hands he said, "Are you going to uncuff me?"

She made no attempt to move, enjoying the rhythmic rise and fall of his solid chest. Her bare thighs were full of goose-bumps against his naked cold skin; a delicious chill in the oppressive heat. Taking the blonde wig off and running her fingers through her own hair, she looked at him with a mischievous grin.

"Well that depends..." she said, eyelashes lowered.

"Don't fuck with me," he snarled, gruffness and unfriendliness back in his tone.

Libby mirrored his stern look.

"Now you listen to me. I'm sick of all your angry bullshit. It seems to me that you're being mean just for the sake of being mean. I keep helping you out, and I'm beginning to wonder why I bloody well bother because you keep shoving it back in my face. You're too pig-headed to realise that we're both after the same thing."

"I hardly think so," he spat.

"See there you go again. It's not that difficult, you know. You need a soul, and I want mine back – it's as good as the same thing."

"No it isn't," he insisted. "There's a *solution* to your problem."

"Not if the solution is detrimental to Rufus there isn't!" she hissed. "Why can't you admit that two heads would be better than one? If you help me out, I'll help you..."

"And how do you propose to do that?" he snapped.

"I don't know," Libby shrugged her shoulders, then relaxing a little, she added, "But I'm great at solving problems. It's one of my many key skills."

She smiled at him and stuck out her bottom lip.

"Don't leave. Stay here and help me."

His expression didn't give a lot away, which was infuriating, because she still couldn't fathom what he was thinking. His mouth remained neutral, and to keep herself from bending to taste his lips with her own, she reached out to take off his sunglasses.

"What are you doing?" he barked, jerking his head away from her.

She retracted her hands as though she'd been burnt, and stuttered, "Don't you ever take them off?" Then trying to make light of it, she added, "It's considered bad manners to wear sunglasses indoors, you know."

"I thought that was *hats*?" he snarled. "And don't *you* know it's rude to sit on a stranger in your underwear?"

Libby looked down suddenly feeling self-conscious, cursing her lazy choice of underwear.

"You're not a stranger though..." she said, tossing her head back, trying to exude an air of confidence. "Just somebody I've still got a lot to learn about."

She was pushing her luck, and she knew it, but it was worth a shot to see if he would respond to her flirting.

He didn't. He just glowered from behind his eye mask.

"So, what does the D on your head stand for?" she asked.

Grim opened his mouth to speak, but before any words had formed, a voice slid in from the doorway, to answer for him.

"Dick."

Libby's head flicked round in alarm, and she was horrified to see that Jarvis Strickler was standing watching them. A wicked smile dominated his scruffy face, and he held a gun in his left hand that was aimed straight at her.

"Come here and say that, Strickler," Grim snarled.

"What do you mean, Dickie Boy?" Strickler feigned surprise. "Did you think I was insinuating that you are a dickhead? After all, your name *is* Richard, is it not?"

Libby looked down at Grim.

"Your real name is Richard?"

"Yeah..."

"Look, as much as I'd love to hang around chatting to you guys, I'm in a bit of a hurry," Strickler said impatiently, moving closer to the bed.

"I know who you are," Libby blurted, still sitting atop Grim but looking at Strickler once again. "And you've got it all wrong. You probably think I'm a vampire or some other type of monster, don't you? Well I'm *not!* You don't have to kill me."

Strickler laughed, a deep throaty noise that sounded like a crow cawing. He motioned for her to get up by flicking his gun in the air.

"That's right, sugar lips, I don't *have* to kill you – and I won't, if you do as I say. Now come on, get down off lover boy, there's a good girl. We're going for a little ride – just me and you."

Libby looked at Grim with uncertainty. She wished she'd unlocked the handcuffs from his wrists when he'd asked her to, now she'd have to leave him hanging there because Strickler would probably shoot her if she attempted to do it now. Instead, she discreetly placed the key near his elbow, signalling it with her eyes – for what good it would do. Then as she slid down from the bed, she reached out and retrieved a white silk dressing gown from the end of a clothes rail.

Strickler glared at her, as she tied the gown at her waist. She looked at him wide-eyed and said, "*What?* You didn't expect me to come with you in my underwear, did you?"

Grabbing her by the nape of the neck, he pushed her toward the door. Then turning around, relishing the sight of Grim shackled to the headboard, he aimed his gun at the bed.

"Sorry Grim, no hard feelings, huh?"

Grim didn't move; didn't say a word.

Libby tried to look round, Strickler's fingers pinching hard at her skin and pulling her hair. She was fearful of what he meant to do and so she strained against him till her head was fully turned – just in time to hear the crack of the gun and see a large red explosion erupt on Grim's chest. Blood sprayed up the curtains behind the bed and spattered the sheets where she'd sat not long since. Grim's head lolled to the side and she clutched her mouth in a silent scream, fighting to keep bile from spewing up her throat. Her eyes stung with the resistance.

She tried to stand firm as Strickler shoved her out onto the landing, but his hand was secured firmly on her neck again and the gun was pushed into the small of her back. Trembling all the way down the stairs, she didn't know why her legs didn't buckle beneath her. The whiskey she'd drunk earlier was scorching her throat like heartburn and she felt sick and dizzy. *It's all my fault*, she thought. *Grim's dead because of me.*

She didn't think he could have survived a wound like that, not with the amount of blood she'd seen anyway. The most she could hope was for Gloria to discover him. If there was a slight possibility he was still alive, she could maybe save him from bleeding to death. But she didn't see Gloria on the way out to let her know, and she didn't even see Gretel, as Strickler pushed her through the kitchen and out of the back door.

Outside in the back street Strickler shoved her towards a battered silver car, and as they drew close to it he suddenly reached around and smothered her face with a cloth. It blocked her mouth and nose, making her light-headed, and it smelt funny. She couldn't get it away from her face because Strickler had clamped his arms around her, crushing her like a boa constrictor. He was surprisingly strong for such a spindly man.

As her legs finally did buckle, and the ground rushed up to meet her, she wondered what colour Grim's eyes were. And then everything went black.

Chapter 17

Rufus had hung around in the kitchen for as long as he could stand – hopes of Gretel dropping some food on the floor a treat not to be missed, especially when she'd started handling cooked meats. She hadn't been much of a conversationalist though and she smoked enough cigarettes to burn a hole in the ozone layer, so when he started to hack and cough, he sneaked off upstairs, following his nose, which led him straight to the second floor.

Despite being a dog, even Rufus was shocked by how grubby and dated the building was. Yet when he entered the exciting domain of the second floor he was taken aback. He discovered that the upper level of Knickerbocker Gloria's was obviously where the money was spent...

A large circular bar stood in the centre of the enormous room in which he found himself. The bar top itself was made of glass and had intermittent starry lights twinkling all the way around, giving a relaxed ambience to the darkened room. The only other light source was a grand arched window, which currently had its blinds pulled up. Grainy shafts of sunshine poured through onto a large leather couch in front, the only tell-tale sign that it was still actually daylight outside.

Three slender chrome poles ran up from the bar top, as though propping the ceiling. Rufus imagined the girls must dance on top of the bar. And for customers' viewing pleasure, there were black leather high-backed stools positioned all the way round. At that moment in time there were three men sitting at the bar, spaced out a fair distance from each other; evidently not a place for idle chit chat. And there was a big bearded man standing behind the bar itself, pouring liqueur of some sort into a crystal cut glass. Rufus wondered whether it was Stan, Gloria's husband. He didn't

look like the sort of man who would be married to Gloria –
he was as large as she was small, and he appeared to be quite
some years her senior. But then, Rufus had wondered what
kind of couple Gloria and Stan would be anyway. It was a
strange business for a married man to run. All those dancing
girls flitting about right under his nose, it would be enough
to make anybody stray.

Along the back wall were six white doors. Each had a
silver star affixed with inscriptions. Sniffing at the air, Rufus
crept along the glossy black floor to the first white door,
which was standing ajar. It looked like a movie star's
dressing room door and the engraved words on its plaque
read *Mitzi & Ragdoll.*

Pawing the door, nudging it open further, Rufus scuffled
inside. His eyes widened when he saw the treacle-haired
dancer, who'd been drinking coffee in the kitchen earlier,
sitting on the edge of a circular stage pulling a silk stocking
up over her knee. He thought she looked nothing short of
beautiful, in a human kind of way. She was positioned just
outside the boundaries of a harsh spotlight that highlighted a
pole in the centre of the stage. The soft light which bled into
the darkness gave her an ethereal quality, and the pole
behind her was flashing intermittently like chaser lights on a
Christmas tree. Soft music played from hidden speakers,
and resting against the wall, blending into the shadows, was
a black leather couch.

"It's Ragdoll, isn't it?" Rufus said.

She looked up, startled.

"Hey fella, what're you doing up here?"

"Oh just stretching my legs, you know."

Ragdoll jumped down from the stage and walked over to
him.

"Poking about then, eh?" she asked with a grin, balancing
a cigarette in the corner of her mouth as she spoke. "That's
okay, I've got a while to kill yet."

Tickling the fur behind his ears, she said, "You didn't by
any chance see another girl out there, did you? Short black
hair..."

133

Rufus shook his head.

Her mouth screwed up in agitation, but before Rufus could ask what was up, the door flew wide open and the big bearded man from behind the bar was filling the entire doorway.

"Doll, can you squeeze in a quick one before the next scheduled punter comes?"

Ragdoll threw her arms up in the air and made a sound of frustration.

"I'm not Wonder Woman, Stan."

Stan made a gesture with his thumb towards the bar area, and Ragdoll looked out over his shoulder. She recognised two Peace & Order Maintenance Officers, who were propped against the bar – and knowing they tipped very well, she huffed loudly as though she was being hugely put upon, but said, "Okay, give me a couple more minutes, yeah?"

Stan smiled and gave her the thumbs up but his expression turned to one of confusion as he was jostled to the side by a slight, but stunning, woman. She had skin the colour of chocolate milkshake and hair that was black, tight and curly. Barging straight past him, she moved him as easily as though he were a skittle and she a bowling ball.

Panting and fanning her face, she said, "Sorry I'm late Stan, got held up in traffic. Peace & Order Maintenance have got the streets nigh-on gridlocked out there. What the hell's going on?"

Stan looked at her through narrowed eyes.

"I've no idea."

Reaching for the door handle, he added sternly, "You two be ready in two minutes flat. Oh and get rid of the dog, it's not professional."

And with that he banged the door shut.

Ragdoll immediately set to unbuttoning the other woman's beige mack, her fingers fumbling impatiently, and Rufus wondered why the new arrival was wearing a coat anyway. He couldn't imagine why anybody in Sunray would feel the need to wear a coat. But when she shrugged it off, it was quite obvious why she'd worn it. A tiny gold two-piece covering her most intimate parts was the extent of her outfit.

"Ta da," she laughed.

Ragdoll slapped the other woman's arm lightly, giving her a look of disdain, and chucked the mack behind the leather couch.

"So where'd you get the dog from?" the dark-haired woman asked, eyeing Rufus. "You didn't mention it before..."

"It's Rufus," Ragdoll said, her smile returning. "Let me introduce you. Mitzi, this is Rufus. Rufus, this is Mitzi."

"Pleased to meet you," Rufus said, bowing his head courteously.

Mitzi gasped and covered her mouth with her hand. Then laughing with delight, which to Rufus's sensitive ears sounded akin to a canary singing, she said, "Pleased to meet you too, Rufus."

She bent down to pet him, and he smelled her skin, which smelt divine.

"Are you Ragdoll's dancing partner?" he asked.

"Yeah." she answered with a nod. "And a bit more than that really..."

"Oh?"

"Come on, Mitzi," Ragdoll snapped. "Get a shift on."

Mitzi rolled her eyes and stood up.

"She's my twin sister. *Bossy* twin sister!"

"*Twin sister?*"

The two women couldn't have looked any more different if they'd tried.

"I thought the penny might have dropped by now," Ragdoll said, smoothing her already smooth hair down with the palms of her hands. "I thought you could smell it...?"

Rufus looked from Ragdoll to Mitzi.

"Smell *what*?"

Ragdoll rolled her eyes and Mitzi grinned, and they said in unison, "We're werewolves, Rufus."

And suddenly the glass to the penny arcade inside Rufus's mind exploded and a whole ream of pennies dropped. It suddenly made perfect sense. His nose had been going into overdrive ever since he'd arrived, distracted slightly by the presence of food, of course, and clouded by cigarette smoke. And twins – even that wasn't such a strange concept any more. Litters of pups weren't always identical.

He stood still, starry-eyed, whilst trying to digest the information he'd just been given, knowing instinctively that there wasn't just Ragdoll and Mitzi either. He could smell it now; strong and engulfing. He was in a loft full of dancing girls – all of whom would be four legged and furry by the time the day was out. The scent all around him was exotic and foreign yet natural and familiar.

Tugging at his collar and disrupting his trance, Ragdoll said, "Come on Rufus, you'll have to leave now. I'll take you down to the kitchen later, see if there's any scraps left over from lunch time."

She opened the door and guided him out into the bar area, and then he watched as she strutted over to the Peace & Order Maintenance Officers. Taking the tallest one by the tie, she dragged him back to hers and Mitzi's showroom, and the other officer followed close behind, like a giddy pup. When the door closed behind them, Rufus turned and noticed Lula, the other dancer who'd been in the kitchen earlier, standing by the window talking to Stan. Her arms and hands were wafting about in the air, and she looked upset. Trotting closer, he heard her say, "...so I'll get kicked out of my flat if I don't pay the last two months' rent."

"And what do you want me to do about it Lula?" Stan replied with his arms folded tight across his bear-sized chest.

"Give me some more hours," she said pleaded. "I'll even work Sundays for just time and a half."

Stan's blue eyes looked at her hard from behind brown-framed glasses.

"I can't let you do time and a half on Sundays Lula, you know that. The other girls get double time. You're all my girls, and you all get treated the same."

"But that's not true," Lula pouted, her shoulders slumping. "Ragdoll and Mitzi get *far* more overtime than the rest of us."

"Don't push it," Stan snapped. "You *know* why that is. The clients love the whole twin thing. It's down to demand, nothing personal."

"Well why don't you let me team me up with Lady or Patches? Who would know the difference?"

Stan's mouth dropped open, and he looked as though he'd been slapped in the face. He turned his head away from her, as though he couldn't bear to look at her. Lula blushed, knowing she'd overstepped the mark. Stan was a good honest man and wasn't into false advertising, not even to make a bit extra cash. Instead of chastising Lula though, he pointed out of the window and said, "What the fuck is *he* doing?"

Lula turned her attention to the street below.

"That's the girl who was down in the kitchen earlier talking to Gloria," she said, angling for a better view.

Rufus scurried past the bar and jumped up onto the leather couch. Planting his front paws on the window sill, he was just in time to see Libby being bundled into the boot of a silver car by the man who'd deprived them of an ice-cream earlier.

Chapter 18

2:06pm: A donkey shed, Sunray Bay

The infusion of hay and horse shit cloyed her senses, and something tickled her nose. Libby tried to rub it, but found she couldn't move her arms to her face. Her stomach heaved and she spluttered until her throat hurt. She struggled to sit up because her arms were bound behind her back, and she groaned because it felt as though her brain was trying to split her skull in two.

Propping herself up against something hard, Libby allowed her eyes to adjust to the darkness, and tried to remember where she was. Her mind was all fuzzy.

And then she saw him.

Strickler; standing in a shaft of light watching her. In that instant it all came rushing back and she pictured Grim lying red, still and dead on the bed.

"You bastard," she hissed. "You killed him."

Bending down, so that his face was only inches away from hers, he asked, "Are you comfortable enough, princess?"

He stank of stale nicotine, and his teeth were long and yellow like a rat's. His watery blue eyes searched hers, and for a moment he actually seemed sincere.

"Are you having a laugh?" she spat.

Strickler smiled, still on his haunches. He gently swept some of her hair behind her ear to see her face better. But she shook her head, making it fall loose again, and scowled at him.

"What do you want with me? And where am I?"

A large hairy head sniffed and grunted to her left, making her jump. When she turned to see what it was she realised it was just a donkey.

"I won't hurt you Elizabeth, I promise," Strickler said, his face and body still invading her personal space.

138

"It's nice to see that you had a good root through my purse," she said. Nobody called her Elizabeth, it was her official name for formal correspondence, like bank cards and her driver's licence – and it used to be her naughty name, which had become obsolete over the years.

"I had to," he said. "Well, okay, no I didn't *have* to, but I just wanted to see if you were who I thought you were. Though, in hindsight, it was silly. I didn't really know what your name would be anyway – and besides, I knew you were who I thought you were just by *looking* at you." His face was deadly serious, and his voice was unnerving. "You should thank me, you know."

Libby looked confused.

"What the hell are you talking about? And why the hell should I *thank* you?" she cried. "I was getting on fine until you came along."

Strickler laughed; a trapped wheezing sound in his chest that rattled at the bottom of his throat.

"Oh I could see that," he sneered.

Libby held her head up high, "Look, you've got it all wrong. I'm not what you think I am. This could all be straightened out if you'd just listen to what I'm saying."

"I know exactly what you are, love."

He ran the backs of his fingers down the side of her face softly. Libby bucked up and down, the touch of his yellowed fingers very unwelcome.

"Untie me now!"

Strickler snatched his hand back and stood up.

"Didn't you hear what I said? You should be thanking me."

Libby stopped thrashing and watched him warily.

"What exactly should I be thanking you for – the part where you stole from me or the part where you kidnapped me?"

She didn't want to antagonise him too much, she was sure he was an all out nutcase, but she was at the end of her tether. The thought didn't elude her that she might end up meeting the same fate as Grim.

Strickler grinned to himself, and then stooped back down to a crouching position in front of her. Perched with his back and neck arched, he reminded her of a vulture.

"You'll know soon enough, and then you can thank me properly."

"Soon enough?" Libby asked, fearful of his drug-addled gaze.

"All in good time, sugar lips."

A lecherous look crept to his face, and he looked down at her exposed flesh where the white dressing gown had come loose at the waist. She gasped when one of his rough calloused hands ran over her thigh, and she wriggled away from him, repulsed.

"Don't flatter yourself," he spat, pulling his hand back and wiping it on his jeans. "Though I bet if I were Grim you wouldn't have objected."

Libby's eyes brimmed with tears and guilt as she thought of Grim.

Strickler rose to his feet again and kicked hay with the toe of his boot. He laughed hoarsely, making some of the donkeys round about jump.

"Just what is it about The Grim Reaper, sugar lips?"

"What do you mean?"

"All the women fall for him. What does he have that the rest of us don't? Tell me, is it those big arms? That gruff voice? Or is it those *pretty eyes*?"

"You're being ridiculous," Libby stuttered. "I didn't fall for him. He was an arsehole just as much as you are."

"Yeah whatever," Strickler said, taking a self-rolled cigarette from behind his ear and running his tongue down the seam.

"Why did you call him The Grim Reaper?" Libby asked.

"It's his name," Strickler shrugged, taking a lighter from his jeans pocket and lighting the end of the rollie.

"But you called him Richard earlier..."

Strickler blew smoke into the musty air of the stable, making Libby wonder whether *all* criminals and monsters had bad smoking habits.

140

"His real name is Richard. Grim's just a nickname, something to do with his reputation."

"What reputation?"

Strickler flicked ash to the floor, and his face became frosty.

"I didn't fetch you here to discuss *him* all day," he snarled. Then taking another draw and breathing smoke down his nostrils like a scrawny dragon, he said, "But I suppose I can spare a couple of minutes.

"I've known some pretty fucked-up characters in my time, especially during my stint in Sunray Bay prison – but Grim went the extra mile, so to speak. In fact, I don't think I've met a man who's killed so many people before."

Libby's eyes widened.

"I don't believe you."

Strickler shrugged.

"I couldn't give a shit."

"Well, hold on, why were *you* in prison?" Libby asked – hoping the answer wouldn't be anything worse than robbery or theft.

He sucked deep on the cigarette again, as though he needed its poisonous fumes in order to function properly, and answered in a billow of smoke, "Murder."

Shit, Libby thought.

"But you're a monster-slayer, you kill all the time, don't you?" she asked, trying to sound indifferent.

"Yes, that's true, but the person I did time for wasn't a monster – she was just a regular woman."

Libby gulped, the sickly feeling she'd experienced when first awaking in the barn suddenly coming back to her.

"Who was she?"

Strickler ground out the unfinished cigarette on the floor with his shoe, his eyes fixed on Libby's.

"She was an old client of mine," he said. "A woman called Sharon Krain."

"*Krain?*" Libby gasped. "Was she any relation to the mayor?"

"Yes," he said, matter-of-factly. "She was his first wife."

141

Libby puffed out her cheeks.

"And she was a client of yours? What were you?" Then shaking her head, she continued, "No, anyway, I don't want to know. I don't want to know anything about it. I hope you get locked up again for murdering Grim, you deserve it because you're round the bloody twist!"

Strickler laughed as though she'd told a *knock, knock* joke.

"I very much doubt it, love. I'd be hero of the day. Nobody would give a monkey's nuts if Grim was dead."

"That's not true," Libby snapped. "Gloria and Stan, they're his friends."

"Hmmm, I wouldn't be so sure about that."

"Why not?"

"Not when they find out what he's been up to. I know he's been capturing werewolves for Krain, and I suspect that when Gloria and Stan find out they'll not be over the moon about it." Strickler guffawed and coughed up a mouthful of phlegm.

"What are you talking about?" Libby asked, recoiling as he spat on the floor next to her feet. "Grim already told Gloria about it this morning, and she was fine."

"In that case she's a frigging idiot."

"Why?"

"Oh you're slow on the uptake, aren't you Elizabeth?" Strickler said. "Didn't you realise? They're big-toothed, hairy-arsed, flea-ridden, mangy werewolves, the pair of them. Stan and Gloria are the alpha male and female of the Knickerbocker Pack."

Libby groaned inwardly.

"Did Grim know that?"

"Of course Grim knew that," Strickler laughed.

"Hang on a minute," Libby said, raising her eyebrow. "If you already knew about Gloria and Stan running a pack of *dancing* werewolves, then how come you haven't killed them? That's what The Ordinaries do, right?"

Strickler leaned against one of the stable doors and rubbed a donkey's proffered nose.

142

"Thanks for pointing that out Miss Marple," Strickler tutted. "The Knickerbocker Pack aren't a threat, they're all fairly domesticated. There's only one male, Stan, and he's an old fart – he likes to think he's an alpha male, but I don't think that applies when you have no competition. So like I say, they're mild enough." Then he winked and added, "Besides, we get a hefty discount for leaving them alone."

Libby gave Strickler a look of disgust.

"But still, *werewolves*? Just how safe can a domesticated werewolf be?"

Strickler laughed without humour, and the whites of his eyes glinted.

"You'll see why they aren't a priority once you've spent a night or two in Sunray Bay. Night time here isn't pleasant, let's put it that way – and you'd better get used to it too, because on average we get around fifteen hours of darkness each and every night. And that's all year round."

"But I'm a monster remember," Libby said sarcastically. "Why should I be worried?"

"Indeed you are, but like the Knickerbocker Pack, you're a drop in the ocean, Elizabeth."

"So what do you want with me?" she screamed in frustration. "Why am I so important to you if I'm so inferior?"

"I didn't say you were inferior. And you'll find out soon enough what I want from you."

Turning around, he walked towards the barn door.

"Now be a good girl and stay calm. Nobody will hear you if you scream, and I don't want you stressing the donkeys."

"Where are you going?" she called after him. "You can't just leave me here!"

"Chill out, sugar lips." Strickler waved a mobile phone in the air. "Just popping out to make a call, that's all."

He grinned to his very core because he'd never heard a woman asking him not to leave before, and it was a sound he could get used to.

"Hang on," Libby said, "I've got one more question."

Strickler turned round, his spiky skeletal shadow already at the doorway.

"Go on then."

"It's about Grim. What was he? I mean, was he a criminal or a monster?"

Strickler was silent for a moment, and Libby wasn't sure whether he was going to reply or not, but then he moved his face into a stream of light, so that his features looked like an emaciated jack-o-lantern, and he said, "Both."

"Well what *kind* of monster was he?"

"The kind of monster who kills hundreds of people single handedly."

"Wouldn't that be classed as criminal?"

Strickler looked thoughtful for a moment.

"Yeah, I suppose so."

Libby had always thought herself to be a good judge of character, and she still couldn't quite believe what Strickler was saying about Grim. In fact, she didn't believe a word of it.

"You're lying to me," she said. "Even if he was a criminal he wasn't a monster, was he?"

Strickler leaned against the barn door and pushed it open. Light burst inside, and Libby saw that her legs and feet were filthy. Before stepping outside, Strickler replied, "Well that depends on what you class as being a monster. I'm not necessarily talking about fangs, cloaks and super powers fuelled by the moon. I'm talking about the kind of monster that would shoot his own wife and baby girl."

And with that, he was gone.

Chapter 19

Krain repeatedly *tick-tacked* his pen on the surface of the desk. He was sitting in a leather swivel chair in the executive meeting room inside the Black Dog Burger Co. factory. He'd called a contingency meeting as soon as he'd left the prison. It comprised of all senior councillors and Peace & Order Maintenance management staff – all of whom were vampires – and the purpose of the meeting was to discuss Operation Dog Catch. It had taken some time for all the attendees to arrive, and the last person had just been seated.

Whilst he'd waited, Krain had made a call to Morgan, notifying her of the situation. She'd been sharp with him, as usual, and had told him that she was more than capable of taking care of herself should any werewolves call at the lighthouse looking for him. Krain found himself wondering whether she might even point them in the right direction, her mood was so black.

He was annoyed that she was annoyed with him. In fact, he was furious. What did she expect him to do? Stand by and let her seduce Grim, just because she felt like it? It was totally unreasonable. He quivered with rage as he recalled the blasé look on her face as she'd said to him, "You know the deal you have with Grim? Well I won't give him a soul unless I can spend a night with him."

"Are you crazy, woman?" He'd yelled back at her. "Was all of that marriage counselling for nothing?"

She'd looked genuinely hurt, as though *he* was being unreasonable, and she'd said, "Well at least I'm not hiding it from you. I could go behind your back, but I don't do that anymore."

"Why *him*?" Krain had asked. She'd never even met the man before, it was ridiculous.

145

"Kitty mentioned he has a reputation. And he sounds unusual – I like unusual," had been her offhand response.

So Kitty had put her up to it, Krain promised himself that he would reprimand her later. He still wasn't quite sure what to do about Morgan though. She'd humiliated him once too often now. Maybe he would have to rethink things when the dust settled down again, when he could think straight – at that moment, he would love to build a huge pyre and burn her at the stake. And as for Grim, he'd kill him twice over for the mess he'd caused him both personally and professionally.

It pained Krain that he'd had to order the Black Dog Burger Co. factory to cease production on the night of a full-moon; its staff now on standby for a full blown attack. Security had been upped, which had required bringing extra men in from Peace & Order Maintenance, and the factory had been locked down as much as possible.

Rapping the pen hard against the desk, the board room quietened, and Krain cleared his throat and addressed the panel.

"Okay, this is where we stand, there's no use in lying. I've absolutely no idea what their plan of action will be, and therefore we need to be prepared. As we all know, werewolves are territorial and don't usually associate with others from outside of their own packs, but in this instance we can't rule it out."

Tapping the side of his head with the pen, he carried on, "In fact, on the contrary, we have to think like they would in this instance, and I can only assume they may well join allegiance with each other and unite packs to form an army."

"How can we be sure that they'll even find us here though?" asked Sebastian Songbird, Councillor of Arts and Performance. His white-blonde hair, wire-framed spectacles and flouncy purple neckerchief made it hard for Krain to take anything he said seriously.

"Well I suppose we *can't* be sure, and that would be a flipping good scenario," Krain replied, impatiently, "But it's a bloody safe bet that they won't be heading down to the

146

library to borrow some books, and they won't be popping round to the local for a good old knees up either."

Sergeant Flatbrook, who was sitting to Krain's immediate left, snickered and Songbird looked daggers at him.

"That's not what I was suggesting, sir," he huffed, fiddling with the knot of his neckerchief subconsciously.

"As soon as the moon is up they'll be out looking for us. And come hell or high water I'm sure they won't stop until they find us...which I'm sure won't be too difficult."

"Till they find *you*," Songbird muttered quietly behind his hand. Krain pretended he hadn't heard. If he bit back now he knew he'd probably end up wiping the floor with the lot of them, which would be counterproductive given the situation.

Dorothy Pallister, Councillor of Public Transport, whose voice was like a washing machine stuck on spin cycle, took the opportunity to speak up, "Then why are we all in here, sir? Shouldn't we split up? What if they kill us all when they find us here? What will happen to our population and all we've built up over the years?"

"How will they kill us all Dorothy?" Krain sighed. "We have the perimeters of the building guarded by our best men. They won't be able to get past the gates. We're in the best place we can be."

"But *what if they do*?" she urged, her eyes signalling that she was on the verge of hysteria.

"They *won't*," Krain insisted. "But if they did happen to, then we have guards in place inside too. *We* need to sit tight within these confines and come up with a good strategy to sort all this mess out by the time the sun rears its ugly head and before the excrement well and truly hits the air conditioning units of Sunray Bay. I want *none* of this in the blasted papers or on the six o' clock news"

"But sir, we have fifteen hours of darkness looming – that's an awful long time," Dorothy shrieked. "What if the guards outside tire and lose concentration? They may become sloppy at holding the fort."

Krain gritted his teeth and rolled his eyes

"Yes, Dorothy, I'm well aware that fifteen hours is a long time – which we can use to our advantage if we're wise. Now if you'd rather head off home and survive the night alone, then be my guest, don't let us keep you. But I think I probably speak for the rest when I say, there's safety in numbers – and like I said, we need to come up with a rollicking good plan!"

Everybody else around the table grunted their agreement and nodded their heads profusely. Dorothy's eyes widened and she shook her head.

"Oh no sir, I'd like to stay. I was just making observations."

"*Observations* that have already been made!" Krain barked. "Now how long do we have till sunset?"

Flatbrook consulted his wristwatch.

"About ninety minutes, sir."

"Okay, call the remaining Peace & Order Maintenance officers in after precisely thirty minutes – even if Grim isn't located by then. The search can continue tomorrow. Right now, he becomes secondary concern – in fact, to hell with him. He's got nowhere to run, and he can't hide forever. If I didn't want to do it myself, I'd say let the werewolves tear him limb from limb – it's more than he deserves."

Flatbrook nodded, fatty deposits beneath his chin wobbling.

"Oh and up the ante on his accomplice. I'd really like that girl fetching into custody immediately," Krain added.

Before he could dish out further instructions, his mobile phone started to vibrate in his trouser pocket. Excusing himself, he left the board room, and standing outside in the bland grey corridor that smelt of new carpet, he fished the phone out of his pocket and raised it to his ear, hoping that it would be Red or Kitty with news about Libby Hood; news that they had taken her into custody.

As he pressed the call retrieve button, he thought to himself how unfortunate it was that she'd arrived on such a bad day. But then wasn't that usually the case. *What is it they call it,* he wondered, *sod's law?*

148

"Krain," he answered.

There was no answer on the other end, but he could hear a hissing background noise. He bristled, feeling slightly unnerved, but before he could hang up a man's voice spoke slowly and clearly.

"Krain, I have something that you'll be very interested in. Now listen carefully..."

Krain instantly recognised Jarvis Strickler's voice. His stomach did a somersault, because he immediately knew what Strickler had. And Strickler was correct – he was *very* interested. So he listened carefully.

Chapter 20

For the second time that day he awoke in a place other than his own bed; the first time was on the beach and this time was in blackness. Light was scarce and he struggled to remember where he was. The air around him had a sweet smell of vanilla, or coconut perhaps.

And then he remembered; it smelt of her. Libby.

With this came the cold realisation of where he was, and he was suddenly overcome with the discomfort of having lain with his hands cuffed to the bed posts for goodness knows how long. Sucking in air through his teeth, he grimaced as he straightened and tried to sit up. He had a crick in his neck that would undoubtedly last for days, and his shoulder was a burning agony.

The spare bedroom at Knickerbocker Gloria's had grown darker still, yet, even though he still wore his sunglasses, Grim could make out dark splotches on the sheets all around him. He didn't bother looking at the wound on his shoulder. It hurt like a bitch, but he wasn't one for sitting around licking his wounds. Never had been.

Now in a sitting position he gathered his strength, and with one sharp yank he tore free from the bed post restraints. A dull tinny noise issued as the thin cheap metal spokes gave way from the headboard and clattered to the bed. He'd known all along he could've broken free easily enough – yet he'd chosen not to. And right then he asked himself why...

He tried to convince himself that he'd been unaffected by her sitting on him like that, in her totally ridiculous underwear. But he was only fooling himself. In reality, he thought she'd looked sexy as hell.

He cursed himself.

In the couple of years that he'd been in Sunray Bay he'd never let his guard down. Not once. Yet he had an unsettling feeling that she'd managed to scrape the surface. She'd created a chink in his armour, and as miniscule as it might have been, he had definitely felt it. He couldn't understand either; he thought she was bloody annoying. Of course, she was attractive, but then so were most of the other women who'd come on to him. Most disturbing though was the fact she had, as Gloria would call it, a slippery soul. Even Ragdoll had as good as said she was a vampire – and her nose was seldom mistaken. Yes, Libby was definitely a vampire, whether she knew it or not. And vampires went against everything he stood for.

Stop thinking about her, he scolded himself. He knew he had to get to The Grey Dustbowl – and fast. It was already dusky outside, and the moon would soon be casting its silvery, spidery rays – and that's when he needed to run like hell.

Right on cue, a shiver-inducing soulful howl cried out in the distance, announcing that the change was beginning already. Grim imagined it would be the sort of night that would be recorded in history books – and he wanted no further part to play in it.

Taking the key that Libby had left on the bed, he unlocked the handcuffs from his wrists, smiling and shaking his head when he realised they were trimmed with black marabou feathers. And again, he thought about her sitting on top of him. Hair blazing red and eyes warm brown – she'd been unmoved by the coldness of his body. There'd been a certain mischief in her eyes and promise in her words. There was a sincerity about her that was endearing, and this made her a breath of fresh air in Sunray Bay. Though he had no doubt Sunray Bay would destroy her carefree spirit and optimism soon enough. She was a nice girl, and he hoped she would be able to get things sorted with her dog and her soul without running into too much trouble.

Scrabbling from the bed he took the shirt Gloria had given him from the clothes rail where he'd hung it earlier. It belonged to Stan. Stan was a broad man, around the chest and the waist, and when Grim shrugged it on, he discovered that the shirt fit okay around his shoulders and chest, but it hung baggy around his midriff. Its paisley pattern also left a lot to be desired, so he took it off and cast it aside. He wasn't the vain type – but all the same, he wasn't going to be seen dead looking like that. Instead, he picked up the plain black thermal vest Gloria had also brought for him – she always worried about him being so cold, despite the fact he kept telling her that he didn't *feel* cold.

Catching a glimpse of himself in the full length mirror hanging on the wall, he decided he could live with the black vest. He wasn't fashion-conscious in the slightest, but he knew where to draw the line when it came to bad shirts. Stan really needed to have a wardrobe rethink if that was the kind of stuff he wore on a daily basis.

Walking nearer to the mirror, he studied his face more closely. His reflection looked dark and detached from real life. Sunglasses blanked out his eyes; eyes that he hadn't looked at in months. He'd heard the expression that eyes were windows to the soul, and he knew it to be true.

He was about to move away from the mirror, when he caught a glimpse of the tattoo on the side of his head. He stopped and touched it lightly. It didn't stand for *Dick* and it didn't stand for *Death*. A lot of people assumed it was the latter because of his nickname – but that was lame.

No, D was much more personal than that.

D was *Della*.

And D was *Daisy*.

Della, his gorgeous wife, and Daisy, his beautiful daughter. His jaw clenched, he wished he could remember Della as she'd been when they'd first met, during happier times. Like when they'd got married, and when she'd found out she was pregnant. But all he could remember was the scared look on her face, a fleeting look of doubt in her eye that he'd never seen before, and the trembling quiver of her bottom lip as he'd held the gun to her temple.

And Daisy, he wished he had better memories of her too. His three-year-old bundle of mischief who'd idolised him and followed him around the house like a shadow. Even her first word had been *dada*. But the look of dejection and confusion as he'd put the gun to her head, having just killed her mother, was enough to scar him for a lifetime and longer.

D was for his two special girls, and there was room for no other. Not in his heart, not anymore. Not after what he'd done.

Or was there?

Libby crept back to his thoughts. Could she be the one to break the relentless grief? Unshakeable, persistent, annoying Libby. He thought Libby was maybe short for Elizabeth – and E comes after D. Could she be a second chance perhaps?

A second chance of what? he thought angrily. *What about Della and Daisy?* He couldn't just forget what happened. And besides, it wasn't right to expect somebody else to take on his burdens. Libby would be better off if he wasn't around anymore.

He punched the mirror hard. His knuckle burst red and it throbbed searing hot with tiny splinters of glass that shattered around him like the fragments of his own life. It felt better now that he was hurting. His head and his heart were in turmoil, and he wasn't sure which he should trust. He was a ruthless, heartless wreck. Reaching for the whiskey, he finished the dregs at the bottom and then threw the empty bottle against the wall.

"Get your arse out of here and just go!" he snarled at himself. The Grey Dustbowl was calling.

Turning to leave, he tripped on a soft mound that lay on the floor, and on closer inspection he realised it was Libby's jeans. Strickler had kidnapped her in nothing much more than underwear. She was out there somewhere with a lunatic ex-convict in not much more than her pants. And what was it she'd said to him earlier? *I've saved your arse three times now, you owe me big,* or something along those lines. It was true. What kind of a prick would walk away from that?

"*Fuck!*" he yelled, kicking the jeans across the room.

Chapter 21

He drove in the rapidly increasing darkness, the headlights of Gloria's car dim like the ends of two cigarettes. Gloria's place had been deserted when he'd come round, it always was with an impending full moon, and so he'd just taken the car without permission. He didn't think she would mind too much.

Heading in the opposite direction, away from The Grey Dustbowl, he knew exactly where he was going. He wound the driver's side window down because the car's interior was airless. Warmth gushed in from the sun-heated streets. The fast approaching night was soaking up some of its wetness and it was a dry heat now, but either way, it still wasn't refreshing. It didn't make much difference to Grim though; usually he opened windows out of habit.

The streets themselves were eerily quiet. Only the odd few stragglers were still making their way to safety. This wasn't such an oddity for the time of month it was, although the more sane residents of Sunray Bay would have already barricaded themselves in their homes by now.

He wondered for a moment where Gloria, Stan and the girls would be – he never asked where they went during a full moon, he'd always figured he was better off not knowing. He liked them enough to turn a blind eye – which in itself was quite hypocritical, given the circumstances. But he could live with that. He lived with a lot of things...

Memories suddenly came to him in a painful flash and he watched them play out in his head like a reel of tape. The day everything changed was now haunting him in full colour complete with sound. Distant and detached as though it was somebody else's life...

Just over two years ago – it had been a warm sunny day and they'd spent the day down by a brook that ran close to their holiday home log cabin in which they were staying probably for the last time before they sold up. Daisy loved to catch sticklebacks in her fishing net, and Della enjoyed family picnics on the grassy bank.

Back then his name was Richard, and he'd taken some annual leave from work in the police force so they could spend some quality family time together, relaxing. His doctor had advised him to take the time out, and his boss had instructed him to. Everyone knew that Richard was stressed. Everyone could see the cracks, and could understand why...

Their family home had been flooded, almost beyond repair, when the nearby river had burst its banks. The insurance company wouldn't pay out, and so he and Della had had to take out a loan to cover costs. Then to top it all off, Richard's younger brother was killed in a car accident on his way to university. Richard just couldn't accept it, he was an emotional wreck.

The day when everything changed was just four days into their break, and Richard had already begun to feel a little better. He knew the time away wasn't fixing their problems, but still, he got to appreciate what he did have – Della and Daisy. He figured as long as the three of them were okay, that was all that mattered. If only he'd realised the irony.

He settled Daisy down for the night, telling her they'd catch more sticklebacks the following day, while Della finished clearing the dining table. And then he took Della out onto the porch where they drank cold beer from bottles and gazed up at stars.

"I was thinking, maybe we should get Daisy a puppy when we get back," Richard said.

Della looked at him and shrieked with excitement, her big blue eyes adult versions of Daisy's. He pulled her close and she laid her head on his chest, her long blonde ponytail tickling his chin.

"That's a great idea, Richie," she said. "She'd love that."

"It's so peaceful, isn't it?" Richard said, stroking Della's hair and looking out at the expanse of thick greenery beyond.

"Yeah," she sighed. "I'm really going to miss it here."

"Maybe when we're back on our feet financially we could get a campervan?"

Della laughed and sat up.

"A campervan?"

"Well okay, you snob," he chided. "We'll get a motorhome. Is that better?"

She hit him on the arm playfully, but before she could answer they heard the sound of glass smashing from somewhere round the back of the log cabin. They both leapt to their feet, and while Della went to make sure Daisy was okay, Richard ran to the airing cupboard to retrieve his shotgun from the top shelf. He wasn't sure why that was his initial reaction, but he had a prickly feeling of dread that crawled over his skin like an intrusion of cockroaches. Common sense told him it could be an animal breaking in, a bird flying into a window or even a tree branch falling against the side of the cabin, but a sickly feeling in his stomach, probably primal instinct, told him that something was seriously wrong.

By the time he got to Daisy's room, the scene that met him was something his mind would never be able to blot out. Glass lay all over the pink carpet like twinkly sequins, denoting that something was very wrong in his little girl's room. And that wrong thing was a strange man who was swaying about like a drunk, banging into furniture, whilst holding something tight to his face. Della was clawing at him like a wild cat, and Richard realised that the thing he was holding to his mouth was Daisy.

Della dragged Daisy from his clutches, and screamed as a chunk of her daughter's neck came away in the man's gnashing teeth. Her cry penetrated Richard's ears, jerking him from his frozen terror. With his ears still wringing, he brought the gun up and aimed it at the stranger, pulling the trigger just as the man bit down hard on Della's arm.

Della yelped and fell to the ground alongside the man, with Daisy clasped to her chest. Daisy was barely conscious, and there was so much blood; blood from everyone but

Richard. He scooped Della and Daisy into his arms and laid them on the pink gingham sheets of Daisy's bed.

"Call for help," Della cried hysterically, covering her daughter's gaping neck with her hands.

Richard ran to the lounge, and dialled emergency services on the telephone. His breath was coming in short, sharp bursts, and he worried he might not be legible to the person on the other end of the line. He'd always been professional and competent in crisis situations as a police officer, yet now his own little girl was bleeding to death, none of that really applied.

Listening to the dialling tone, he looked out of the window. And what he saw outside made him realise that it wouldn't matter what he sounded like on the phone at all – it was game over...

3:42pm: The streets of Sunray Bay

If Grim had had any tears left, he would have wept. But he was all cried out, as though his eyes had dried up. He mentally shook himself and refused to relive the rest of that night. Not now anyway. He'd arrived at his intended destination, and he needed a relatively clear head for his next move. The lights were on, which meant somebody was in. He was standing outside The Ordinaries' headquarters.

Chapter 22

3:43pm: The Ordinaries Headquarters, Sunray Bay
The Ordinaries' headquarters was actually just a pokey storeroom at the back of Booze 'N' Stuff. Thad Daniels was the founder and chairperson of the small, close-knit army, and he also ran the convenience store. By day he was a general dealer of milk, bread and other essentials and by night he was a knife-wielding, gun-toting monster-killer.

He'd been operating for close to ten years now in both businesses, since his release from prison, where he'd served a short spell for petty theft. He'd seen some tough times inside, mostly at the hands of monsters, and since then he thought about nothing but vengeance. It hadn't taken him long to gather a small group of like-minded people together – others who thought that killing monsters for fun was a worthy cause. Officially, by Krain's rules, The Ordinaries were allowed to execute only monsters that posed a threat to the safety and wellbeing of the law-abiding citizens of Sunray Bay. This was impossible to police, however, and in truth nobody gave a shit enough to even attempt to. So, in practice, The Ordinaries killed whoever they wanted – apart from Krain's own group of sophisticates.

Krain didn't seem to care that Jarvis Strickler, the man who'd been jailed for the murder of his first wife Sharon, was working within The Ordinaries. Strickler was a mere blast from the past as far as he was concerned, and Krain had never liked his first wife anyway – and besides, it was common knowledge that Strickler had gone as nutty as a fruitcake during his stint in prison. He was well and truly away with the show folk, and Krain hadn't see him as any kind of threat.

Grim rapped on the back door of Booze 'N' Stuff five times and waited. He heard movement from inside, followed by clanking bolts and jangling chains, and then the door creaked open a few inches. A dark blue eye peered out.

"Daniels," Grim rasped.

The door cranked fully open to reveal a middle-aged man with a ponytail and balled-up fists. His face was hardened brown with sharp silver whiskers scattered along his jaw-line like iron filings and faded green-black tattoos crept up his neck. His one dark blue eye stared hard at Grim; the other one was white and cloudy like a piece of opal.

"Grim." Daniels snarled back. "What the fuck're you doin' 'ere?"

Two others appeared behind him, Jimmy Clyde and Frank Murphy, and they both looked displeased to see Grim standing there.

"Long time no see," Clyde sneered. He was a tall black man whose neck was as thick as a tree trunk, and he stood with his arms folded. "What brings you crawlin' back?"

Grim ignored Clyde and instead addressed Daniels.

"Thad, I need your help."

Daniels roared with laughter and slapped his hand against the metal door.

"You've come runnin' back for *help*? Whassup? You had enough o' Krain and want back in now?"

"I'm not working for Krain anymore," Grim said, then nodding towards the storeroom behind Daniels, he said, "Can I come in? It's not ideal talking on the doorstep like a couple of sitting ducks."

Daniels poked his head outside and glanced around suspiciously.

"What's goin' on?"

"I'll tell you," Grim said, "If you let me come in."

Inside, the storeroom was still the same as Grim had remembered it. A cramped space filled with boxes, crates, Gil Elvgren style pin-up girls and a massive metal cabinet where the weapons were stored.

"So, what's up? Why've you decided to show your ugly face round 'ere again?" Daniels asked, planting his foot on top of a crate.

Grim had been a member of The Ordinaries for around nine months before Krain had made the elusive offer that he hadn't been able to resist. When he'd left to join the Peace & Order Maintenance team, The Ordinaries hadn't been sympathetic with regard to his reasons for leaving them behind. In fact, they'd been pissed off – and evidently still were.

"It's going to get hairy out there pretty soon," Grim said.

"No shit, Sherlock, that's 'cause there's a fucking full moon."

"Well yeah." Grim's jaw tightened. "But that's not the only reason..."

Daniels' eyes narrowed.

"Yeah? Well, what's the other reason?"

Grim went on to tell Daniels, Clyde and Murphy all about the Black Dog Burger Co. revelations and the prison breakout.

"You've got some balls doin' that, Grim, I'll give you that," Daniels said, smirking and shaking his head in wonderment. But then his face became serious, his narrowed eyes and sharp nose lending him a fox-like appearance, and he said, "And you've got some balls showin' up round 'ere again too."

Grim looked down at his own feet. He was hardly surprised, he certainly hadn't expected a welcome back hug. And as Clyde and Murphy edged closer, their bulky frames emitting animosity, he wondered if he'd end up tackling all three of them in a physical one on three – which was the last thing he needed.

Sighing, he met Daniels's good eye again, and said, "I'll come back. I'll join up again..."

"What, like before?" Murphy sneered; he was a squat man who looked like he should pull buses for a living.

"And how long would it be before you ran off again, leavin' us on our arses?" Clyde asked, his eyes watchful and dubious.

"I wouldn't, it'd be for good."

"What makes you think we'd want you back?" Daniels asked. He folded his arms across his chest, taking a dominant stance.

Grim smiled wryly and shrugged his shoulders.

"Because I'm the best there is. Why wouldn't you want me on side?"

A disgruntled silence followed. Nobody disputed what he said.

"You can't tell me you just missed us and got homesick. Or that you need us to fight this battle for you. What's the reason for all this Grim? What's your ulterior motive?"

"Yeah, you're right," Grim said, holding his hands in the air. "I thought I'd lay my cards on the table before I asked you a favour."

"*A favour*? You have a fuckin' nerve," Daniels said, his lip curling like a vexed dog guarding his turf. But he looked intrigued nonetheless "Go on then, what is it?"

"Where's Strickler?" Grim asked. "I want to know where he is."

"Why?" Daniels didn't look very cooperative.

"I want to know why he's been hell bent on tracking down a new arrival."

Daniels looked perplexed.

"How the fuck should I know? The crazy bastard's been sellin' donkey rides down on the beach, as per usual, as far as I'm aware. Who's the new arrival?"

"A woman. He came and took her from Gloria's a while ago, and I want to know where he's taken her and why he's so keen on her in particular."

Daniels stood with a lop-sided grin, saying nothing at first. Shaking his head, one of his gold teeth flickered yellow underneath the bare sixty-watt light bulb hanging down above his head.

"Never thought I'd see the day you were chasin' after a tart, Grim. And Gloria's place, you've been there all day? "

"No. It's not like that," Grim snapped.

"Don't talk bollocks. You don't put yourself out for anyone."

161

That was true. Grim squared his shoulders and tried not to look guilty.

"Stop fucking about, Daniels. You're wasting time. Do you know anything or not?"

"Like I said, I haven't seen Strickler all day," Daniels replied. "And I've no idea who your bit stuff is either. Do you know *what* she is? I take it werewolf if she's been hanging round Gloria's place?"

"I'm not sure. Possibly vampire," Grim replied. "And she's not my bit stuff."

Daniels face grew serious and he said, "Vampire, huh? There is one possibility, perhaps. We knew somethin' was up with Krain and the werewolves – he'd warned us to lay off 'em, see – but we, along with just about everyone else in Sunray Bay, had noticed how the numbers of full moon killings were dwindlin' each month. And I suppose all that makes sense now after what you just told us. But anyway, all of that's by the by. We weren't too interested in the werewolves anyhow, 'cause we've been pretty tied up with somethin' else. Somethin' pretty fuckin' big actually..."

He let his words hang in the air, enjoying the fact that Grim's curiosity had been ignited.

"There's a group of vampires who've just turned up in Sunray Bay from outta nowhere. It's like they've just appeared from thin air."

"How do you mean?" Grim asked. "Who are they?"

"No idea." Daniels shrugged. "We know they're not part of Krain's lot though, and they're not from the usual mob of anti-Krain ferals either."

"How do you know?"

"Because they're a different breed altogether from the neck-suckers we're used to. In fact, they're pretty fuckin' cool in their own messed up kinda way."

"How so?"

"These ones feed on *vampires*!" Daniels laughed out loud. "They're cannibalistic, shape-shifting vampires."

"*Shape-shifting?*" Grim asked incredulously.

Daniels nodded and grabbed a can of beer from on top of a crate, its tinny sides dimpling as he took a big mouthful.

"Aye – bats, eagles, rats, wolves – any of them things they can turn into, and that's just what we know so far. Oh and get this, sneaky bastards can even mimic fog!"

"How did you find out about them?" Grim asked, leaning against a stack of dusty fruit boxes.

"We've been watchin' 'em for a while now. We *think* they're comin' in from The Grey Dustbowl."

"Does Krain know about them?"

"Oh yeah. He's got his balls in a right old uproar about it. So much so, he's even been discussin' things with us. See, these shape-shifters broke into the archives yesterday and took off with some top-secret documents. And that's not before they killed all Krain's workers in there. Bled them completely dry, so we're led to believe."

"What documents did they take?"

"Dunno, Krain wouldn't say. But his code name for this new strain of vampire is Phoenix."

"*Phoenix?* Why?"

"Because they appear to have *risen from the ashes of the dustbowl*," Daniels said, rolling his eyes and mimicking Krain's voice. "Somethin' airy-fairy like that, anyway. You know what he's like."

"So how come you're communicating with Krain so much about the issue?"

"We're in negotiations," Daniels said, smugly. "If we capture even just one of them and hand it over to him, we get to have our own digs instead of usin' this scratty room out the back o' my grocery store. Krain'll also provide us with annual fundin' every year from the council's budget."

Grim almost scoffed, he wanted to laugh – he'd learned the hard way about Krain's negotiations, but he held his tongue. He didn't want to rile Daniels. Instead he said, "That's great, Daniels, but remind me – what does all this have to do with Strickler?"

Daniels downed the rest of his can, balled it up in his fist as easily as though it were paper, then tossed it into a crate on the floor by the door.

"Well, it's just a suggestion, but maybe your bit stuff is a Phoenix..."

Grim found it hard to believe – but then, he didn't know what he was thinking any more.

"Of course, I'd be royally pissed off if Strickler's gone and bagged a Phoenix without havin' consulted me first," Daniels said, before belching loudly. Wiping the back of his hand across his mouth, he narrowed his eyes and asked, "Is she a looker?"

"*What?*"

"Well, we all know that Strickler's appreciation of the fairer sex borders on the verge of creepy," Daniels said, his face thoughtful – and concerned. "And I'll kick seven kinds of shite out of him if he's taken a Phoenix without tellin' me on the basis that she's a bit of a looker."

Murphy stepped closer to Grim and breathed hard in his face.

"Well is she?" he grunted.

Grim, not in the least bit intimidated, stuck his neck out so that his nose was millimetres away from Murphy's and said, "Yes, she is."

Clyde laughed out loud and wolf-whistled. "Sounds like Strickler could've gone off on a tangent, the dirty dog."

Daniels didn't laugh. He walked towards the weapon cabinet, and said, "Let's go find out who this bit of fluff is that Strickler's gone and caught himself. And let's hope she's not a Phoenix – for his sake."

"Her name's Libby," Grim snarled, the muscles all over his body tensed. He was becoming increasingly concerned for her wellbeing.

As he followed Daniels to the cabinet, he asked, "How will you know where to look for him?"

"I don't," Daniels replied. "You got any ideas?"

He didn't. So he waited until the other three had loaded themselves with enough guns and ammunition to fight a world war, then followed them out of the back door.

Chapter 23

2:48pm: A donkey shed, Sunray Bay
Strickler was standing over her once again, his hands tucked behind his back.

"Sorry, sugar lips, gotta move you again. We have to get a move on – places to go, people to see and all that."

"Where are we going now?" Libby asked, worried by his sudden urgency. Her eyes tried to determine the look on his face in the dim light, wondering whether he meant to harm her or not. His face was completely cast in shadow, but when he brought his hands round from behind his back she could see a dark rag in them.

"Ugh, please don't knock me out again," she groaned, pushing her head away. "I'm still feeling sick to the stomach off last time."

"It'd be best if you didn't see where we're going though," he said, sounding genuinely sorry.

"Well, I won't look then, I promise," she pleaded. "And I won't make a noise either."

He stood up straight again, holding the rag out. Agitated, he tapped his foot on the floor.

"*Please*," she implored, hoping she was breaking through to his conscience – if he had one.

He cursed quietly and tossed aside the rag. Then stooping down, he hoisted her body up onto his shoulder, relishing the feel of her soft, warm skin on his fingers.

"Okay, but if you misbehave, I'll break your arms and legs."

Despite being scrawny, Strickler was surprisingly strong, so she didn't bother putting up a fight – she didn't see the point at that moment in time. She imagined he'd quite capably throw her about like a ragdoll if he wanted to, especially with her hands and legs being bound. She worried that if she resisted, even the tiniest bit, she'd piss him off –

and she'd rather not find out whether he was being serious about carrying out his threat or not. So instead she bided her time, waiting for the right opportunity to make a break for it, putting up with his fingertips digging into her thighs and his bony shoulder digging into her stomach.

Strickler breathed heavily with the exertion, but nonetheless he carried her swiftly. He'd always been a puny kid but when he'd grown up his job as a postman had built his upper body strength significantly. He still *looked* weedy, but lugging heavy bags around all day, six days a week, had made him a lot stronger than people would have expected. He'd never looked a picture of health. But then that was partially down to the drugs.

Even in Sunray Bay he was still partial to taking drugs now and again. He'd gone through his entire existence with people thinking he was crazy; puggled by the drugs – but he couldn't *not* take them. He'd had his fair share of problems in life, but in death he felt hollow. In fact, sometimes he thought maybe he *was* hollow. The continuation of drug usage had been an attempt to fill that void; his escapism. But now, bizarrely enough, he'd found a way to fill the wide gaping hole at last – at least he was hopeful. It had been a stroke of pure luck when Libby had walked past him earlier that day, luck that he almost couldn't believe. He wondered if the gods were in fact looking down on him at last and giving him the break he'd been waiting years for. They'd been nothing but cruel up until now.

Strickler couldn't remember a time in his life when he'd ever been truly happy and not reliant on drugs – not even a sliver of contentedness came to mind. He'd always been a loner, a complete outcast, with no loving support from family either. The Strickler household had been a volatile one throughout his early childhood. And three days after his twelfth birthday his father had killed his heavily pregnant mother in a drunken rage. He was amazed that it hadn't happened sooner, the way his dad used to knock her about – and he still felt inadequate and pathetic for having done nothing about it. He'd always wondered whether he could

167

have prevented it, often fantasising about the life he *could* have had with just his mother and his little brother or sister. But it was never to be, because the truth of it was, he'd been scared of his dad – absolutely petrified. He'd never have stood up to him. But that didn't mean he didn't regret his choice every single day. What he would give to change all of that. He'd take the knife instead of his mother every single time. Hindsight was a wonderful thing.

When his father had been locked up and his mother buried in the ground underneath a stone that he couldn't bring himself to visit, he'd gone on to reside in numerous foster homes, never really bonding with anyone. He'd entered his teenage years more withdrawn than he'd ever been, and nobody was surprised when he'd started taking drugs by the age of fourteen – everyone around him wrongly assuming that he'd fallen in with a bad crowd. But if they'd taken the time to get to know him properly, if they'd persevered, then they would have discovered that just wasn't true – he hadn't fallen in with *any* crowd. The drugs were just a coping mechanism.

By the time he'd reached adulthood, he'd managed to secure himself a job as a postman, which suited him fine. Doing his rounds early while the streets were quiet was always a good thing, it meant he could get on without having to chat to too many people – and also, because he was always out and about, he didn't have to worry about socialising with colleagues either. In the evenings he worked as a self-employed private detective – which had afforded him extra money to subsidise his ever-increasing drug habits. He'd been a bloody good private detective too. One of the best – if not *the* best.

As well as delivering post during the day, solving problems for clients at night, and using drugs, he'd harboured a fondness for women. Watching them and listening to them, from afar, was one of his favourite pastimes. Yet, tragically, when he died at the age of twenty-eight he'd never once been with a woman. There were a couple of horny housewives on his postal route who often tried to lure him into the realms of their homes with flashes of bare breasts and glimpses of knicker lace, but he'd never taken any of them up on their offers. As ever, he'd been too scared of consequences. Though, again in hindsight, given half the chance he'd go right back to his old life and shag them all senseless. Each and every one of them. In all his time spent in Sunray Bay, he'd never had any such offers; nobody had so much as batted an eye at him. As far as the womenfolk of Sunray Bay were concerned he was just the nutter who worked on the beach with the donkeys, who'd done time for killing the mayor's wife. But it was all just a big misunderstanding. That was the problem with Strickler; his whole life was just one big misunderstanding.

He remembered the day he'd died quite vividly. He'd got a call from Sharon Krain, the morning after he'd discussed his findings with her...

"Sorry I had to cut you off last night, but *he* came home. Anyway, I just thought I'd call you back to thank you for all the hard work you've done, Jarvis. You've done well. I'll send a cheque out in the post."

Strickler should have left it at that – but he hadn't.

"Are you okay? What are you going to do now?"

"Oh don't you worry about me," she'd laughed wryly. "I'm going to stay home today, and get things sorted. As you can imagine, I have a few *things* to deal with."

That's what Strickler had been afraid of, and for once in his life he chose that moment to act upon impulse. He'd stood by and watched his mother get stabbed to death, he'd stood by and let numerous women flash their underwear at him – and every time he'd done absolutely nothing about it. Not anymore though – this time, for whatever reason, he'd jumped into action. He'd decided it was the time to grow some balls. With military precision, he'd waited until the right moment, and then he'd headed round to the Krain household – unaware that it would be his undoing.

He'd arrived the same time as student Merilyn Stockner, having spied on her and followed her there in his car. Imagining himself as a heroic advocate in brightly coloured

169

spandex, he thought that, unlike his mother, he could save this beautiful young woman – which at least, for all his efforts, he could say that he had. If his life was worth one measly jot, it was because he'd saved Merilyn Stockner. But that was all such a long time ago...

Setting Libby down on the ground in front of the door, he took hold of the dressing gown's wide satin sash that was tied around her waist and tugged at it, flicking it from the loops that held it in place. Libby gasped as the gown fell open, but she saw no malice in his expression as he leant forward and tied the sash over her eyes like a blindfold. Lifting her again, he heaved her onto the back of Polly the donkey, and simply said, "Don't make a noise, or I'll kill you."

Before he covered her with a rough hessian throw, he looked at her face and smiled to himself. She was the result of his one good deed. And it was funny, he thought, because she looked exactly the same as Merilyn – yet this time *she* would be *his* saviour.

He was a firm believer in karma – as of that moment.

Chapter 24

"Meet me in front of the pier in an hour," Strickler ordered.

"*Are you crazy?*" Krain barked. "I can't do that!"

"You know, all my life people have asked me that," Strickler said, "So maybe I am. Therefore it would be in your best interests to make your way to the pier as soon as possible, otherwise I very much doubt you'll ever get to meet little Miss Hood, and I think I'd be correct in saying that you'd very much like to meet her."

"Look, I already know about Libby Hood..."

Strickler chuckled, "Great, it's good to know that we're both singing from the same hymn sheet – makes my job so much easier now. Let's just cut to the chase, shall we? I'm ready to negotiate."

"How do I know you really have her?"

"Oh I have her alright," Strickler replied. Then delighting in rubbing salt in the wound, he added, "I found her half-naked with an employee of yours – Grim."

Krain gritted his teeth. Grim seemed to be at the centre of all his problems, one way or another.

"Alright, I'll meet you," Krain said reluctantly. "But give me till tomorrow, okay?"

"That wouldn't be wise, sorry. I'd say you have about three hours, tops, to sort this out – otherwise your chances of meeting her are very slim..."

Strickler rang off.

Krain couldn't have imagined a worse day – a worse week for that matter. His post-adulterous wife had reverted back to her old ways, and the man who had set her off on a wanton path of marriage destruction had released all hell into the streets, for which Krain would pay the price. A group of shape-shifting, blood-thirsty vampires had turned up out of the blue, and were already causing havoc. Then, to top it all

171

off, Libby Hood had arrived in Sunray Bay – and despite his best men trying to locate her, they'd been beaten to it by mental case Jarvis Strickler – who had now kidnapped her and was presumably threatening to kill her.

Krain grabbed fistfuls of his own hair in frustration. Going red in the face he rattled vulgar swear words around inside his head. After a moment or two, he composed himself and stepped back into the boardroom.

"Let's resume this meeting, shall we? And could somebody call Red and Kitty? Have them meet me round by the back doors in about an hour," he said to nobody in particular. "I have to go out later."

Dorothy Pallister's face drained of colour and Flatbrook sat up straight.

"What's going on?" Dorothy asked. "I thought you said we should all stay in here together..?"

"Do you need any assistance, sir?" Flatbrook asked, talking over the top of her.

"No Flatbrook, just tell Red and Kitty to meet me. Everything's in hand."

In truth, Krain would have loved more assistance, but he didn't want any more of his personal life made public. Thanks to Morgan, enough of that was going on as it was. And so, he decided to tackle the mess by himself, along with Red and Kitty.

It was still dusky outside but soon it would be dark, so he needed to plan how on earth they'd make it to the pier without encountering any werewolves along the way. Then, of course, there was the Phoenix strain to consider as well.

He sucked in a deep breath and allowed thoughts of Grim to overcome him, which fed his anger and drove his determination. Allowing his fury to build, he told himself that he was the mayor, Sunray Bay was *his* town, and he was damned if he was going to shy away from other vampires.

And besides, Libby Hood was worth putting himself at risk for – she'd prove invaluable to the greater good, if he could just obtain her from Strickler.

172

Chapter 25

The north pier was deserted, and waves lashed the shore somewhere down on the darkened beach. White lights stretched and swung like glorified skipping ropes all the way down the pier, highlighting the wooden boardwalk right up to the amusement area and beyond. The ferris wheel was like a large skeleton at the end; still and waiting. None of the fairground rides would be opening for a while yet. Even a full moon wasn't enough to dissuade ride operators from making a few quid, it'd be business as usual later on; it always was – 365 days a year.

Krain, Red and Kitty had made it to the beachfront unharmed, and stealth-like, in Red's car with Kitty driving. She drove without headlights, claiming that she could see perfectly in the dark. Krain didn't doubt it either, the way she'd handled corners and alleyways – on a few occasions he'd held his hand over his eyes.

Once at the pier, they stepped down onto the sand and walked to the barnacle-encrusted posts beneath, crouched and catlike, watching for four-legged trouble as they went. The night had a certain peaceful quality to it, like the quiet before the storm – Krain imagined the thunder clouds were already collecting. He made large peculiar strides, trying to prevent sand from getting into his shoes and socks whilst crouching low. It wasn't long before he spotted Strickler half-submerged in shadows underneath the pier. The end of his cigarette glowed orange each time he took a draw.

"Stay here," Krain said to Red and Kitty, with a warning glare. "I'll be alright from here." He didn't want them hearing any of the forthcoming conversation between himself and Strickler. They nodded their understanding and remained still, each with a machine gun perched on their arm, as he moved off again. When Krain got within spitting distance of Strickler, he growled, "Where is she? And what is it you'd like to negotiate exactly?"

Strickler flicked his cigarette butt away and confronted Krain.

"Oh I think you know very well what I want. Stop mucking about. How could you *forget*? Or do you want to do a little reminiscing, perhaps? Go over all the ways in which you've royally fucked me over. It wasn't enough that you stole from me, but you framed me for the murder of Sharon too. Do you have *any* idea what my life's been like?"

"Oh my heart bleeds," Krain spat. "None of us would even be in Sunray Bay if it hadn't been for you. You deserved all you got."

"*I* was trying to stop Sharon from killing Merilyn Stockner!" Strickler yelled, his eyes bulging in their sockets.

"You were sticking your nose in where it didn't belong."

"And I wouldn't have had to if you hadn't been sticking your dick where it didn't belong!"

"How dare you!" Krain barked, his eyes were wild with outrage.

Somewhere behind, Kitty stifled a giggle. It was hard for her and Red not to hear the conversation, both Krain's and Stickler's voices had risen as their disagreement had progressed. Krain flashed a look of disdain at her, and she immediately hushed up and turned away from him.

Strickler sneered, "A man of your age shagging one of your nineteen-year-old students, I bet you thought you were a right Casanova, didn't you? In fact I bet you loved the fact that you were having your cake and eating it. Tell me, what pisses you off more Krain? That Sharon knew all about your sordid affair, or that it was me who gave her the gory details? She'd had her suspicions for a long while – she just hired me to confirm what she thought she already knew. See, she'd given me a neck tie that belonged to you and, oh my God, the images that thing brought to mind when I touched it..." Strickler grimaced and shuddered. "I felt dirty after handling it. It showed me enough to make poor Merilyn blush if she'd known. Anyway, I told Sharon all about your lunchtime romps within the marital bed."

"Bastard!" Krain hissed.

"No, I think that's rather unfair of you to say. You see, as well as seeing all of your sordid little shagfests running through my head, I also saw *what* you were. Sharon never ever knew that you were a vampire, did she Krain? I spared her those details at least."

Krain edged closer to Strickler, his voice low.

"And why's that Strickler, because she hadn't *paid* for that bit of information? Get off your moralistic high-horse, will you? You ruined all of our lives that day, so stop trying to convince yourself otherwise."

"I was saving lives that day!" Strickler growled. "I heard Sharon's voice when she called me that morning. I *heard* the murder in her voice."

"And why did you care?" Krain bit back. "You'd got your money, and you'd stirred the excrement up well and truly. So why? Were you having it away with her or something?"

"Don't be ridiculous," Strickler said, screwing his face up in disgust. "I had no qualms about you being killed, and I had no qualms about Sharon doing the deed and being locked up for it. No. It was Merilyn I was bothered about; I couldn't stand by and let Sharon kill Merilyn. There's no denying, she was beautiful – too good for you. In fact, she was wasted on you. She was very precious. I used to deliver her post every day, you know..."

Krain's jaw jutted forward and fire burned in his pupils.

"It was by chance that a few mornings before the incident, she'd dropped one of her study folders on the garden path. I'd picked it up to chase after her, and that's when I knew, when I felt it in my gut – that the poor little cow had only got herself pregnant by her pervy old university lecturer."

"So you've known all these years that I had a child?" Krain asked, ignoring the insult, with his mouth gaping open.

175

"Of course I did," Strickler grinned. "Touché – isn't that what they say? Now, where were we? Ah yes, you have something of mine and I have something of yours – let's negotiate hmmm? But do be hasty, she doesn't have much longer. It'd be such a waste for you not to get to meet your long lost daughter, and she's such a pleasure she truly is."

"I get the point, Strickler. Where is she? Show me, and then we can see about these negotiations."

Strickler laughed, and held his stomach for effect.

"Very funny, Krain, do you think I'm stupid enough to fall for that old chestnut? *I'm* calling the shots here. First you give back that little part of me you stole, and *then* you can have your daughter. But be quick – time's ticking, and she doesn't have long." He emphasised the point by looking at his wrist watch and making a whistling noise.

"Why, what will happen? And how long do we have?"

"Hmmm I'd say maybe an hour – an hour and a half if you're lucky."

"How am I supposed to sort everything out in that time?" Krain yelled. "I'm not a bloody miracle worker. In fact, I don't even know if it can be done..."

"That's your problem," Strickler said, deathly serious. "It's up to you to find a way."

Not for the first time, Krain cursed Sharon. Even in death she was ruining his life. None of this would have happened if she hadn't been so irritatingly annoying in the first place, he would never have had the affair with Merilyn. And then there'd been her meddling and nosing, she'd started this whole mess by hiring a bloody psychic private detective.

Krain had planned on leaving Sharon all those years ago; back when he'd been a university lecturer – back when he was still alive. He'd been waiting for the right time – when Merilyn had left university and was no longer a student of his. He could have lived with Merilyn, she'd been an intelligent and captivating young woman, unlike Sharon – and unbeknown to him, until now, she'd mothered his only child.

He remembered the day he'd died alongside Strickler and Sharon – the last time he'd seen Merilyn. He'd snuck her into the house, as usual, and had led her upstairs for one of their usual lunch-break steamy sessions – not realising that Sharon was lying in wait for them. Merilyn's eyes had glowed with mischief and youth as he'd pressed her against the wall at the top of the stairs, and he'd kissed her hungrily on the lips – and that's when Sharon had jumped out of the landing airing cupboard with a carving knife in her hand. Merilyn had screamed and barricaded herself behind the bedroom door, whilst he had grappled with Sharon and her silver, pointed ally. Strickler had arrived at that very moment, barging up the stairs like a man on a mission. The skinny, blundering fool had smashed into them headfirst, knocking them off balance. Then, in a bundle of arms and legs, all three of them had crashed through the wooden banister at the top of the stairs, tumbling down onto the hard granite floor below in the hallway. All of them dead outright; Sharon and Krain with broken necks and Strickler impaled on the carving knife.

Upon awaking in Sunray Bay, the first thing he'd been aware of was Strickler chanting, "I can't see, I can't see..." and then he saw him sitting in a corner looking almost comatose, with saliva dripping from the corners of his mouth and his eyes rolled back in their sockets. And Sharon was moving around erratically. She was saying that she felt different – that she could *see* things, that she felt weird, and that she was thirsty – *really, really* thirsty but for what, she didn't know. He had immediately compared his own feelings of pitiful weakness and lack of senses to how Sharon said she was feeling – and he'd wondered at the possible connection. When she'd charged him like an angry pit bull, teeth chomping, going straight for his jugular, he'd suddenly understood – and had crushed her throat with his bare hands.

That was his first lesson in abnormal souls – that his soul had somehow broken free, finding its way into Sharon. But that wasn't the extent of it. After he'd strangled her, he'd felt his own strength gushing back – his hearing defined again,

177

his sense of smell finely tuned once more, his vision perfected, all his vampire qualities rightfully restored – and yet there was something else, something *strange*. He could *see* confusing images in his mind, flashing lights and movements, like photograph negatives in colour – coupled with a splitting headache. And, after a few moments of contemplation, he realised that the sensation belonged to Strickler; it was his psychic ability. Suddenly, he understood Strickler's own comatose and docile state of mind. Having had such a deep and overbearing power stripped from him, no wonder he was slavering in the corner. It was because of this that Krain had ingeniously used Strickler's unfortunate state of debilitation to his own advantage, framing him for the murder of Sharon. Though how he'd managed to function properly enough to be able to do this was still a small wonder, his newfound psychic ability having hit him like a million migraines all at once. Thankfully, there'd already been quite a strong vampire influence in Sunray Bay, so he'd been taken under their wings, so to speak.

In the aftermath of that whole horrible incident, he'd had to deal with the fact that not only had he absorbed Strickler's psychic inner-self, but Sharon's soul too – he'd discovered the complexities of soul absorption to its full extent. And as a result, he found he had a new love of net curtains and china teapots, thanks to his wife, which was devastating to his manliness – but a small price to pay for the repossession of his own powers.

Now, fast forward twenty-three years, and here Strickler was, standing in front of him making absurd demands. It wasn't that he was particularly precious about the psychic ability he'd nurtured and adapted to over the years – if anything some days he wished he could have a break from it. But separating it from his own soul, he really wasn't sure it was viable – which meant that, one way or another, somebody would probably have to die. And it wouldn't be him. His face puckered in frustration and his mind raced furiously, he wanted to kill Strickler right there and then, but if he did he might never know where Libby was.

Discreetly removing his gloves behind his back, Krain inched towards Strickler, a plan forming in his mind. Strickler, who was already on the same train of thought, moved backwards and wagged his finger out in front.

"You forget, Krain, I was psychic for all those years – it was *my* power. I know how it works better than anybody. You lay your hands on me and I'll..."

His words hung in the air, and he gulped hard.

"And you'll what?" Krain laughed.

Strickler pushed his hand into his jeans pocket and pulled out his penknife. Holding it to his own throat, he said, "I'll kill myself."

"You *really are* crazy," Krain murmured, not doubting for a second that Strickler would willingly slit his own throat to prove a point.

"Touch me and we both die – me and Elizabeth."

Krain knew he needed to act, and he needed to act fast, if he was to see his daughter. And he hated to admit it but the only person he could think of who might be able to help him was Morgan – his angry second wife, who at that point in time wasn't even speaking to him.

Oh bloody fucking fiddlesticks, he thought to himself as he pulled his mobile from his trouser pocket.

Chapter 26

Grim, Daniels, Clyde and Murphy sped through the streets in Gloria's car, heading to the seafront and watching out for signs of Strickler along the way. Daniels, who'd sat in the passenger seat, had suggested Strickler's donkey shed as a good starting point to begin the search, so that's where they'd gone.

The donkey shed was near to the promenade wall, around half way between the beach access point and the funfair pier. There were no streetlamps to light up that stretch of beach, but just behind, affixed to each beach hut, were watery yellow lanterns which afforded enough light for unfortunates who were just arriving in Sunray Bay to see – yet not enough light for Grim to see far enough into the donkey shed to tell whether Strickler or Libby were there.

He walked down the length of the stable checking each donkey-filled cubicle, ensuring a thorough search.

"Any luck?" Daniels called out. He stood by the barn door with Clyde and Murphy, his night vision goggles a strange looking contraption strapped to his head.

Grim shook his head and was about to reply, but a loud banging, scratching noise pounded down the side of the barn from the outside. He jumped in alarm and listened intently as the banging ceased and a pattering, scuttling noise came from above, and then a dull *whump* as something hit the floor on the other side.

"What the fuck's that?" Murphy rasped.

They all bristled, each of them unsure whether to move or not. After a moment's pause, Daniels carefully cracked open the door and peered out. When he saw nothing there he motioned for them all to follow. They ventured outside, curiosity piqued and adrenaline thumping through them. Grim and Daniels shifted round to the side of the barn together, Grim ready to grapple with his bare hands and Daniels with a semi-automatic pistol poised and ready to go. The beach was black-dark because a thick grey blanket of cloud cover was hiding the moon. Unfriendliness laced the air, which would have been more appropriate for a cold, windy night – not the warm and balmy one it was.

"Shouldn't Strickler have these animals locked up a bit better on a night like tonight?" Grim asked quietly, thinking how easily they'd accessed the barn and wondering if whatever had trampled all over the roof had come for an easy supper.

"If they were mine, I'd have 'em locked up better, yeah." Daniels agreed. "But you know Strickler. And to be fair, the werewolves don't seem to bother with the donkeys at all. It's them poor bastards up there who need to run for their lives." Daniels tipped his head towards the beach huts, where new arrivals walked aimlessly around the promenade. "They're much more excitin' prey."

They could see nothing unusual round the side of the barn, and Daniels started retreating back round to the front. As Grim went to follow, a low throaty growl came from just above his head; a noise deep and rich like a motorbike engine ticking over. Whatever had run across the barn was now back on the roof.

Grim looked up slowly and saw two gleaming eyes and a set of pointy teeth staring back at him. Bracing himself for action, he bared his own teeth and snarled, "Come on then, you sneaky bastard!"

The creature, which had been crouched low, rose up onto its haunches, ready to pounce, and Grim saw that it was a werewolf. Saliva glistened from its jowls in a long silvery string, and it was ready to take Grim up on his invitation. It snarled louder, its teeth as big as a baboon's, but just as it was about to leap into the air Murphy came charging round the corner, wailing like a banshee with a knife held high. The werewolf fleetingly weighed up the situation and backed off. Turning quickly it scarpered, clearing the barn's roof easily and landing at the other side as though the barn was just a wendy-house.

"Fuck me, Murphy," Daniels cried. "You scared the shit out of me there."

Murphy grinned like a loon, but then looked perplexed.

"Why didn't you bleedin' well shoot it?"

Daniels grinned back and said, "I was just seein' if Grim still had it in him."

Grim grunted; it seemed Daniels was busting his balls, no doubt some kind of initiation to get him to prove his worth within The Ordinaries once more.

"What if it'd been one of them Phoenix vampire thingies?" Clyde asked, joining them.

"So what if it had?" Daniels shrugged.

"Well we don't know much about 'em yet. What if it's not even possible to take them on in a physical fight?"

"Then Grim would 'ave found out for us, wouldn't he?" Daniels laughed and cracked Grim on the back with his hand.

"What did you say they shape-shift into again?" Grim asked.

"Lots of different stuff, including wolves," Clyde said, tipping his head in the direction in which the werewolf had run, "Which I suppose could get bloody confusing at times. Mostly they seem to prefer bats though, from what we can gather."

"Well that's not too bad," Grim said.

"Ah, but I'm not talkin' piddly Pipistrelle bats, I'm talking bats twice the size of fruit bats with teeth that'll rip your throat out."

"Well I haven't seen any around," Grim said, dismissing Clyde's worries. "There can't be many of them."

Which was true enough.

"Well, let's find Strickler and we might find out. You two head back into town, check in The Lost Sailor and ask the old boys in there if they've seen him about," Daniels said to Clyde and Murphy. "Me and Grim'll check out the pier. Call me if you find him, okay?"

Clyde and Murphy both nodded and moved off.

"Hey, thanks for this," Grim said to Daniels.

"Don't thank me, we're not doin' this as a favour to you. We're doing it for the thrill – and because, I'm gonna enjoy killin' Strickler if he *has* got a Phoenix."

They walked the length of the beach towards the pier, keeping close to the promenade wall and keeping a conscious eye on the black shadows of the shore, Grim relying on Daniels and his night vision to warn him if anything untoward was heading their way.

They'd walked about a hundred metres when they heard a munching, snorting sound, like a pig sniffing for truffles. Peering over the promenade wall they saw some kind of ghoul sitting on the floor feasting on the flesh of a man's body; a man who didn't look like he'd been dead all that long. The ghoul's bloated grey face was disgusting and gluttonous as it tore into the piece of thigh it was clutching. Oblivious to its spectators, its teeth ripped into the limb as though it were a chicken drumstick, tearing off bits of trouser material too. Not fussy about the mix of flesh and nylon, it swallowed greedily in big gulps. Grim wrinkled his nose and sniffed the air, trying to place what the ghoul's offensive stench reminded him of. Possibly rotten meat or maggots left in a bait box. Shaking his head in disgust, he turned to carry on walking; he'd seen and smelt enough. Usually he or Daniels would have killed it outright, but it was the ghoul's lucky day because they just left it alone, thinking they could do without drawing any attention to themselves – and besides, the person it was dining on was past saving anyhow. Grim made a mental note of its brown corduroy trousers though; he'd get it later, just for being so revolting.

They moved off again, like a couple of snipers, and Daniels halted after they'd only walked for a few more minutes. He whispered, "Hold up. There're figures beneath the pier up ahead."

Grim froze. Daniels was right, he could hear voices, faint but drifting over from where he'd pointed. Grim motioned with his arm across the beach, down towards the sea, and Daniels nodded his understanding. They both scurried silently seaward, hoping to approach the figures from the darkness of the water's edge. The extra blanket of black would be used to their advantage.

"I think we could be in luck. I think the lanky streak of piss beneath the pier might've been Strickler, you know," Daniels said excitedly as they stooped low and ran towards the sea. When they reached the water's edge, they made the rest of the way over to the pier and slowly crept back up the beach underneath the boardwalk, until they were within hearing distance. Two figures stood just ahead and another two were set back a little further on the actual beach.

"It is. It's Strickler and Krain," Daniels confirmed in a harsh whisper.

Grim nodded. "Let's see if we can get a little closer, find out what they're talking about."

They both crept closer still, till neither dared go any further. Positioning themselves behind one of the pier's posts they listened.

"What will happen to her? And how long do we have?" they heard Krain's voice ask.

"Hmmm I'd say maybe an hour – an hour and a half if you're lucky," Strickler replied.

Grim's mind raced, he wondered what Strickler's time frame signified. He looked to Daniels and asked, "What do you reckon?"

"I reckon we've got to find her before Krain does," Daniels replied, shrugging his shoulders. "We can't go marchin' up there demandin' to know where she is, we'd get ourselves killed."

Grim knew he was right. With his back against the scratchy surface of the pier post he continued to watch Strickler and Krain, hoping more information would be divulged, and he almost jumped out of his skin when something wet and bristly touched his arm. In quick retaliation, he snapped round to confront whatever it was that had touched him. With his fist raised high and ready to

184

punch, he managed to stop himself just in the nick of time when he realised it was only a donkey.

Daniels pinched his nose and fought back laughter, the thought of Grim decking a donkey apparently too funny. Grim gave him a menacing glare and patted the donkey on the neck. It snorted and ground its hooves into the sand, rubbing its nose against his hip.

Further up the beach, one of the figures who was holding a gun bristled and looked down to where they stood.

"Shit," Grim cursed. The donkey had drawn attention to them all. He signalled for Daniels to move back down toward the sea. The last thing they needed was for Red and Kitty to come mooching around. Unarmed, Grim wouldn't stand a chance.

As they moved past the donkey, Grim noticed something white and shiny draped over its back. Picking it up, he stroked the soft fabric curiously and held it aloft. It was a silk dressing gown, hanging in tatters.

Balling it into his fist, his face twisted and he whispered, "She must be around here somewhere."

Chapter 27

3:32pm: A dark place, Sunray Bay

There was a definite chill in the air as though she was somewhere the sun never shone. Goose-bumps stood to attention all over her body. Strickler had transported her on the back of a donkey at first, then when they'd come to a stop he'd lifted her down onto the ground. She'd tried resisting by wriggling and lashing out at him, but he'd been too strong, easily dominating her. In fact, the attempt to break free had done her no good whatsoever and she'd even lost the dressing gown in the process – when she'd tried to hop away, Strickler had grabbed a handful of the slippery fabric, and as he'd wrenched her back the garment had torn from her body in one ripping movement. And then he'd been down on the floor next to her before she even knew what was happening, his arm around her neck in a choke hold. Before she'd blacked out she could remember him saying, "I warned you not to play silly buggers, didn't I?" But at least he hadn't broken her arms and legs. At least, she didn't think so.

The next thing she remembered was being doubled over his shoulder again, as he'd carried her to wherever she lay now, and she couldn't even hazard a guess as to where that might be. The dressing gown sash was still firmly affixed across her eyes, and her arms were now bound to her sides, as well as her hands being tied behind her back still. She could hardly move at all. The ground beneath her was lumpy and hard, and very unpleasant against her naked skin. She would just have to trust that Strickler would come back for her and set her free like he'd promised.

Lying still she listened for noises, anything that might give her a clue as to where she might be, but the quietness was so complete it buzzed in her ears. There was a fusty smell of damp in the air and with growing paranoia she

186

hoped there were no rats around. Scratchy little feet and tickly whiskers and tails were the last thing she wanted crawling all over her body.

Her nostrils flared, and she suddenly allowed herself to grow angry again. If, or when, she saw Strickler again, she promised herself that she was going to kick his head in. She was having a really bad day.

"*Hello*?" she called out in a hushed tone, the sound of her voice sounding strange and childlike. Chastising herself for being so ridiculous, she then yelled, "Is anybody there?"

Her question was met by more silence.

She had a feeling she was in for a long night, and it was only at that moment she wondered where Rufus must be. *Shit!* She hadn't seen him since she'd left him in the kitchen at Knickerbocker Gloria's. Hopefully Gloria would take care of him – if Gretel hadn't already made him into dog stew or something. That thought made her throat feel dry; she really hoped he was okay.

And what of Grim?

She writhed frantically, trying to move but getting nowhere, feeling two hard ridges to either side that ran the length of her body. These combined with the uneven bits which felt like slats beneath her immediately made her think of tracks of some kind. And that idea swamped her with a horrid, tingly feeling of dread. Rubbing her head against the floor, until it hurt, she managed to slacken the blindfold, but when it moved up and away from her eyes, she still couldn't see a thing. All around her was pitch blackness. She wondered if perhaps she was tied to train tracks down in a coal mine, suddenly imagining herself as a damsel in distress in one of those old black and white movies where the villain ties the hero's love interest to train tracks – then just in the nick of time said hero comes along and saves her. She hoped this wasn't the case, because there was nobody to come along and save her from the mercy of a runaway train. And as much as she hated being pathetic, she could do little else but lie there waiting. She knew, as useless as it was, she needed rescuing though. Bollocks to feminism, she wasn't

187

afraid to admit that she needed a knight in shining armour to gallop in on horseback. Or, better still, for Grim to march in with his buff body glistening and for him to sweep her up into his sturdy arms. Not that that was ever going to happen. It was a crying shame that all of her hopes were pinned on a small elderly terrier and a dead, or at least seriously injured, man to come and save her.

She closed her eyes and wondered what time the train would come...

Chapter 28

Morgan answered on the fourth ring.

"Krain. What do you want now?"

Krain bit his tongue for a moment.

"Sweetheart..."

"*Sweetheart*?! What are you after?"

"Just a favour..."

"I don't know how you dare," she sniped. "That's all you want from me isn't it? Favours! Well I'm sick of it, and I won't do anything else for you, Krain. You can take your favours and shove them up your..."

"Hang on a minute, darling," Krain cut her off. "I'll make it worth your while."

There was silence for a moment.

"*Oh?* And how exactly?"

Krain smiled; she was pissed off, but intrigued enough to hear more.

"I'll let you have what you wanted," he said.

"And what's that? A new fitted wardrobe?"

"No, darling," Krain sighed. "Well, yes, if that's what you want. But I was talking about Grim."

"*Grim?*" He could imagine her grinning now. "*Really?*"

"Yes, really."

"Good. When?"

"As soon as you like, sweetheart."

"Okay, I want him right now in that case."

He'd expected as much, his wife was a complete and utter whore.

"Okay, okay. Have it your way. Is it a deal then?"

"I suppose so," she said, her voice softening slightly. "So what was it you wanted from me?"

"I want you to find out where somebody is for me. Please."

"Why can't you do it? You're the psychic one."

Krain clenched his teeth and held his breath for a moment.

"I know, darling, but I can't right now. Can you just read your tea leaves or get your dowsing rods out – or whatever it is you do?"

"Okay," she huffed. "But I won't tell you anything until Grim arrives, mind you."

Krain realised at that exact moment their relationship didn't have one scrap of trust left in it. She didn't trust him one jot and he wouldn't trust her as far as he could throw her.

"Okay okay, just brew your tea or whatever you need to do and be ready with the information – I don't have much time."

"So who is it I'm I trying to find?"

"A woman. She's called Elizabeth Hood."

"Oh?" Morgan sounded even more intrigued. "Who is she?"

"I'll explain later."

"But, *Finn*, who is she...?"

"Not now Morgan," he said, snapping his mobile phone shut. He suddenly couldn't bear the sound of her voice anymore.

Chapter 29

4:38pm: The North Pier, Sunray Bay
Grim let the white silk fall from his hands to the ground. For the first time in a long, long while he felt a grip of fearful discomfort in his chest; a fear for what had already happened, and for what *would* happen or *could* happen. She'd awoken something within. And even though the fear wasn't a pleasant feeling, he welcomed it nonetheless. It meant that he wasn't completely dead.

Looking up at the sky, he wondered again what an hour meant in terms of how safe Libby was. If he could figure it out and if he could save her, he thought it might be a chance for him to redeem himself. Not that it was all about him, he was doing it for her too.

Aware only of the sound of waves breaking the shore, he suddenly had an idea. The water – it was coming closer.

"What time will the tide be in?" he asked Daniels suddenly.

Daniels shrugged. "Dunno, maybe half an hour, an hour? I'm really not sure."

Grim took off back down to the shore, sprinting silently. Sand kicked up behind him and he checked the pier posts on his way.

"Where're you goin'?" Daniels hissed, following close behind.

"I dunno," Grim answered. "I suppose it's a shot in the dark, but what if he has her tied to one of these posts? She might drown if the tide comes in."

"Bloody hell, Grim." Daniels panted. "That *is* a shot in the dark, mate."

"Can you see her on any of these ones up here?" Grim asked.

Daniels looked about at the posts.

"No, but I'll go and check them all if you'd like me to?"

"Yeah, I'm gonna go and check the ones further out, just in case."

Leaving Daniels behind, he ran out into the frothing sea, not sure whether he was doing the right thing or not. Wading in, he began the futile task of trying to find Libby. Torrents of dark salty water battered his legs, knocking him off balance. He fell down and waves dragged him in further, pummelling his face. And once again, he was transported back to that warm summer's night over two years ago...

Della and Daisy on the bed in a tussle of blonde hair and blood; he hadn't bothered making the call to the emergency services. It would have been pointless. Whatever Della had seen in his face when he'd returned to the bedroom he'd never be sure, but the thought haunted him at every given opportunity. Her blue eyes hadn't seemed to recognise him at first, but when they did he'd seen a flash of distrust and wariness in them, and that broke his heart. What had he expected, standing over her with a gun in his hands? It had all happened so quick, he hadn't had time to plan it out properly.

"I love you," he'd sighed, tears streaming down his cheeks.

He'd wanted everything to happen quickly, so she and Daisy wouldn't have time to know what he was about to do. Though in hindsight, the thought was nonsensical. The man they'd known and loved was standing over them like a demented maniac. In his defence, he hadn't wanted to tell them what was *really* happening, that truth was even scarier. And he couldn't fetch himself to hug them good bye either, if he'd faltered it would only have made the choice even harder to make – and he may never have done what he'd done.

Raising the gun, without dwelling too much, he'd pulled the trigger, shooting Della in the head. This was when he learned the hard truth that hasty plans seldom pan out properly. He'd mistakenly thought Daisy was unconscious, hence the decision to kill her mother first; and it was the biggest error he'd ever made. As Della's body rolled back lifeless, little Daisy had looked up at him in horror. The look on her face was to be the foundation of all his future nightmares, and he knew it would haunt him for all eternity. Pulling the trigger for a second time, he knew that nothing would ever hurt him even close to the pain he felt when shooting his own little girl in the head. He'd sat sobbing and cradling them both in his arms; his two special girls. Consoling himself that at least he'd made them safe. He'd sat with them for as long as he'd dared, while all around him the windows of the log cabin had smashed in...

And finally the zombies had arrived.

Hundreds of them.

His little family hadn't stood a chance, especially since Della and Daisy had already been infected – they'd been just as good as dead. But he'd saved his girls from being members of the walking dead, both of them were too special for that. Their place was in heaven, not amongst the stinking corpses of the earth.

With a blood-souring wail he'd ran through the house, aiming to kill as many zombies as feasibly possible. And he had. There hadn't been a square inch of his skin that wasn't covered in blood by the time he'd finished. When he'd grown tired and afraid for his own fate he'd taken his machete and, whilst screaming for Della, for Daisy and for himself, had stabbed himself through the heart.

He was to learn in Sunray Bay that his hate-filled vengeance had come at a huge price. Having been bitten himself, he'd allowed the infection to run through his veins for far too long, and the change had already begun by the time he'd taken his own life. His soul had already rotted away. Inside he was blackened and barren. His only saving grace was that he'd killed himself before the infection had wasted his mind – although most days he thought that was a curse in itself. Things might have been a lot easier had he awoken in Sunray Bay a brain-dead zombie, but as it was, he was suspended in purgatory instead; a state of existence that held no sense of hope or ending. He allowed himself some small comfort in the knowledge that he'd killed Della and

Daisy soon after they'd had zombie contact, allowing them to bypass Sunray Bay with their clean souls intact.

But that didn't change the fact that he'd failed to protect them in the first place. And now, what of Libby? She wasn't his responsibility, yet he felt some duty towards her. At least, he told himself it was duty.

Checking the last post at the end of the pier, he was surprised to find that for the first time in a long while he felt a glimmer of hope. He wasn't sure of the reason, but Libby had undoubtedly roused a sense of optimism in him. It felt weird, but good. And the feeling wasn't even dashed when he found that Libby wasn't strapped to any of the posts. He knew he still had time, albeit very little of it, a fighting chance to find her before whatever fate Strickler had left her to.

He fought his way back to shore, hoisting himself onto the wet sand, where Daniels rushed to meet him. Daniels was shaking his head. His search had been fruitless too. Grim used Daniels's proffered arm and heaved himself up onto his feet, panting and gasping for breath. When he raised his head and looked towards the promenade, he noticed a solid wall of hulking black figures on the beach. Large and fast, they pounded closer and closer to where he and Daniels stood, their paws nimble and silent on the sand.

"Ah shit. Get back in the water, Grim," Daniels instructed. "There're too many of them."

Grim stood still. He'd face up to whatever he was due; he was sick and tired of running. If the dozen or so werewolves had come for him, he couldn't say he blamed them. Sucking in air through his mouth, he braced himself for the onslaught.

In a line of thick fur and curling snouts, the werewolves all halted just feet away from him and Daniels, and as Daniels stepped back in the water and cocked his gun, a familiar voice said, "Grim? Where's Libby? Have you seen her?"

Grim watched as a small, black figure emerged from behind the rest of the pack.

"Rufus?"

Rufus stopped at Grim's booted feet and looked up.

"Yes soldier, 'tis I," he said, face beaming. "So do you have any idea where she is? That scruffy-looking wazzock with the donkeys took her from Gloria's."

"I know..." Grim replied. He then went on to give a quick recap of the preceding events.

The clouds were now starting to shift and the moon kept poking through, silvery white and enough for Grim to see that Rufus's eyes were shining with worry. He wondered if his would be the same, underneath his sunglasses – but he doubted it.

"Crikey, we don't have long to find her then, do we?" Rufus gasped.

Grim shook his head solemnly.

One of the werewolves slid close to Grim, overstepping the boundaries of his personal space, its wet nose just inches from his. Its fur stank of damp earth and wet dog, to an extent that Grim found it dizzying. Not intimidated, he stared back into its massive blue eyes (which would have been more fitting on a husky), and he silently dared it to make a move.

"You need to leave, Grim," it snarled through massive pointed teeth. "I can protect you for a short while but, as you well know, the Knickerbocker Pack isn't exactly the largest or most revered in Sunray Bay. The larger packs will kill you as soon as they see you."

Grim looked stunned.

"Gloria?"

The wolf before him remained balanced on hind legs and nodded its head.

"Yes, it's me."

He'd never seen her in wolf form before, he'd never wanted to.

"I can't go yet, Gloria. I have to know that Libby is okay."

Gloria nodded her understanding.

"Well just know that I can't protect you. I'm very fond of you Grim, but I won't put my pack in danger for your sake. So unless you leave now, you're on your own."

"Then so be it," Grim said.

He stepped past her and started moving up the beach. The other werewolves parted to allow him past, watching with great interest.

"Wait! Where are you going?" Rufus called out.

"To find Libby," Grim replied. And as he started to run up the beach, he yelled back, "And I suggest you do the same."

Chapter 30

5:06pm: The streets of Sunray Bay

Kitty drove Strickler to Prospect Point Lighthouse in Red's car; the entire journey in silence. Strickler had been too busy trying to fathom whether Krain had tricked him or not to make conversation (he knew he wasn't the sharpest tool in the shed, especially since he'd lost his psychic prowess) – besides, he was too awkward around women anyway. As for Kitty, she wouldn't have spoken to him even if he was the last man standing in a post-apocalyptic scenario.

Under the pier Krain had instructed Kitty to take Strickler round to the lighthouse.

"What will happen there?" Strickler had asked.

"Morgan will use some of her hocus pocus on you to give you back what is rightfully yours, of course."

Krain's grin had been too smug, and Strickler wasn't imbecile enough to fall for it.

"But what about you? Where will you be? Shouldn't you be there too, since you have my... psychic-ness?"

"Ah Strickler, you crazy fool," Krain had laughed, light-heartedly. "I will be waiting right here for instructions on where to find Libby – time is ticking, you know. Fear not, I'm not trying to trick you. What would I gain from sending you away, when I have no idea where my daughter is? And don't be ridiculous, Morgan is a *witch*, she doesn't need me present to perform the deed."

And so, that had sounded good enough to him. Strickler had been sold on the deal, hoping that Morgan would be able to pull off her magic in a timely fashion so Libby wouldn't be harmed. He'd already begun to feel a little unsettled at what he'd actually done to her – though he knew there was no going back now.

When Kitty pulled up at the gates to the lighthouse, she keyed some numbers into the security panel and waited for the gates to open up. The gates swung open slowly, and the car crawled up close to the lighthouse. Coming to a stop, Kitty remained facing front. Strickler looked at her.

"Are you coming in?"

Kitty's eyes narrowed and she huffed, "You're a grown man, surely you don't need me to hold your hand? Now get out and hurry up, you numbskull."

Strickler gulped and looked up at the looming lighthouse.

"Is Krain's wife okay? I mean, does she definitely know I'm coming? Will I be safe in there?"

"You'll be fine," Kitty sighed impatiently. "Morgan loves men. Probably even you."

With his eyebrows arched, Strickler stepped from the car and strode cautiously to the door of the lighthouse. Again he was filled with self-doubt as to whether he'd made the right decision in doing as Krain had instructed, realising that ultimately, Krain had called the shots after all. *Manipulative bastard*, he thought. But before he could go back on his choice the door to the lighthouse opened, as though his arrival had been eagerly anticipated, and Krain's wife greeted him with a large white smile.

She wasn't how he had imagined. Not at all. He thought Krain was a camp, middle-aged tosspot, and had wrongly assumed that his wife wouldn't be up to much either. Before now he'd always conjured up images of her being an old hag with customary witches' warts and all, but Krain's wife had none of that going on. Her skin was the colour of latte, smooth and unblemished, and her black hair fell in masses around her young, pretty face. And she had the body of a goddess, standing there in a black lacy negligee. He gasped, suddenly not knowing what to say – all thoughts of why he was even there had flown from his head. *Why am I here?* he wondered. *To seduce Krain's wife?* In that moment, it was all he could think about. He thought it was no wonder Krain kept her locked up in the lighthouse all the time – she was magnificent.

"You aren't exactly as I expected," she said, looking him up and down, but smiling nonetheless. "But, never mind, you'll do."

She reached out and grabbed his arm, pulling him into the lighthouse hallway. Cupping his face in her hand, she licked her lips as a sheen formed on his top lip. A woman had never touched him like that before, and so he just stood gawping at her.

"What's the matter? The cat got your tongue?" she asked.

Strickler shook his head, his eyes stinging because he hadn't yet blinked.

"You *are* Grim aren't you?"

Strickler instantly forgot about his missing psychic power, about Libby's peril, and about the last twenty odd miserable years he'd spent in Sunray Bay – seeing instead a new opportunity present itself. This time he wasn't turning down the advances of a woman in her underwear, especially not when the advances were coming from this one in particular. If he could shag Krain's wife silly that would be repayment enough for all his troubles. In fact, afterwards he would be happy to just die and cease to exist.

"I'm anybody you want me to be," he finally answered, nodding his head a little too vigorously.

"Good." Morgan kissed him lightly on the lips and said, "Now wait there like a good boy, I need to make a quick call. Then you're all mine."

Strickler wondered if he'd already died and gone to heaven.

Chapter 31

Prospect Point Lighthouse looked like a glowing stick of candy in the distance, and Krain imagined Strickler would be inside by now. As soon as Strickler and Kitty had left, he'd scaled up to the top of the helter skelter to await Morgan's phone call, which he expected any time soon – that is, if things had gone according to plan. He worried about whether it had, though he had no reason to think otherwise – so long as Kitty had done as he'd instructed, and so long as Morgan was still as horny for Grim as she'd been earlier. With that thought Krain's mouth dropped at the sides in revulsion. Divorce was definitely on the cards this time around. The last time he'd found out she'd been unfaithful he hadn't had sex with her for a full two months, because he hadn't been able to bring himself to touch her tainted body. And now, well, he just couldn't be bothered with her antics anymore. He'd rather remain celibate for the rest of his years than suffer the humiliation and degradation she brought about for him.

Interlacing his fingers the fabric of his gloves tightened, and he thought fondly of Merilyn Strickler, his beautiful, young student. He wished things could have been different. But it had all gone so horribly wrong. Sighing in anger, he kicked the orange plastic at the top of the slide and cursed Strickler and his first wife Sharon for having ruined his entire life. Red, who was standing at the foot of the helter skelter on werewolf patrol, looked up to see what the clatter was. Krain growled down at him. Sulking like a grounded teenager, he scanned the area down below, noting how the fairground looked hostile even now with its flashing lights. He imagined Scooby Doo and his friends wouldn't have looked out of place running about trying to capture villainous ride-operators and giant land-walking squids – in fact, he thought the big snickering hound would have an all-out field day in Sunray Bay in general.

Letting his gaze wander to the swirling iron gates beneath the Pleasant Point Funfair sign, he saw there was already a small group of people congregating there, waiting as the park attendant jangled keys in the locks. Krain presumed the crowd was most likely made up of teenagers who had no real fear of the dark, feral vampires, werewolves or any other night time beasties – or in the same breath, he considered they may be teenagers who *were* feral vampires, werewolves and other night time beasties. He shook his head and clicked his tongue – he despised other monsters, always had done, even going so far as to harbour an inherent dislike for his own kind. Readily willing to admit that he was a snob in that respect, he could never understand the allure of biting a person and drinking their blood. His mother had always told him not to put sweets in his mouth after he'd dropped them on the ground – so why would he want to put a complete stranger's skin in his mouth? Yuck. He wished he could get out of Sunray Bay and leave it all behind, but he'd made his bed when he'd killed Sharon, and now he'd have to lie in it. In all the years he'd been in Sunray Bay, he'd never once had his soul weighed. The sophisticated scales would have picked up on the fact that he was in possession of more than just his own soul, which would, in effect, show him up for the murderer that he really was. In that instance, he'd lose everything and be thrown into prison. So, he figured he'd rather just stay at the top of his game, albeit in a place he hated, and try to eradicate the dirty vampiric need for blood, ultimately sanitising Sunray Bay once and for all. And who knew, he thought he might even invest more time and money into The Ordinaries if they proved their worth by stamping out the new Phoenix strain of vampires, whoever the hell they were. Which was another thing, once the drama of that night was over he knew he must continue the search for the documents that had been stolen from the archives; the

201

blueprints for the scales at the courthouse, a top secret map of The Grey Dustbowl and the deeds to his own home.

Scanning the skyline, he searched for dark, flying shapes that didn't resemble sea birds – annoyed that he'd resorted to hiding at the top of a children's slide; annoyed that he had to hide at all.

To console himself he took his thoughts back to Libby, believing that not all was lost if he could reach her before she suffered whatever unpleasantness Strickler had chosen for her. He had a trick up his sleeve, and although a long, tough night undoubtedly lay ahead, he knew that if he could pull his plan off, a brighter future lay ahead.

Just as the corners of his mouth lifted slightly, his mobile phone rang.

"Morgan?"

"Krain."

"Is everything okay, darling?" he asked, his tongue suddenly feeling too big in his dry mouth.

"I'm really not happy with you still," she snarled back. "But thank you for sending Grim, he's here with me now. It was a really nice gesture, Krain."

Krain's temples throbbed and his eyes would have glared red, had he been able to make them do so. At that moment he couldn't bring himself to say anything because he was afraid of saying the wrong thing and ruining his plans.

"Anyway, I suppose I'd better help you with your little game of hide and seek now," Morgan said, not sensing the tension at the other end of the line. "I know where Elizabeth Hood is..."

About bloody time, he thought. The helter skelter would open any minute now.

Chapter 32

5:46pm: Somewhere dark, Sunray Bay

It was still dark, but something had changed. There was a greenish tinge to the shadows, and Libby wasn't sure if it was because her eyes were adjusting, or because lights had been switched on somewhere. An added chill crept over her body like a blanket of ice as though a door had opened up somewhere creating a draught. She wondered whether Strickler had come back for her – or whether she was going to find out that the vampire and werewolf populations of Sunray Bay were in actual fact a reality. Holding her breath, she didn't dare make a sound in case it was the latter. She'd had about as much as she could take, and she felt like crying. What a shitty day. Not knowing how long she'd been tied up already was disconcerting, but not knowing how much longer she'd stay there was frightening. Hot tears glazed her eyes and she blinked them away, cursing herself for being so weak.

As she turned her head to rub her damp cheek on to her shoulder, she was shocked to see the outline of a figure standing nearby. It was hard to tell whether the person was male or female, but whoever or whatever it was they were stooped low with rounded shoulders; hunched and still. She hadn't noticed anybody there before, and she tried shrinking her own body down flat to the ground hoping she wouldn't be spotted – if she hadn't been already. There was still no sound despite how close the figure stood; she couldn't even hear it breathing. And the black cloak it wore shimmered in the gloom like bin liners.

She took a slow, deep gulp of air, willing herself to be quiet and not wanting her own breathing to be detected. But it all came back out again in a long rasping noise when the figure turned to her, its eyes glowing red. From its green lips it issued a high, chilling cackle. Libby's mind was consumed with terror.

And it was then that she screamed and passed out.

Chapter 33

5:29pm: The North Pier, Sunray Bay

Grim raced up onto the pier and headed straight for Pleasant Point Funfair. It would be opening soon, and he didn't know why he hadn't thought of it before, it seemed glaringly obvious that Libby *had* to be there somewhere. When he arrived at the gates, they were already open and people were now milling around inside. Teenage boys were queuing up to whack the strongman attraction that stood nearby; a high-pitched *ting-a-ling* would mark their masculinity and impress their girlfriends. A small boy, who appeared to be alone, was trying to hook plastic ducks with his magnetic fishing rod. His coordination was not the best and, each time the hook-a-duck stall owner turned his back, he tried to give the dangling magnet on the end of his line a helping hand. And a carousel of brightly coloured horses spun round, their saddles all empty and their hand-painted faces evil. The evil seemed to power the carnival music that drifted out from the well-lit canopy that their bodies slid up and down under. Grim hated coming to Pleasant Point Funfair, it inspired painful memories of Daisy.

Turning to Daniels, who had followed him, he said, "Let's split up. Look for Strickler and Krain as well as Libby, okay?"

Daniels was gasping for breath, clutching his thighs as he bent double trying to alleviate the pain in his chest, but he nodded his head anyway. And then Grim was off again running towards the red and white flashing lights of the indoor arcades behind the carousel. He knew he had to get into the mindset of Strickler. Wherever she was, it had to be somewhere that would have dire results at opening time, once the punters had made their way in. Halting outside the arcades, he saw teenagers playing penny slots and jiggling about on flight simulators inside. Loud jingles and space invader bleeps constantly rang out, and Grim didn't believe he was looking in the right place. There was nothing unseemly about the arcade, apart from the money hoarding, junk-spewing machines themselves.

At the end of the pier, in the distance, he watched as the big wheel's lights flashed on, dancing yellow around its frame. He didn't think that was the answer either. It didn't make sense; there was nothing any more treacherous about the ferris wheel than the arcades – not that he could think of anyway.

But it was as he stepped around a pair of kissing teenagers that he saw it – Zoltan's Passage to Hell, the pier's ghost train. Looming behind a hotdog stall, it was modelled on a haunted mansion with crooked windows, grey brickwork and creeping ivy. An idea struck a chord in his mind instantly, and part of him hoped he was wrong.

Spurred into action once again, he sprinted over to the ghost train's barriers where two teenagers stood guarding their spot at the front of the queue. They were waiting for an old man, who was fiddling with the admission shutters, to take their fare and let them in. Grim barged straight past, clipping their shoulders and knocking them both round almost three hundred and sixty degrees.

"Hey, watch it," one of them spat, his spotty face twisted with attitude and his hormones ready to fight. Sizing Grim up, he shrank back, his pluckiness shrivelling before his friend's eyes in a matter of seconds. The old cantankerous ride attendant stopped rattling the shutters in their frames and turned around.

"Will you lot behave, else I'll give y'all a good hiding!" he snarled, shaking his fist for effect. Grim ignored him and jumped over the barrier onto the ride's tracks and, parting long strands of tattered black fabric which was hanging down in the entranceway, stepped into the darkness beyond.

"Oi, where the hell do you think you're going?" the old man yelled after him, the gruffness in his voice now tinged with a higher pitched urgency.

Grim poked his head back outside and pointed up to the ride's sign. "To hell, of course. Now hold the ride five minutes."

"Crazy bastard," the old man grumbled to himself, shaking his head and setting to work on the jammed shutter again with renewed vigour.

Grim edged his way further and further into the blackness feeling his way by tapping his feet against the tracks, and just as he was about to call out Libby's name he heard a woman's scream echo all around him. With a quickened heartbeat, he increased his pace as much as he dared to, so as not to obtain a sprained ankle.

"*Libby?* Are you there?"

There was no answer; just silence that filled Grim with foreboding. The sickening scream was still ringing in his ears. Huffing, he cursed, not so certain of his own convictions anymore. He realised the scream could have been part of the ghost train's sound system. In fact, the more he thought about it the more he thought that was probably the case; the ride attendant most likely trying to scare the shit out of him. His pace slowed down again, and for the umpteenth time that day he started to feel defeated.

Before he had time to turn around and give up, he felt a sudden movement in the air, and a large, shrieking object flapped down into his face, smothering him with leathery wings. Knocking it away, he swung his arm wide and punched it hard. It hung suspended in mid-air, rocking back and forth like a weird pendulum. He could only presume, in the dark, that it was some kind of giant plastic bat perhaps, whose squawk had now been reduced to a tinny and pathetic mechanical drone. Batting it out of the way using the back of his hand, he proceeded further into the depths of Zoltan's tunnel of doom, his anger renewed.

The track began to dip down on a steep decline, which was enough to make him slow right down to almost a crawl. He wished he'd brought a torch because the most he could see were pin pricks of red light on the walls and ceiling,

207

intended to be gleaming droplets of blood or glowing eyes perhaps.

Once the track had levelled out again, he called out, "Libby, are you in here?"

Still there was only silence.

His feet met a soft mound on the tracks and he stumbled forward, just managing to steady himself before falling. He swore loudly, but the soft mound groaned louder still.

"Strickler? Is that you?"

"No, Libby," Grim replied with relief. "It's me."

"Grim?! You're alive?"

They both bristled when they heard *clink-clanking* of machinery, followed by vibrations running through the tracks.

"For the time being, yeah," he replied.

"Quick, untie me!"

Wasting no time, Grim set about struggling with the rope that bound her upper body to the track, and after a few sharp tugs it fell loose and Libby sat bolt upright.

"My feet, *undo my feet*," she cried frantically, her hands still tied behind her back.

Grim pulled blindly at the rope around her ankles, feeling pressure growing more and more with every heartbeat that jumped. Neither of them could see the ghost train yet, but its thundering wheels announced its imminent arrival.

After a few moments more Libby suddenly yelled, "Get off the tracks. Here it is!"

Grim looked up and saw the outline of a cart at the top of the incline, and his heart completely stopped. With one last frantic pull, the rope gave way and he yanked Libby up into the air. They both tumbled hard to the side, as whooshing air issued from the cart that whizzed past. Libby's hair whipped back, and she scrunched her eyes shut. Grim's head hit the side of the fibre glass tunnel, and Libby groaned as though it was hers. Shaking fake cobwebs away from her face, she asked, "Are you okay?"

Grim lay on his back, and when he looked up he realised, for the second time that day, Libby was on top of him in her underwear.

"Yeah," he said, managing a smile. "And you?"

Before she could answer, dim lights flickered on all around them. They saw the cart that had narrowly avoided them was now at a standstill further down the track, and an empty one was balanced at the top of the incline. The two teenagers Grim had met in the queue outside jumped from the first cart and scarpered in the opposite direction, and one of them yelled back to Grim, "Hey, get out of here man. He's coming!"

Libby looked at Grim. They were both breathing heavily from exertion and adrenaline and under different circumstances she would have relished the feel of his angry whumping heart.

"Who the hell are they?" she wheezed. "And what are they talking about?"

Grim rolled Libby carefully onto the floor so that he could stand up.

"We need to get out of here. Now!"

But as he helped Libby up onto her feet, a shiver-inducing voice bellowed down the tunnel.

"Ah Grim, how very convenient."

They both looked up and saw two figures standing at the top of the incline.

"Who the hell is *that*?" Libby asked. "This is getting bloody ridiculous."

"It's your first acquaintance with a Sunray Bay vampire," Grim groaned. "It's Finnbane Krain."

Libby rolled her eyes.

"Oh *great*!"

209

Chapter 34

Krain and Red stepped around the stationary ghost train cart at the top of the incline and walked down to meet Libby and Grim. Krain's eyes darted back and forth between the two of them, and Red's eyes focussed solely on Libby's body.

"What do you want with her, Krain?" Grim asked; his hard body poised and ready for action. "Let her go and I'll hand myself over."

"You bloody fool," Krain laughed. He and Red had stopped several yards away. "She's the *only* reason I'm in here. I didn't take a stroll through Zoltan's lousy back passage to come looking for you as well. Quite frankly, I'm bored with you already. In fact, if you hand her over I'll let you just walk away."

Grim put his hand on Libby's shoulder and shook his head, keeping a watchful eye on Red and the gun that he held aloft.

"What do you want with *me*?" Libby asked. "Is this to do with Strickler?"

In a surprising gesture, Krain shrugged his suit jacket off and tossed it over to her.

"Cover yourself up, darling."

It landed on the floor by her feet, and she stood looking at it, her hands behind her back with a piece of rope still binding her wrists. She didn't want to accept hospitality from a vampire, but she didn't want to stand around in her smalls any longer either – not that she had much choice in the matter.

"I can't," she spat.

Realising her plight, Grim stooped down and picked up the jacket, swinging it around her shoulders.

"There, that's better," Krain beamed. Red gave him a sideways glance of disdain.

210

"Now then, to answer your question, yes, I suppose this is to do with Strickler, in a roundabout kind of way."

"There's been some kind of mistake," said Libby, who was now swamped beneath expensive black fabric and large square shoulder pads. "I'm not like you, I'm not a vampire."

"She's not one of the Phoenix strain either," Grim lied, he hadn't even had chance to speak to her about it yet.

"One of the *who*?" Libby looked to him for an explanation. But Grim didn't give her one; he kept his eyes on Krain.

"Of course she's not," Krain guffawed. "But how did you know about – oh never mind." He wafted his hand in the air and dismissed Grim. "She's much more special than that."

This time Grim did look at Libby, confusion marking his brow.

Krain clapped his hands together and smiled smugly, taking pride in his next announcement.

"She's a vampae."

"What the fuck's a *vampae*?" Grim asked, before Libby could.

Krain's neatly aligned teeth still shone in a brilliant smile.

"A vampae is a hybrid. A mixture of vampire and faery."

Libby laughed out loud. And Grim snorted, "Did you just make that up?"

Krain chuckled, mischief playing in his eyes.

"Yes actually, I did. But it's got a nice ring to it, don't you think? See Libby is a rarity, quite possibly one of a kind."

"This is the most ridiculous day of my whole life," Libby said. "So now I'm not just your average run of the mill vampire – I've been promoted to a vampae? What's wrong with everybody here? Are you all insane?"

Krain's face grew serious.

"Look, let's get this straight," she spat, tired of being messed around. "I'm not a vampire because I don't drink blood, and I'm not a faery because I don't have a tutu let alone a wand. And besides the fact that nobody else in my

211

family has wings or fangs either, I'm a bloody vegetarian. *Okay!*"

Krain looked almost sympathetic and stepped forward awkwardly.

"My poor girl, it's as I feared. You've never been told the truth."

"The truth about *what*?"

Libby felt Grim's hand tighten on her shoulder.

"The truth about your mother."

"*My mother?* What about her?"

Krain looked skyward while he thought of the right words to say. But then he just came right out with it, "That she was one of the last faeries."

Libby would have thrown her hands up in the air, had she been able to. She was losing her patience – and the will to live.

"What the hell are you talking about? My mother isn't a bloody faery!" she cried. Then remembering the feather trimmed marigolds she wore to do the washing-up in, she said, "Well, she has her moments, I suppose."

Krain laughed a little this time, a sparkle of warmth in his cold black eyes.

"Merilyn was from the fine Stockner lineage. She was really quite special."

Libby's mouth dropped open.

"How do you know my mother's name?"

"He's psychic," Grim said, unimpressed with Krain's revelation.

Krain held up his gloved hands.

"Indeed I am, but this is all above board, I swear. Merilyn was a student of mine a long, long time ago, you see." His face fogged over as he recalled. "It's true. I was a lecturer in the sciences, and she was a brainy young thing. My star pupil."

"So I've heard," Red muttered quietly with a smile.

Ignoring Red's remark, Krain moved close to Libby, reaching out his hand to touch her. She flinched away and

Grim stepped between them. Lowering his hands to his side, Krain then said, "You look just like her."

Libby's face was sour and full of scepticism.

"What, so you're saying, my dad is a vampire?"

"Yes."

"And I suppose you knew him too?"

"Of course," Krain laughed. "I knew nobody better. Quite a charming chap really. And, of course, he was from a rare bloodline himself."

Libby rolled her eyes.

"I suppose he was from the fine Hood bloodline, was he?"

"Don't be ridiculous Libby, darling," Krain tutted and wagged his finger at her. "He's from the Krain bloodline."

Libby felt woozy, and Grim gripped her tight. Krain held out both of his arms wide, as though he meant to hug her, and said, "I'm your father, my dear girl."

Chapter 35

Grim kept hold of Libby for support, although it was probably reasonable to say he was almost as shocked as she was. He wouldn't have seen *that* coming in a million years.

"You're lying," Libby spat, rage dancing in her eyes. "My dad is Dennis Hood."

Krain bit his lip. Keeping a calm voice, he said "Dennis Hood might be the poor sap who picked up the pieces after I was gone – but *biologically*, I'm your father."

"No!" Libby yelled. "You're a liar."

"Well supposing it *is* true," Grim said. "What are you expecting, Krain? A happy family reunion?"

Krain smirked, cruelness returning to his face.

"Indeed, Grim, you're hardly one to talk. What you'd give for a family reunion, I'll bet."

"*Bastard,*" Grim snarled. He clenched his fists ready to take a shot at Krain, but Red was standing with the gun aimed straight at his head.

"Keep your comments to yourself, you Neanderthal," Krain said. "People in glass houses shouldn't throw stones."

Libby looked between Krain and Grim for a moment, not sure what they were talking about, but before she could ask, Krain said to her, "I was having an affair with your mother – that is, *I* was married and she was single at the time."

"Spare me the details," Libby spat in disgust.

"I'd have left my wife for her eventually, you know." Krain admitted, his face becoming distant once again. "I loved her."

"Well that's very gallant of you," Grim chided. "And is that meant to make her feel better?"

Krain glared at him, his snake eyes warning that he was close to the edge, but instead of biting back, he continued

214

talking to Libby. "I didn't realise Merilyn was a faery at first, I mean, that's not why we began seeing each other."

Libby rolled her eyes with impatience, she'd heard enough.

"Come on, Grim," she said. "I'm leaving."

As she made to move, Krain stepped forward and grabbed her upper arms, a little harder than he meant to.

"Wait. Don't you want to hear more?" His voice was urgent and almost pleading.

"No thanks." She tried to shrug him off.

"But your powers, if you tap into them, the possibilities that would open up... Don't you want me to teach you?"

"My *powers*?" Libby asked becoming still, and allowing him to keep his grip on her.

"Of course, I'll give you a few examples. If you've taken after me, you'll possess great physical strength, have an ability to heal yourself quicker than normal folk, and you will also have great powers of persuasion – you'll be able to get pretty much whatever you want, within logical reason, that is."

Libby turned her head and looked at Grim, one of her eyebrows cocked.

"I hardly think so. And, anyway, what if I've taken after my mother?" she asked, humouring him.

"I can't be completely certain, but we can find out together what the extent of your faery powers are," he said, panic rising in his voice again at the thought of losing her attention. "I'll help you..."

Libby shook her head and laughed. "This is all too ridiculous, I *really* have heard enough now." She scowled at Red and his gun.

"But your blood could potentially save an entire population..."

"Ah, now we're getting to the crux of the issue," Grim said, sardonically. "I knew there'd be some ulterior motive behind your newfound kindliness."

215

"How so?" Libby asked, suspicious yet intrigued by the man in front of her who was not only claiming to be a vampire, but also her father.

"Okay, let's start with the basics, shall we? I'm not sure how much you know, but it's true that Vampires need a steady diet of blood."

Libby looked flummoxed.

"And the blood we consume provides us with that all important iron intake – it's essential for our sustenance. Forget about what you *think* you know about vampires from films and comic books," Krain said, rolling his eyes. "We all have different capabilities, depending on what bloodline we're from and what strain of vampire we are – but when it boils down to it, we *all* need a diet that's high in iron."

Libby didn't look convinced. "So why don't you just eat lots of red meat and breakfast cereal?"

Krain chuckled and shook his head. "The iron we require has to be sourced from a *living thing*, I'm afraid. It must have a soulful essence."

"Okay," Libby sighed, playing along. "So where do I come into this?"

"Well, faeries, on the other hand, are very sensitive to iron – in fact, in complete contrast, they're actually allergic to it. If you gave a faery a drop of normal blood, she'd go into anaphylactic shock and her head would blow up to the size of a balloon."

Libby tapped her foot impatiently.

"Again, what does this have to do with me?"

"It means, Libby darling, that, theoretically, you *should* be neutralised to both extremes. If I'm correct, you will not need iron for sustenance, and neither will you be sensitive to it. You're a very special girl."

"That sounds anything but special." Libby rolled her eyes again. "In fact, it sounds pretty normal to me."

"But you have no idea what it could mean for the entire vampire society, sweetheart. What your blood could do," Krain said, with a maniacal look on his face, which made the hairs on Libby's neck stand on end.

216

"What *my blood* can do for the vampire society?" she cried. "I'm not sure I want to know."

"Don't be so alarmed," he replied, trying to look reassuring, but achieving instead a look of sheer lunacy. "With your blood, I could make a special serum. I could inject it into all vampires so they would no longer require iron – no longer require blood!"

"You're absolutely round the twist," Grim said. Even Red, who'd lowered his gun slightly, didn't look too sure about Krain's master plan.

"Isn't that the point in being a vampire though?" Libby asked, looking more confused than scared once again. "That you're *meant* to bite people and drink their blood."

Krain cringed inwardly.

"Yes, but it's our downfall, all the same. Infection amongst vampires is rife, it's spreading like the clap at a sixties festival."

Libby was again stunned into silence.

"If I can eradicate *that* problem vampires will be more likely to achieve immortality. We'd become a super race then, the race we've always dreamed of becoming. I'd be like a God. And all I'd need is some of your blood."

Libby stepped away from him.

"Think about it Libby, we could rule Sunray Bay together. We'd be a great father/daughter team. I'll help you reclaim your soul as well; I know it's with your dog."

With renewed interest, Libby looked her supposed biological father in the eye, and seeing nothing at all of herself there, she said, "How? How do I get it back? If you tell me, I'll think about helping you."

"*Libby...*" Grim was ruffled, perturbed about what she was suggesting.

"You'll have to kill the dog, I'm afraid, darling," Krain said matter-of-factly, as though he was telling her not to forget her umbrella because it was raining outside.

"*Kill him?*" she yelled. "Are you kidding?"

Grim sighed intolerably and growled, "I could have told her to do that..."

"Ah, but I can offer her comfort. And I can get her a new dog afterwards if it means that much."

Grim laughed derisively. "And I could've done both of those things too. You're obviously too numb and heartless to understand the complexities involved. How could you even suggest she kills her own pet dog?"

Libby looked at them both wide-eyed.

"Look, I'm *not* killing Rufus, okay? And I'm not taking part in any of your crazy plans either. I'm not a vampire or a faery, and I'm certainly not a bloody *vampae*! I'm just a normal girl, I don't care if what you say is true or not. If I have any powers, then I relinquish them. And what's more, Rufus can have my soul if that's what it takes for him to stay alive. I'm not even sure I want it back. If you *are* telling the truth, then my whole life has been a complete lie." Her eyes filled up, glassy and fragile. Straining to keep her voice from breaking, she said, "I will *not* kill Rufus."

From somewhere up above a voice cried out, "Well I'm jolly well pleased to hear that!"

They all looked up and saw a small four-legged figure standing in front of the ghost train cart, and beside it stood the Knickerbocker Pack, looking like a mangy set of Alsatians standing on their hind legs, bared teeth white and sharp in the dimness, with their hackles raised.

Libby gasped. Although she'd already been acquainted with her very first monster, Krain – who looked decidedly human – now that she was faced with a whole pack of werewolves who were balanced capably on two legs there was no denying that monsters *were* a reality in Sunray Bay.

"*Rufus!*" she cried. "What the hell are you doing? Why didn't you stay at Gloria's?"

"It's okay," Grim said calmly, "That *is* Gloria."

Libby's mouth opened in wonder as the werewolf directly behind Rufus stepped forward. Its familiar blue eyes were big and babyish, and Libby noticed the crown of its head bore a streak of shaggier fur that was peroxide blonde.

Libby could hardly believe it, Strickler had been telling her the truth – there was such a thing as the Knickerbocker Pack.

Rufus's tail wagged excitedly as he trotted down towards Libby, his small dumpy legs negotiating the tracks. But before he reached her, Krain stooped and plucked him easily into the air by the scuff of his neck. Krain's expression was no longer friendly. One of his hands was placed firmly around Rufus's neck in a threatening manner, and Rufus whimpered.

"Are you ready to work with me yet?" he asked Libby.

Shocked, she involuntarily expelled air from her mouth as though she'd been punched in the stomach.

"Don't you dare involve my dog in this, how could you?"

Krain shrugged nonchalantly.

"If I don't, it's only a matter of time before someone else does. You can't just let a dog saunter about with your soul, for goodness sake girl."

Rufus's ears were pinned back to his head, and he watched Libby with doe eyes.

"Don't you dare harm him," Gloria barked at Krain. A larger hulking werewolf, presumably Stan, edged forwards to back her words. "He's part of our pack now, so put him down."

Libby raised her eyebrows at Rufus.

"You're part of the Knickerbocker Pack?"

Rufus nodded his head sheepishly.

"Look, just put the dog down, Krain," Grim said. "Stop this charade. You have no intentions of killing him – if you did, you'd absorb Libby's soul. Would you *really* stoop so low as to deprive your own daughter of a soul?"

Krain opened his mouth and laughed; a maniacal laugh, filled with humour.

"Have you learnt absolutely nothing about me in all this time, you buffoon?"

Before Grim could respond, Rufus's nose shot up in the air and he sniffed loudly and fervently. The rest of the Knickerbocker Pack also prickled and shifted restlessly in the tunnel, their fur standing on end, and excitable looks played in their eyes. They were suddenly like a pack of terriers sensing a small, furry animal nearby.

A loud cracking noise echoed throughout the tunnel and without warning Red flopped to the ground with a dull *whump*. Unmoving he lay crumpled in a heap, and from the darkness, a glowing white figure stepped out, holding a gun that was aimed at Krain.

"And have *you* learnt nothing about Morgan in all these years, you imbecile?" the new arrival purred mockingly.

Chapter 36

"*Kitty?* What are you doing?" Krain gasped.

The sound of his voice broke the tension, and the werewolves jumped about excitedly, as though, up until that point, they'd been spellbound by Kitty's arrival. Kitty kept the gun trained on Krain with one hand, and in the other she waved a samurai sword in the air.

"Nobody move." Her dark eyes reflected the dim light, and she looked positively deranged.

Not needing to be told twice, nobody stepped closer. Krain looked anxious, he had a feeling he knew why she'd arrived.

"I've wanted to do that for a long time," Kitty spat, nodding her head in Red's direction. "And now it's your turn. You tried to trick me, didn't you? And you tried to trick Morgan."

Not once had she taken her eyes off Krain, and she appeared to be completely unperturbed by the werewolves.

"Ah," was all Krain could muster.

Kitty rolled her eyes and said, "You aren't as clever as you'd like to think you are, are you? Maybe if you didn't wear those ridiculous gloves you might not be *so* stupid."

Krain looked dumbfounded as though he was trying to work out what she meant. Words failed him.

"You silly man," she pointed out. "You've been married all these years to a witch and you never once wondered who her familiar was?"

And suddenly it was all clear to him.

Looking dejected, he nodded and said, "Ah, it would appear I *have* been blindingly stupid in that case."

Kitty threw her head back and laughed. It was an unexpectedly hoarse laugh, which made Libby flinch. Tipping her head in Grim's direction, she added, "You

221

promised you'd send *him*, didn't you? But no – instead, you thought you'd be scheming and clever. You thought you could get away with sending Strickler to her instead."

Grim's face darkened, but Libby on the other hand choked on her own laughter. Everyone looked at her as though she'd broken wind during a funeral service.

"*What?*" she asked defensively, shrugging her shoulders. "It's just, how the *hell* could you get Strickler and Grim confused? Is Morgan *blind*? There's absolutely no comparison. Strickler is a weedy thug, and Grim – well, Grim is..." she clammed up, not quite sure what to say. "Er, well – you know..."

Grim looked back at her, his expression deadly serious, and she fell silent.

"Morgan is housebound," Kitty retaliated. "She does not know what he looks like, she only knows of his reputation."

"I thought she was a witch," Libby said. "Wouldn't she just *know* these things?"

Kitty grunted impatiently.

"She is not like Krain, she does not possess the third eye. Morgan relies purely on nature's resources, she is not a freak like he is."

Libby looked confused.

"That means she has a big cauldron," Krain offered, sardonically. "For making lotions and potions in."

"She uses only natural ingredients," Kitty butted in. Her voice was still bitter, but her expression had transformed and softened with pride. "She can tell the future from reading tea leaves, but that doesn't mean to say she *sees* the future. Knowing and seeing are two different things."

Libby nodded her head, pretending she understood.

"Well, I can imagine how disappointed she must have been when Strickler turned up, that's all I'm saying."

"Shut your mouth, you insolent girl," Kitty hissed. "And that's another thing!" She directed her attention back to Krain. "After all these years you have never given her a child."

Krain groaned loudly and rubbed his temple.

"Could you have picked a more public place to discuss this perhaps?"

Kitty sneered at him, ignoring his sarcasm.

"You told her all along you did not want children, that you had *never* wanted children. Even all the potions in the world that Morgan used didn't help."

Krain's mouth snapped open and he looked at her wide-eyed. "*Really?* She used potions on me for *that*?"

Kitty again ignored him and continued where she'd left off. "Then just as Morgan makes peace with your decision, and your inability to have children, along comes *this woman*."

She pointed the sharp edge of the sword in Libby's direction. "And so it turns out you've been lying all along. You *already have* children!"

"Er, there's just the one," Krain corrected, holding up his right index finger. "And really, I must object. I'd rather we didn't air my dirty laundry in public any further thank you very much."

"Don't worry," Kitty spat. "I wasn't planning on doing a full cycle, just a quick rinse before I put a bullet through your head. I'm going to do Morgan a favour by making her a widow. Let's face it, it'll be less hassle than divorce proceedings. Oh and while I'm here, I'll take back what *you* promised her in the first place."

She looked over to Grim. He smiled sourly back at her and shook his head.

"Well I hate to disappoint, but I hope she doesn't have any baby-making plans for me," he said, "because it's not going to happen. I'm not going anywhere with you."

"You will do as you're told," Kitty ordered, her pencilled-on eyebrows creasing in the middle, lending her a cartoon-ish quality. "You will stay at Prospect Point Lighthouse for however long Morgan sees fit, and you will do whatever she says. You'll stay there for an eternity and longer if that's what she wants."

Libby's face crumpled in outrage and she rushed forward, Krain's jacket falling from her shoulders. Not yet sure what

223

she intended to do, with her hands tied behind her back, she yelled, "You're not taking him anywhere, you weird-haired freak!"

Kitty effortlessly realigned the gun to Libby's head and squeezed the trigger without a moment's hesitation, but Grim had already propelled himself forward, shoving Libby to the side as the gun's sound cracked the air like a whip. The bullet tore through the thin material of his vest and penetrated the hard flesh of his chest. Blood sprayed out as it pierced his heart, and in a long drawn out moment of horror, Libby watched as his body flopped to the floor; still and lifeless.

"Look what you made me do!" Kitty roared, stalking over and kicking Grim's body in anger.

Libby lifted herself awkwardly up onto her knees, blood seeping from scuff marks on her shoulder, and shuffling herself over on grazed knees, she flung herself across his motionless body.

"*Grim?*" she whispered, willing him to move or groan in response. "Grim? Can you hear me?"

Tears spilt down her cheeks onto his vest, and her chest heaved painfully with each silent sob as she realised the inevitable truth. It was ironic, she thought, that he'd died protecting her. After all that's what they'd been doing all day – saving each other. Now it was over. That was the last time. And she realised with renewed bitterness she'd never even had the chance to proclaim her feelings for him. True enough, her feelings were based on lust alone – but isn't that where things usually start out? The lust would have been a good foundation for further development surely. She knew it.

Krain set Rufus down on the ground, and edged his way into the shadows, hopeful that Kitty, who had now refocused her gun on Libby, wouldn't see him. As soon as Rufus touched the floor he bared his teeth and snarled.

"Tell your mutt to back off," Kitty snarled at Libby.

Libby looked up glassy eyed and saw Rufus shaking with anger. The fur on his neck was standing up, and he had a wild look in his eyes.

"Rufus, back off," she squeaked. A newfound fear burnt within her eyes, soaking up the lingering tears somewhat. "Go and wait with Gloria."

Rufus didn't appear to hear what she said though; all of his senses were tuned into the feline figure in front of him who was pointing a gun. He hated cats, and he didn't like loud bangs either, and with one more open-mouthed snarl he pounced at Kitty as though she'd tried to steal his favourite bone. When his teeth found purchase on the flesh of her hand he clamped his jaw tight and ragged his head from left to right, in the way he'd throttle a rabbit.

Kitty immediately dropped the gun in shock, and looked down at her mauled hand which was spurting blood. Rufus was still firmly attached, and she shook her hand furiously, trying to loosen his grip. Sheer panic as the werewolves started bounding down urged her into action, and she brought the samurai sword round, dragging its shiny surface across Rufus's flank. He immediately let go and fell to the ground with a whimper. Kitty swaggered about on her feet, disorientated and now at a disadvantage. The Knickerbocker Pack were already within swiping distance. She turned and fled. Bolting down the tracks towards the exit, pursued by the mob of angry canines.

Libby thrust herself away from Grim's cold body and knelt beside Rufus.

"Oh God, Rufus," she sobbed. Banging her arms up and down behind her back she cried in frustration, realising she couldn't even hold him. Rufus coughed weakly, a wet rattling noise in his throat, and his big brown eyes looked up at her.

"Sorry, Libby," he whimpered, his face pained. "I've messed it up for you now."

She wanted to bundle him up into her arms and tell him that everything would be alright. But she could do neither of those things.

"No you haven't," she said, lying down on her side, so that her face was inches away from his. Her bottom lip quivered, and through blurry eyes she could see his breathing becoming slower and weaker. "You haven't at all, do you hear me?"

" Yes I have," he said quietly, air and blood hissing through his teeth. "I've gone and lost your soul..."

"*Rufus?*"

His eyes stopped blinking and his chest fell still. Leaning over, she kissed his face softly. "Don't you dare leave me here on my own. Hang on!"

Burying her face into the wiry fur on his neck, she breathed in his smell and whispered, "*Please*."

When he didn't respond, she wailed loudly, filling the tunnel with her profound grief. Her shoulders lurched and her heart felt heavy. She couldn't imagine life in Sunray Bay without him. And Grim, he wasn't even there to console her.

Suddenly she had nobody.

Not even a soul.

Chapter 37

7:04pm: Zoltan's Passage to Hell, Sunray Bay

Libby lay next to Rufus for what seemed like hours, but in reality it was only minutes. Sadness enveloped her, and she heaved in deep breaths that physically hurt her chest. Remembering all the good times, she couldn't quite accept Rufus wouldn't be there by her side anymore. She'd known the day would arrive eventually, it had been one of her biggest worries since becoming a dog owner – but that certainly didn't make things any easier. And she'd never imagined that it would end this way either – she thought she'd lose Rufus to the graceful whim of old age, not through a mindless act of violence.

A hand touched her shoulder, and she hardly noticed, until she heard a voice say, "I'm so sorry Libby, I realise now how much the dog meant to you."

Lifting her head she saw Finnbane Krain standing over her, a look of concern etched onto his regal-looking face. He offered his arms, and Libby wasn't sure whether he was proffering them to comfort her or whether he just wanted to pull her up from the floor – she rejected them either way.

"You have *no* idea," she hissed, blinking her red puffy eyes rapidly in an attempt to shake away the remnants of tears.

"I do, darling." Krain nodded his head, solemnly. He stroked her hair, watching the fiery strands as they fell through his fingers. "I knew something like this would happen..." He looked thoughtful and saddened, as though trying to find the right words to continue. But failing to find anything suitable to say, he said, "And now your soul is gone."

Sitting up, Libby could feel hatred welling up inside.

"How dare you even say those things, *you* were threatening to harm him before Kitty even arrived on the scene!"

Krain flinched and said, "It was just a lesson in love, sweetheart, that was all. I wouldn't have harmed him really. I was proving a point..."

"*What point?* That you're a bully?" She shook her head, not believing his brazen faced lie. "To hell with my soul, anyway," she snapped. "She can keep it."

Krain shook his head.

"No darling, Kitty doesn't have your soul. That only works if you kill somebody with your bare hands."

"So what does that mean? Where *has* it gone?"

"Your soul, as well as Rufus's, has more or less vanished into thin air – irretrievable now, unfortunately."

Libby hung her head, it seemed like she was in deeper shit than she cared to imagine.

"I can help you though," Krain said, forcefully taking hold of Libby's upper arms and hoisting her to her feet. As her bare feet balanced uncomfortably on the uneven ground, she tore herself free and looked at him with deep loathing. He'd turned her whole world upside down.

"Why would I want help from you? I've lost everything because of you!"

Krain grasped at his chest theatrically, to show that her words were cutting.

"Am I *really* so bad?"

Libby recoiled. She wasn't even sure. After all, it was her mother who had concealed the truth for all those years; for all of her life. She just didn't know what to think anymore.

Krain's eyes narrowed, and a smile that almost looked sincere crept back onto his face. He walked behind her and took hold of her hands, then went about untying the rope. His fingers worked gently, tugging at the knots, so as not to hurt her chaffed skin underneath. She stood and allowed him to.

"You look so much like your mother, it takes my breath away," he said softly. "I'd forgotten how beautiful she was."

228

"She still *is*," Libby snapped. "She's very much alive and well."

Krain nodded his head and bit his lip.

"I'm pleased for her. That is, I'm pleased she found happiness."

Libby felt awkward, unsure as to whether he was thinking of bundling her into his arms for a hug. She hoped that he wasn't.

"We could catch up on all those lost years, you know. Get to know each other properly," he said, coming back round to study her face.

"I don't think so," Libby shook her head.

Krain looked wistful and put his hands on her shoulders, forcing her to meet his eyes.

"Why not?" he urged.

"Because you're a cold-blooded killer," she said without emotion, whilst rubbing her wrists. "I heard what you did to those werewolves, and quite frankly, you make me sick."

A fleeting look of something new that Libby hadn't seen before, something calculating perhaps, flashed across his face, and he snarled, "And what do you think werewolves are? *Pets?*"

Quickly remembering himself, he loosened his stance and kept his anger in check. He suddenly went back to looking doleful.

"You're quick to judge me, aren't you? Yet you accepted Grim just like that!" he snapped his fingers together, the fabric of his gloves muffling the snapping noise.

Fire burned in Libby's eyes.

"Don't bring him into this. He wasn't a vampire like you are. I want nothing to do with you, you make my skin crawl."

"You can't run away from the fact that *you're* a vampire too, Libby," Krain's voice was becoming cold and impatient.

"Yes I can. Just watch me."

"Well what about Grim, what *did* you think he was exactly?"

229

A rumble suddenly echoed through the tunnel, making Libby feel as though they were arguing inside the stomach of a hibernating dragon. They both looked around.

"Certainly not a vampire, at least that much was clear. And anyway, this is about me and you."

Fresh, new tears formed a sheen over her eyes, and she said, "Grim's dead now, it doesn't matter what he was."

"You're right, this is about me and you, Libby, and, you know, I'm not the bad person you'd like to think I am. We can't help who it is we're born as." With a shifty smile, he raised one of his eyebrows and added, "Can we...?"

Libby huffed, "I don't care who you are. You're *not* my dad."

Krain let his hands drop to his side, and his jaw clenched tight.

"I can see that, what's his name...Dennis? Yes, Dennis did a sterling job of bringing you up. But as much as you want it to be true, he isn't your real father. We can have DNA tests done if that would help convince you."

"You aren't listening to me. I don't want *anything* from you, and I don't want to know you."

Right at that moment she was terrified because when she looked into his face, seeing his jaw jutting forward and stubbornness dominating his eyes, she saw a tiny bit of herself there.

"I don't care if you are my real father."

As quickly as she could have flicked a light switch, Krain's face turned stony cold and he put his gloved hands into his pockets. Rocking on his heels he chewed on the inside of his mouth, and his dark eyes glared.

"Very well, suit yourself. You can't ever say I didn't try, but if that's how you want to play it, so be it."

Libby yelped as he pulled a syringe from his pocket.

"Now, you wouldn't mind if I took some blood from you, would you? Just a small amount will do. You won't feel a thing – I promise," he chuckled.

Libby backed away, scanning the ground for suitable weapon options.

"Don't you *dare* touch me!"

Matching her steps and moving forward, he said, "Oh I *dare*."

A further loud grumbling noise echoed once again through the tunnel and Libby's eyes widened.

"Dodgems," Krain said calmly. "Up on the boardwalk."

Tapping the syringe in his palm, he looked nothing like the doting father now.

"Now, about this blood, are you going to make it easy or hard?"

Libby braced herself for a fight, balling her fists up as tight as she could. She wasn't confident that she could beat him in a physical fight, especially not with his so-called vampire strength – but she had no choice but to have a damn good go of it anyway. She wouldn't let him take anything from her easily, and she wanted no part to play in his vampire super race scheme.

He bore down on her, and even though he was actually only a few inches taller than she was, it seemed more like a whole foot. With the needle gripped in his hand, its silver tip pointing menacingly at her, she wondered if he'd ever really wanted to build bridges with her in the first place. His promises all seemed shallow now, and she wondered if Morgan was right – he had no paternal impulses whatsoever. She was dashed from her thoughts when he lunged forward reaching for her arm. Rearing her foot back, she brought it crashing forward into his crotch just as the needle point scraped down her skin.

Tears erupted in his eyes and he fell down to his knees, clutching his groin with one hand and holding the syringe in the other. Just as Libby was about to comment on the fact she hoped he'd never be able to bear children again, she looked over his shoulder and was stunned into silence. As another roar reverberated through the tunnel, the ghost train cart at the top of the incline teetered on the brink for a brief moment before tipping over the edge of the slope. Her mouth dried up. She stood stock still, watching as the cart careened towards them. Her mind was willing her to move, but her legs were refusing to budge.

Krain looked up at her with a mixture of pain, confusion and anger on his face. Licking his lips nervously, he turned around to see what she was transfixed by just in time to see the cart as it crashed into his body. Libby saw the look of shock horror on his face. It was as though the whole incident was taking place in slow motion, and she braced herself for the impact. It was the second time that day she was about to be knocked over, and she kind of knew what to expect.

Feeling a rush of air as the cart came for her, she was surprised when the impact actually hit her side on. Knocked through the air and dropping to the ground, hard, the cart narrowly missed her feet, and she felt as though she had a tonne weight on her chest.

Spluttering and coughing, she was winded and hurt – but alive. And when she looked up, she saw a pair of brilliant white eyes looking back at her.

"Grim?"

But she passed out before he could answer.

Chapter 38

Libby awoke in soft darkness. Twelve hours had passed since she'd died the first time around. She wondered if she was in hospital and whether the events of the past day had been a very vivid dream, but as her eyes adjusted she saw rails of clothes, feather boas and other props at the foot of the bed and realised she was back in Gloria's spare room.

Propping herself up onto her elbows she looked round and saw Grim sitting on the floor by the bed with his back leaning against the wall. His chest was bare, and bandaged in a haphazard fashion, and his arms were resting on his knees. His face, as ever, was shielded by sunglasses.

Scrambling up onto her knees, Libby winced at the pain, but bent down to look at him regardless of how much it hurt to do so.

"Grim? You saved me. But how? I saw Kitty shoot you. You were dead..."

Grim's mouth curved up at the sides, in a sad, yet endearing way. "I'm *already* dead, Libby. I can't be killed no more than I already am."

"But, I don't understand, we're all technically dead..." Libby started. But Grim shook his head dismally.

"Don't Libby, let's not do this now, eh?"

Despite looking disappointed, she nodded her head and said, "Sure, you can tell me about it when you're ready to." And leaning forward she touched his arm in reassurance, keeping her fingers on his icy skin even when he flinched.

"Thank you," she said, smiling. "For saving me, that is."

He didn't reply, but he moved his arm and grasped her hand in his.

"So what happens now?" she asked, relishing the feel of her hand in his large grip.

233

"How do you mean?" Standing up and clutching the bandaged wound on his chest he grimaced. "What would you like to happen?"

Libby watched him with concern. "Well what happened to Krain? I mean, is he dead? And what about the werewolves?"

Grim sat down on the side of the bed next to her, eyebrows protruding from the top of his shades, and said, "Oh Krain's definitely dead, there's no doubt about that. And the werewolves are still going berserk outside. At a guess, I'd say they're still pretty pissed off with me."

"So what will you do?" Libby asked, scared of what his answer would be.

"I'm heading off into The Grey Dust Bowl soon. I'm not wanted here anymore."

Fear flashed across her face, and her voice broke as she said, "No, that's not true. You don't have to go."

"Why? What else will I do? Why would I stay?"

"You should stay because you don't have to keep running." Grabbing his hand again, she squeezed it tight, and added, "And because I'm here."

"You don't know *who* or *what* I am though Libby, you've only just met me." His face darkened, and her heart fluttered.

"I'm willing to find out," she said, stroking his hand with her fingers.

"But I'm not willing to talk about it," he snapped.

"I know that," she said, putting her face in front of his so he could see the sincerity in her eyes. "And I'm willing to wait until you *are* ready to talk to me about it."

Grim sighed; her offer was tempting. Libby could sense that he was already swaying.

"Actually, what ever happened to *Strickler*?" she laughed, abruptly changing the subject. Buying more time in case he made his mind up that he was leaving. She couldn't stand that right now.

"Who knows," Grim said, puffing out his cheeks and shaking his head. "If Morgan was the last to have her hands on him – I dread to think."

234

Libby winced, but laughed all the same.

"What about you?" Grim asked, splaying his fingers and fitting hers in between. "What will you do?"

Libby cocked her head to the side and thought for a moment. "Well I rather like the idea of The Ordinaries – only if it was done properly and above board, you know. It's a worthy cause, and I think I have some monster arse to kick."

"*Oh?*" Grim's eyebrows poked above his sunglasses once again.

"Yeah, Kitty – I'll start with her."

Grim shook his head sympathetically, and clasped her hand between both of his. "Hey, I'm really sorry about Rufus..."

Libby smiled back at him, "I know."

They sat in silence for a few moments, thoughts of Rufus fresh and sore in Libby's mind and heart. Then suddenly she piped up, "So are you in?"

When he gave her a look of utter bewilderment, she said, "The *refined* Ordinaries."

Laughing, he asked, "*Me?*"

"Yeah, we'd make a great team," she giggled, reaching over and pinching his arm.

Although he couldn't deny what she said, trepidation filled his face.

"Come on," Libby urged, batting her eyelids at him. "How could you refuse? And besides, we're both officially soulless. Maybe we could do some soul searching together?"

His smile widened.

"I'm liking the sound of this idea more and more. Keep at it, you're twisting my arm."

"Thank God for that," she laughed, "I was beginning to think I'd have to actually get you into an arm wrestling match."

"Well now I am scared, so I'd better agree."

Libby sat up straighter and edged closer to him. The tension in the air between them silently crackled. Raising her hands she tentatively took hold of his sunglasses – and this time he didn't flinch.

"Can I take them off?" she asked, nervous that she was being too forward.

There was a slight moment of resistance, but finally he nodded his head and sighed. Slowly removing the black shield from his face, Libby unveiled his stark white eyes. Tiny black pupils, that seemed lost amidst so much white, stared back at her, desolate and empty. He held her gaze and didn't look away, gauging her reaction.

"That's better," she said, stroking the side of his face with her fingers. Then casting the sunglasses away, she lied, "You've got the most beautiful eyes I've ever seen."

He didn't believe her for one second, but he appreciated the sentiment.

"So when are we going to go and find that skanky hell-cat?" Libby asked, diverting the conversation in case he felt self-conscious.

"Right after this..." he replied.

Putting his hand on the back of her head and burying his fingers in her hair, he pulled her towards him. The sensation of his cool breath on her face prompted goose-bumps to prick up all over her entire body, and Libby shuddered with glee. When their lips met he kissed her hard, and she kissed him back with a greater urgency. The room around them was stifling, but Libby found that his lips were deliciously cold. Falling backwards onto the bed, she pulled him down on top of her, her hands exploring his hard body as he tugged at her bra strap. She groaned in pleasure and sighed, "Yeah okay, we have forever, don't we?"

Epilogue

He sat in the dark wondering if she'd ever come back. He had no way of knowing, but he reckoned he must have been left alone for hours already – maybe even days. She'd taken him to the brink of insanity and had left him hanging out to dry, just like that.

The time he'd spent with her had been worth giving everything up for though. Despite losing the opportunity to regain the psychic part of his soul, he'd gained the opportunity to pop his cherry – and boy had she popped it. There'd been no satiating her hunger, but then, he certainly wasn't complaining. He'd have been happy enough to go at it with her non-stop for the rest of his life. Who wouldn't? She was stunning.

But then Kitty had arrived, screaming and yelling and spoiling his fun – and that's when Morgan had left him alone.

He hated dogs, and they hated him (some things never get past a dog's nose, including the scent of an ex-postman), and so he'd always claimed to be a cat person whenever anybody presented him with the bizarre question '*are you a dog or a cat person?*' But now, as he dangled from chains, he thought of Kitty and he realised that he hated cats too.

He guessed he was neither a dog nor cat person after all.

Hanging suspended in the air, he waited and waited and waited, realising that he wasn't a fearless Bengal anymore – he was a twitching bug caught up in the witch's spider web...

About the Author

Rachael H Dixon lives in the northeast of England with her husband Derek and their furry, four-legged son Marvin. She's been writing pretty much ever since she could hold, albeit strangely, a pen, and her favourite subjects are anything to do with horror and/or the paranormal. Her love for the macabre stems from late nights spent watching black and white Vincent Price films as a young child.

She has a degree in Graphic Design, and when she's not busy writing and reading she enjoys drawing and painting. And, as with lots of other creative types, she loves a glass of red wine now and then.

To contact Rachael, to enter competitions and to keep updated with news of subsequent releases in the Sunray Bay series, please visit her website: **www.slipperysouls.co.uk**.